I0544311

The Shadow of Her

Aspen Bassett

This is a work of fiction. Names, characters, places, and incidents are products of the author's imagination or are used fictitiously and are not to be construed as real. Any resemblance to actual events, locations, organizations, or persons, living or dead, is entirely coincidental.

World Castle Publishing, LLC
Pensacola, Florida
Copyright © Aspen Bassett 2021
Hardback ISBN: 9781953271570
Paperback ISBN: 9781953271587
eBook ISBN: 9781953271594
First Edition World Castle Publishing, LLC, February 15, 2021
http://www.worldcastlepublishing.com

Licensing Notes
All rights reserved. No part of this book may be used or reproduced in any manner whatsoever without written permission, except in the case of brief quotations embodied in articles and reviews.
Cover: Karen Fuller
Editor: Maxine Bringenberg

To all my siblings. Through blood, marriage, and choice.

Chapter 1

The sun above me blared mercilessly as the desert wind blew layers of heat across my skin. I lay on my back, blinking at the blue and yellow, and wondered how far I'd fallen, literally and figuratively. Traveling through time and space had been a norm for me the past few months, ever since I'd fallen through a crack in time and learned to control the darkness slipping into our world to create doors between the moments. Usually, I landed on level ground, just like walking through a normal door. But this travel had been different. Where I needed to go, my powers couldn't make a connection. The sand was the problem, tiny pebbles and larger stones of petrified wood which interfered with the dark energy. So I had to go higher. Then I stepped through and hoped for the best.

"Ow." I moaned and rolled to my side.

A metal ship deck had broken my fall, so at least I'd gotten the location right. The ship made for a strange sight, stranded in the middle of the Arizona Petrified Forest during the American Wild West period. It was my fault the ship was there. The Pirate Ship Noble had once sailed the seas, but that was before I ticked off a being ten times stronger than I could ever be. I had run, and

I took the occupants with me, several of whom were running up from below deck, to find out what that noise was. I'm sure me hitting the metal at a free fall must have echoed. The first one up was a girl my age with long brown hair and a futuristic take on traditional Indian clothing. Her name was Shreya, and her parents captained this ship.

"Penny?" She gasped when she recognized me. "Everyone! Penny came back!"

I nodded like *yeah yeah, I'm here*, and forced myself to move. Pain radiated from my side as if something had broken, but I gave it a second to correct itself. An upside to my current fifty-percent-dark-energy condition was rapid healing. The downside was anyone who didn't know about the darkness would forget me as soon as I wasn't in sight. Thankfully, I was among fellow believers.

Shreya reached me and helped me up. The pain was softer this time around. I'd be fine in a few minutes but wouldn't have lived through that without this new healing. Life, it seemed, had tiny ups to the many downs.

"How long have I been gone?" I asked. In my memory, I'd left them only forty-eight hours ago to get The Shadow off their back. But time travel was iffy.

"You've been gone a week," Shreya said. "Mom and Dad left to see if they could find a nearby town. Provisions are okay, but our water filter broke, and the Wild West doesn't have the tech to fix it."

Limited water. That was not good. "When will they be back?"

"They said they'd be gone three days max, so I'm hoping to see them this evening."

"Okay." I limped to a plastic lawn chair that belonged in the eighties and sat down.

Shreya glanced around. "Where's the rest of your group?"

Ah, there it was. The one question more painful than breaking my...let's go with everything in that fall. I leaned back into the chair and considered how I should answer. In the end, the simpler, the better. "Mission completed. We saved Jack. Luke stayed with him."

Shreya frowned. "Luke?"

Everyone knew him as Stranger. It had been a nickname at first because he lost his memory, and then he'd refused to tell me his name once he'd gotten his memories back. But we'd gotten in a fight. Him telling me his name was the end of something. The end of us dating definitely, but a core trust had been broken with that fight. It was the end of a friendship too.

"Oh," Shreya said. She must have read my expression because she noted, "His name is Luke, huh?"

"Yeah."

"And Dinah?"

My twin sister. We didn't say goodbye. I'd taken her back to her time, back to friends and a family who loved her, who'd remembered her as they couldn't me, and then I slipped out the door and out of time before she noticed. "She's home."

"Okay." Shreya didn't push it. "Max, go get Penny here some water and a sandwich."

"No thank you," I said. I wasn't sure how I'd get out of there again, but I wasn't going to take their rations. "I'm fine. Really."

I skimmed through the crowd for a familiar face. Tall, same black hair and ebony eyes as me, same skin and same smile, but we weren't related. He belonged to another world and had created a body based on my own to live on Earth. It was a long story, and I didn't know much of it myself. We had a rocky relationship. He'd tried to kill me, save me, and manipulate me, but he had the same powers as me, and lived under the same rules. A creature named The Shadow mixed their dark energy with mine in hopes of stopping me from changing the timeline. This boy, once a bodyless creature, had learned how The Shadow changed me and created a body for himself. We were both fifty percent this world and fifty percent the darkness. But I didn't see him anywhere.

"Did Kyle go with your parents?"

Shreya shook her head, and concern wrinkled her brow. "He went into a deep meditation the morning after you left, and he hasn't woken up since. We tried loud noises, shaking him, and little Davy tossed water in his face even though everyone told him not to. His breathing is really shallow, and he feels...cold."

That wasn't good. I tried to recall what I knew about the situation. "The Shadow had cornered us when we were going to change Jack's timeline, and it had me beat, but then it stopped, said something about Kyle coming home, and left."

"Coming home." Shreya frowned. "You mean the dark world?"

"I think so."

"How can he be there if he's here?"

"I was hoping he'd merely created an illusion, tricked The Shadow. But if he's not waking up...."

"It would be a waste to lose a face as perfect as his."

I made a face. "Ah, gross!"

She giggled. "I'm sorry, but he looks like a bad boy biker teen, and that's *so* my type." She lightly slapped my knee and motioned me to get up. "Come on, I'll take you to Kyle. He's in the spare bedroom."

I followed her down the deck, where family photos lined the staircase, and into the narrow halls. The ship used to be a prison ship with cells and bags, but the Noble family had long ago taken them out and created rooms out of curtains and makeshift walls. Shreya led me to the second room to the right. Coloring pages and homemade kid-style get well cards balanced on the side table next to one solitary bed. The boy was there, blankets tucked along his sides. Shreya was right. He did look like some tragic rebellious biker guy, but the polished, overly perfect kind you'd only see on TV. He was too aesthetically perfect. I had the sneaking suspicion he'd done some research on Western ideals before creating his body. There was something off about him now, though. His skin didn't glow with health, and when I touched him, he felt chilled.

"He's not doing too well, is he?" I asked.

Shreya shook her head. "Gets worse every time we check on him. The younger ones have been making 'get well' cards. They want him to get better. Of course, they do. We all do." She frowned. "Right? I mean, he did a good thing, especially if it stopped The Shadow from killing you. And I believe we should default on helping people...."

"But?" I asked.

"I mean, isn't he...?" Shreya leaned closer and whispered, "The Void? As in the reason our world and the dark world are colliding? Isn't he kind of the source of our problems? What would happen if he didn't...you know, come back? Would that be bad? Or good?" Shreya looked guilty, but her question had been sincere.

And I didn't have a good answer. "It's complicated, I think. If The Void/Kyle hadn't messed with time, I'd still have my family. They'd remember me. But also, your father would have died an orphan kid on the streets of Shakespearean England, and your mom wouldn't have been born until almost a millennia later."

Shreya rose an eyebrow. "So I wouldn't exist at all. None of my siblings would have been adopted into the family. Whoa." She stared at the shallow breathing body in front of us. "Think he did it on purpose? Some kind of insurance to make sure we didn't turn him in?"

"I don't know," I admitted. "Sometimes I think he's got a plan of his own that he refuses to share and that every single word he says is to manipulate us like we're pieces on his chess game against The Shadow. And sometimes...." I shrugged. "I wonder if he's pretending to know what he's doing, and he's actually scared and alone and came to our world for something better."

Shreya nodded. "Cool. So our options are a manipulative

enemy or a guy who needs our help."

"Pretty much." I pulled a fold out chair from the corner and set it up next to Kyle's bed. "Either way, we can't let The Shadow get him. I don't know if The Shadow can erase what's happened, how time has changed, but I don't want to take that chance."

Shreya hesitated. "Why not, though? I know it would stink for me, not existing and all that, but you'd get your family back, right? Your parents would remember you."

I sighed. Being home, eating dinner with my parents and twin sister, making jokes and sharing stories about our days, it just didn't appeal to me as much as it used to. Before, I would think about my family and get homesick. But now? It just made me numb. I didn't want to hurt anymore. It wasn't okay yet, but....

"I don't think my home is there anymore. It's time to move on."

I wrapped my fingers around Kyle's still hand. Physically he was cold, but energetically he felt empty.

Kyle's energy had always felt different from everyone else on earth. Take Shreya, for example. Her aura had nervous reds and creative purples intertwining like braids around her. She had a warm, excited energy, like the feeling of stepping to a table filled with delightful paints, brand new brushes, and a blank canvas. On a good day, Kyle's aura felt like a void—hence the nickname—like a gap where energy should be. Since I'd been born with psychic abilities to see energies, I could see exactly where our world ended, and the dark aura of his world began. But now? As he lay there on that bed, his chest barely rising with each inhale, I saw no gap between the worlds. No darkness. Nothing. Energetically, it was as if I stared at an empty bed.

"He's gone," I realized.

"What?!" Shreya jumped up and checked his pulse, then cursed at me. "He's still alive. Don't scare me like that."

"No, I mean his soul." I scooted my chair closer as if my empathic sight might be getting nearsighted. Nothing. "It's gone.

Could he…?" I thought my theory through in my head before testing it out loud as if thinking it would show how obviously ridiculous it was. "This ship is surrounded by petrified wood, which stops me from using the dark energy in any way outside of my body. So traveling is impossible. And yet we know Kyle traveled to get The Shadow away from me that day. What if he made a portal inside himself? Just traveled in spirit. Is that possible?"

"I have no idea what's possible or not with you two," Shreya admitted apologetically.

I let go of Kyle's hand and leaned back. "I could give it a try, I guess. I worry that he hasn't come back, but if The Shadow had captured him, I think we'd notice."

"Everything we know fading from existence would turn a few heads," Shreya agreed.

Still, I hesitated. "What if the petrified wood is keeping him from coming back?" Because on the off chance that I could separate my darkened soul from my body, I'd prefer to return to it.

"Oh…." Shreya's eyes widened. "Maybe, don't do anything until my parents come back."

I thought about what would happen if my twin sister Dinah was there. She'd probably hit my arm with her knuckles to make a point and warn me never to think about separating my soul from my body until she was long dead of old age. It was a threat she'd used before. Now my Stranger Luke, on the other hand, was a completely different story. He'd say he trusted me, that I could do it. Then he'd say if I wasn't back in an hour, he'd carry my body right out of this forest and away from any petrified wood so I could come back. That was Luke—one-hundred percent faith and a plan B. Just in case. Like a catching net under a trapeze artist. The kind of thing one would immediately miss while standing several feet in the air. But dealing with my future chaos sans Luke had been my choice. I couldn't start complaining about it half an hour after leaving him.

I took a deep breath and nodded to myself in encouragement. "Okay. I'm doing this."

"Um.... No, let's wait for Mom and Dad."

But I closed my eyes and settled into my chair. It had become a habit to quiet the mind and block out the physical world so I could focus on the darkness. Shreya's reds and purples in her aura were swirling with a nervous twist. In other rooms of the ship, blots of energy of various colors marked the locations of several kids going about their day. Three souls leaned against the door to the hall, listening to Shreya and me talk.

Where I sat was pure black, a gap of color — a point of soreness in conversation, but exactly what I needed to travel. In all previous attempts to travel through time and space, I would gather the darkness like a door in front of me and connect that energy to the energies of another place. I would use something specific as an anchor, like a person, an emotion. But this time, I brought my awareness deep within myself instead, deep within my chest, my core. Then I thought of Kyle. At first, I focused on my memories of him, his smug grin or manipulative conversations. One time he blew up a building full of people after they'd kidnapped him, only to run back in with me to save them. Or the time he asked me why I cared so much for humans when none of them seemed to care back. But no moments lit up to connect.

Then one specific memory came to mind. I had asked him why he fought so hard to leave his world and be a part of ours. He'd waved at the sun in our faces and the sand at our feet, and said "Because it's beautiful." As annoying, untrustworthy, and suspicious as I saw Kyle, that's who he was. That longing desire to be a part of a world in color.

There. A little spark of connection deep within the darkness. I mentally tapped on it, and a rush of emotions ran through me. Fear. Fight or flight. And voices.

Shhh.

Is the coast — ?

Shhh! No wonder the girl named you Void. You're empty where you should have common sense.

I smirked. Yeah, that's the right spot. I formed a connection and imagined a portal the same as I always did, but this time I made it within me. The sensation was strange, like butterflies in my stomach at first, and then it grew around my body. I felt my body relax beyond my control as I slipped through the portal within. The last thing I physically experienced was my legs slipping off the chair and Shreya's shriek in surprise as she caught me. And then...nothing.

Chapter 2

Nothing surrounded me. No light. No air. No smells or touch. Just me, my thoughts, and the darkness. I had experienced the dark world only once before, and completely against my will. The Shadow had torn me from my body to threaten me. It pretended to be the good guy, but I didn't trust it. I had a tendency not to trust anyone who took me against my will, even if they claimed to be fighting the good fight.

At first, I thought I was alone in the darkness. Then a strange wave tugged me back.

Penny?

I couldn't see Kyle, but I knew he was there directly in front of me. The darkness changed from an empty chill to a warmth, like surprise and gratitude and…life. As if I had my eyes closed and could feel the heat of the body next to me. Strange, how human his soul felt. I'd never noticed that before.

Kyle's voice rang, not in the darkness, but in my mind. *What are you doing here?*

Getting you, I replied. *You've been missing for days. Shreya and I figured you couldn't connect your body because of all of the petrified wood.*

I haven't even been able to get that far, he admitted. *I'm afraid we've got a bigger problem blocking our way.*

This is, as you humans would say, a code red situation.

The new voice took me by surprise, and I tensed. But I felt none of Kyle's manipulation or The Shadow's rage. This voice was calm, light, had a touch of humor and an eager seriousness to it, like a smile of excitement in a battlefield. I mentally focused on the space where the voice originated. The soul, if that's what it was, felt like a shield. No wonder Kyle hid here with it. If The Shadow was down here with us, a shield was exactly what we needed.

My name is Penny, I introduced myself.

Names are human constructs, the other soul said. *We were all one before your Kyle's rebellion. Individuality was and technically continues to be illegal. Which, of course, makes it all the more intriguing. Perhaps you can give me a nickname.* Instinct told me this new soul had moved closer, as its voice continued to ring in my mind. *It is a curious thing that you are here, in our world, to rescue one of ours. I didn't expect that. Our mutual friend here is correct, perhaps, about the familial bond between you two.*

No bond, I denied. *Kyle still has a mess to clean up in my world. I'm not letting him get away that easily.*

The other one chuckled. *You blame your Kyle for the collision of our worlds?*

Kyle spoke up, almost like a whisper. *I've learned what I could about why our worlds are colliding, Penny. I need to update you on a few things.*

Do you think the opening I created for Kyle to escape through was unstable? The other one laughed again, and it was a cocky laugh. It reminded me of Dinah whenever somebody doubted her history knowledge. *You're the expert around here.*

I could answer to that name.

I chuckled. Something about this soul was endearing to me. *Expert it is, then. Now how to—* A whisper rolled through the darkness, but when it reached me, instead of sound, a wave of fear shot through me.

The Shadow, The Expert said. *Penny, I sure hope you know how to empty your mind. One thought, and I can't hide you.*

And then it was there. Everywhere. A large, imposing mass. In my world, if I needed to quiet my mind, I would focus on my breathing. Inhale. Exhale. But here, there was no breath. My lungs were back on the noble ship. So I focused on the silence, imagined it washing over me as if me and the darkness were the same. The energy shifted to my right as if Kyle moved to be by my side. To protect me, comfort me, or hide behind me, I didn't know.

Report. The Shadow's empty menacing voice rang in my mind, and I shuddered, but the order was not meant for me.

All clear, The Expert replied. *No signs of the traitor.*

And what of your investigation into the one who helped it escape?

They continue to elude us.

Then you continue to disappoint.

Yes. The Expert's tone lost all humor, but there was no fear there either. Or annoyance. It sounded emotionless as if trained to keep the truth of its personality silent when needed. *What of the human?* The Expert asked. I knew it meant me and paid extra attention to the roaring silence around me in fear that a mere thought would give away my presence, and then afraid that fear would be enough. *Last I heard, you planned to appeal to her sympathies regarding the drowning of our people as the two worlds collide.*

She chose to save one over the many.

Then perhaps it would be wise to simply close the gaps and end it ourselves.

And let the traitors go without punishment?

No. Of course not, The Expert replied. Only then did I note the slight venom to its tone. *I will double my efforts.*

Ideas, thoughts, connections threatened to come to light my

mind, so I doubled my focus on the silence around us. I needed a hug or a look to assure me, to direct me. Mind alone could not release the ever building stress of what I'd heard and who spoke the words. Of what it could mean and what would happen if I was found.

Capture the traitors, The Shadow warned. *While we still have souls left to save.* Like a whoosh, the opposing force faded. The energies around me changed to relief. The Shadow was gone.

Good work blending in with the silence, The Expert said to me. *You have strong control — rare for a human.*

But I'd held my questions in for too long, so I ignored its compliment and went straight for the point. *The gaps between our worlds, the entire reason for the apocalypse — are they accidents like I originally thought, or...? Surely The Shadow wouldn't intentionally open them, let its own people drown just to punish one soul for wanting a different life.*

Like I said, Kyle answered. *I have a lot to catch you up on.*

First, we need to get you out of here, The Expert interrupted. *Making a direct portal out of this world is not an option.*

Why? I asked.

No physical material. You need both. I'm sure you took for granted the constant access to the physical realm, but here it kills first.

Like the darkness in our world, unless controlled, it burns our world, I said.

Yes, only your world drowns us.

But I'm from the physical world. It wouldn't drown me, I said. *I can control it and get us out.*

Silence followed my declaration. Why, I didn't understand. It seemed obvious.

Point me in the right direction, I said. *I'm sure Kyle and I can take it from there.*

Penny, you don't have a body either, Kyle pointed out. *You touch that water, and you'll be lost to the tide. Just like us. I'm sorry, but I'm afraid the rescue mission was a one-way trip.*

No, I replied without hesitation. *That's not an option for me.*

Unfortunately, it's the fact, The Expert said.

I did not survive everything I've gone through and sacrificed so much to believe that. The silence after my declaration was ripe with tension and awkward curiosity.

About that.... Kyle's voice trailed off. *You're alive despite the current soul/body separation. I guess that means....*

I knew what he was asking, and since the awkward tension came from both sides of me, Kyle had filled The Expert in on my impossible choice: save Jack and die myself, or live by letting him meet his fatal destiny. I chose my answer carefully. *It means never underestimate me. Jack is alive, and so am I.*

What? Kyle responded with a low emotional whisper. It wasn't just disbelief, although I couldn't quite place what lingered behind the shock. Hope perhaps, although I couldn't understand why. *You overcame a paradox?*

Yeah. Turns out I existed outside of the paradox. It would have occurred without me, so my actions couldn't trigger it.

The tense silence changed from shock to a whispering kind of whir. I wished I had my colors so I could read if the two souls around me were tense with dread, fear, or analyzing blue. All I saw was black, and I couldn't understand any of it.

Wait a minute. If you could— The Expert started, but Kyle interrupted it.

I can take us to the nearest source of your world. If what you say is true, then it's worth a shot.

What were you gonna say? I asked The Expert.

Nothing. He responded too quickly. I immediately got suspicious. *I'm just in shock. No one's ever outsmarted a paradox before. It might never happen again. Someday, when we are all safe, I'd love to hear of your tales.*

It was a pleasure to meet you, I said. Something about the openness to the darkness, how every single one of our thoughts were projected as words into the minds of others, made me hesitant to delve into deeper conversations. Better to play along and talk to Kyle once we had our bodies back. *So how do you all move without a body?*

The Expert chuckled. *With intention. I'll keep The Shadow busy for as long as I can. Follow your brother. He knows the way.*

And with that, the energy of The Expert slipped away. This time the stunned silence came for me. Brother? Did The Expert actually think Kyle was my brother?

My kind doesn't have families, Kyle's voice chimed in my mind. *Your so-called Expert misused the term. Don't get all offended. Come on.*

And with that, he dragged me to the darkness. I never doubted following him, which took me by surprise. I reasoned I was too tired and ready to get moving to bother with my usual cynicism toward Kyle's plans. But really, he was there because of me. The one thing he wanted to do was to get out of there, and yet he came back to make sure I was safe. And then I realized something they had said earlier.

Kyle? I asked as we moved to the darkness.

What? He sounded preoccupied.

What was your original plan out of here? No answer. *Kyle?*

I didn't have one.

That answer took me by surprise, and the shock rippled through my exposed soul. That meant he came here to stop The Shadow from killing us without any way out. A complete sacrifice. *Why?*

Can we not do this here?

He had a point, but it frustrated me. The Void was a frightening terror, the lingering fear that kept me running, but I came here to protect Kyle. I never even hesitated. The two seemed so different to me. The monster and the teammate. I couldn't wrap my head around the fact that they were the same being. But not two hours ago I ran away from home and broke up with my boyfriend. Since then, my default setting had been confused. Maybe that was my new norm. Maybe confusion was just how things were now. And maybe there were multiple sides to people. Luke had described me as a superhero many times, and I'd betrayed him. So somebody I considered a villain could be a hero too.

Penny, can you hold off on the inner crisis? Kyle's voice gritted in my mind. *You're kind of loud, and I'm trying to focus on getting us out of here before we get captured.*

Sorry, I forgot, I thought to him. *Heard everything?*

Yeah. Good to know your feelings about me are just as cynical as ever.

Sorry, I repeated.

A moment of pause. *I get it. Humans believe thoughts to be private. Here it's like a scream. It radiates to everyone around you. The only way to be private is to be thoughtless. And in doing so, one could lose themselves.*

I'd probably go crazy if down here for too long. Or make the souls around me crazy, I joked, expecting him to tease my blabbering humanity. But his response was sober.

This place makes me desperate. I could feel the anxiety from where he was in front of me as his thoughts entered my mind. *This is my worst case scenario, trapped down here again.* And the connection once again slipped into my mind that he came here voluntarily for me. *Don't get used to it,* he said. And then, *There.*

I felt the terror in the air before I became aware of the rushing waves of light which splintered through waves. Water spilled from my world to the darkness, and as it created new currents, the intelligent souls nearby were washed away with the waves. I had been here before and witnessed a similar massacre. The waves of core souls eroding away against the watery onslaught horrified me. The remaining souls learned to stay away, and yet the more water that splashed in, the less room was left for the survivors.

Kyle got us as close as he dared. *There. Material from your world. But I don't recommend touching it.*

It's just water, I thought, and yet I knew to be scared. I may have survived the water with my body and some decent swimming lessons in my world, but here with my energies alone? I would be like one drop of food dye in a river. Gone in the second, diluted to nothing. And yet I said, *We gotta get out of here.*

I agree, Kyle said. *I tried it once, and it almost pulled me in. The current is strong. Maybe it'll be different for you since you know how it could act, understand it more.*

When Luke, Dinah, and I went to save Jack, the paradox nearly killed me, splitting the darkness from my body. It was like being torn in half. I didn't want to experience that again. *Maybe if I had an anchor,* I thought. *Something to hold onto. I could connect to the water and use it to get home.*

Penny, I have no hands to grab you, no legs to pull you back.

You pulled me here, didn't you?

It's just intention. I chose it, and so you followed.

So choose to be my solid anchor.

I'm not solid.

You know what I mean.

And you're not listening to me. Think about it, Penny. When all I am here are my thoughts, and I am in doubt, how could I possibly do it? It's not like in your world where life can prove you wrong. We are only our thoughts here. Which means right now, all I am is my doubts.

I frowned, and a large part of me felt the loss of Luke's optimism. But if what Kyle said was true, then the opposite must also be true. If I believed I could anchor myself against the current, would I become immovable?

Penny, don't risk it, Kyle warned. *There are worse things than being stuck here, and you being torn apart would be one of them.*

I have to try. I chose to get just a little closer and felt the movement. The energy here whooshed with a dizzying confusion, not the intelligence of souls, but what I could only define as air. Not oxygen, but this world's equivalent, the space between whatever existed. I mentally reached out and tapped the edge of the water. Like a spoon under a faucet, the current sprayed everywhere. On me—no, *through* me. No burst of physical pain, but a stabbing loss to my conscious. Like a core part of what made me *me* got swirled around and almost lost to the drops running through me. Almost. Disheveled and disoriented, I was still me.

I tried again, more gingerly. A tiny stream of droplets ran through me. A connection. *I got it,* I said. *Let's get —*

Ah, traitor and enemy together.

The Shadow's voice rattled through my head. Behind me, Kyle's soul vibrated like a scream, and my own soon joined in. The last time The Shadow and I met, it nearly squashed me like a bug. I was nothing compared to it. Especially here, especially now when all I was were my thoughts. The doubt took over, and water washed through me. I wanted to scream but had no lungs, needed to swim away but had no limbs. The current took me, overwhelmed me.

Penny, no, Kyle shouted. There was a tug, like someone trying to pull me out of the current. I needed safety. I needed air. *You have the connection to your world. Think! Get us out of here!* Kyle pleaded.

All I am are my thoughts. As soon as the sentence entered my mind, I knew I couldn't run. Instead, I pulled my attention from the flowing current, turned, and faced The Shadow head on.

Chapter 3

The energy went still. Shock, surprise, and bewilderment quieted every consciousness in the area. I used that to my advantage.

You made a mistake threatening me here, I warned.

Mistake? The Shadow sneered. *This is my world. You are an invader.*

I am Penelope Grace, and if I am my thoughts, then you better get out of my way.

I felt the energy pull back, like a tide lowering before the wave, and then a rush of darkness slammed into me. But I was too ticked to be afraid, so instead of becoming lost to the attack, I chose to be stronger and barely felt it rush around me.

I defied a paradox. I have seen your kind and learned how to control your darkness. I will NOT be pushed around or threatened!

I imagined my own wave of energy shooting away from my mind, empowered by my defensive stance, and felt The Shadow's domineering soul stutter in a moment of question. And in that moment, that split second of question, The Shadow was no bigger than a child. A scared, trembling child watching in horror as the monster of its nightmares finally escaped the closet and leered down at it.

The strange reaction caught me off guard, and I knew I wasn't the only one. The Shadow grew in power as if puffing its chest, and the loss of energy whooshed past me with too much energy. Time to go. I grabbed Kyle's soul and jumped into the water. The second the earthly water hit my mind, I wrapped a portal around us.

For the second time that day, the floor came rushing at me — carpet this time. I braced myself for painful impact as light and air flooded my senses. But the impact never came. Instead, I slowed to a stop, hovering about a foot above the floor. Right, I thought as I remembered, no body.

This feels really weird, I thought as I straightened up. Instead of a solid step, my soul slowly whooshed into position. I reached out my arm and saw only darkness. *I think I might be a ghost right now.*

We both are. Kyle stood up next to me, the pitch black silhouette. I had seen that before. He was all Void right now. *Think we're safe?*

From The Shadow, yes, I believed so. But would I ever feel safe with The Void? And yet, I felt guilty for my continued distrust after what he'd risked. If only I could shake the feeling that he was still manipulating me. Before, when I first met him, he used fear. Then we made deals. Who knows what he would try next to get what he wanted. The silhouette stepped in a circle, gesturing around us. *Should've guessed we would land here — your default safe zone.*

I'd been so busy trying to size Kyle up that I'd never noticed where we had landed. But as I took in the large study table, the whiteboard full of equations, and bookshelves of science books, a longing dread weighed down my heart. This was where it all started. Time traveling, meeting The Void, getting literally pulled into the darkness. But it also held memories of easy conversations, flirtatious glances, and lingering touches. This was where I first said I love you to a boy. This was where I left him alone and betrayed. My Stranger's basement.

I went to the equations on the whiteboard. No longer did it hold theories about time travel, dark energy, anything we could find to get an upper hand against the darkness. Gone were any signs of our experiments. The whiteboard had school work now. Luke was homeschooled, and the papers on the tables held only class notes. Everything connected to me was gone. I went to the calendar stuck to the board. Two weeks after I left. *He didn't waste any time, did he?* I said, and regret slammed into my gut. I wished I had my body so I could cry and get rid of it, but here it lingered and strangled my core. I was so easy to forget—friends at school, even my own parents. But Luke Hendricks had always been different. Or maybe not. Maybe me leaving him hadn't hurt him at all. I had been flattering myself, thinking he took the breakup as hard as me. I'd never even considered it might be easy for him to forget me. Seeing the proof in front of me made me want to crawl into a ball and cry to breakup songs. It was the final nail in a coffin. If someone like him could let go of me so easily, I must not be worth remembering.

Penny? Kyle came to my side, concern distorting his voice. *You okay? This place doesn't usually make you sad.*

But I didn't have time to answer him because a door upstairs slammed shut, and a familiar laugh tangled my emotions as footsteps started down the stairs. And then there he was, just a little taller than me, dusty blond hair, and compassionate pale blue eyes, built like a soccer player. Luke Hendricks had always been attractive, but it was his sunshine soul I missed the most, as bright as mine was dark, and in that moment, it was stronger than I'd ever seen. The black grief, which once sliced into his optimism, had softened to a mere speck. His brother came back to life. He was happy as he listened to the caller on his cell. Proof I'd made the right choice to leave him. Which hurt like hell.

"Hold up, I gotta find my wallet." Luke stepped to the desk

and started going to the piles. "Where did I put that? Wait, where?" He listened to the caller for a second and then turned to the bookcase and smiled. "You're right." He stepped to it and grabbed a small brown wallet, slipped it into his back pocket, and then rolled his eyes to something the speaker said. "Yes, Dinah, you're always right. Okay, I'll meet you at the theater, but I was serious about what I said before. If you're dragging me to this, then I'm going to make you watch the next investigating YouTubers my parents are so obsessed with. And if you're so bored waiting for me, buy us some popcorn and drinks. I can pay you back with cash." He laughed at her response. "Deal. Hey, I forgot to ask you, do you have the notes from that seminar — ?"

Luke stopped dead in his tracks as he stepped past the whiteboard, where Kyle and I lurked in our ghostly forms. Luke's eyes widened, and he snapped his gaze to us. Did he see me? No, his eyes whipped around, looking for something.

"Dinah, I need to call you back."

Luke hung up his phone. I felt frozen, desperate to see his response. Did he know I was there? When I first met him, he had zero psychic abilities but had developed a strong psychic touch since then. Could he feel me?

He squinted and stepped forward, a mere foot away from me. His breathing quickened, and he swallowed hard. That sunshine order spiraled with hopeful pinks, soft reasoning blues, and curious purples. He felt me. He remembered me. But then the soft blue of reason turned darker and spread around him like a suffocating blanket, killing the hopeful pink completely. He straightened up, blinked, and frowned with a sigh before returning his phone to his ear.

"I'm on my way." He glanced at us one more time, shook his head, and left.

You definitely need to catch me up on some things, Kyle whispered.

I watched the top of the stairs where Luke disappeared, and it took me a moment to register what Kyle had said. *Later. First, we need to get back into our bodies.*

It was an easy trip, really. The second I focused on creating a portal, a little time popped in my mind, my physical body open and waiting for the return of its own soul. I connected, and the whoosh of movement faded into a jerk of muscles as if I were falling. I snapped my eyes open, adrenaline pumping as if I'd woken from a dream. The energetic world held my eyesight as Shreya's aura flicked red, and the scream of surprise came from her direction. I blinked and waited for reality to return. Slowly, Shreya's concerned face sharpened into view.

"Ugh." I sighed and grabbed my head. Dizziness and the return of the petrified wood saturated air made me feel weak.

"You alive?" She asked.

"Yeah." I croaked and gestured weakly at the bed. "I found Kyle."

But the body on the bed remained still. She helped me to my feet, and we waited, watching. After a few moments, Shreya poked his cheek. "You sure he got out?" Crap. What if The Shadow got to him? He came with me when I connected back to our bodies, right? What else would he have done?

But then he shot up, making both of us jump back as he gasped for air and immediately groaned. "Ow, everything hurts." He eased back onto the bed. "My muscles, my poor knotted up muscles."

"You've been out for a couple of days." Shreya handed him a glass of water, which he drank too fast and sputtered.

"So my muscles revolt?" He moaned as he stretched his neck.

Sharia raised an eyebrow. "You've got a low threshold for pain," she noted. "Guess that makes sense. You've only been human what, a few months?"

He glared at her. Kyle was a lot of things, and having an easily bruised ego was top of the list. He stopped complaining and sat up, maintaining that glare as he stretched his arms. "My body is at least a year old," he said in defense.

"Oh," Shreya snorted. "Excuse me."

Kyle looked at her like he wanted to say something else but chose against it. They had a bit of a staring contest for a moment, as Shreya wordlessly dared him to say what was on his mind. Instead, he gave her a not-falling-for-that smirk before turning his attention to me. "I need you to tell me everything that happened when you saved Jack."

It wasn't exactly a story I liked going over, but I knew Kyle wasn't asking about the emotional side of things. He wanted the facts. Paradoxes were impossible, or so he thought. He had once told me there was no way both Jack and I could live, and I don't think he meant it to be rude. He was preparing me for a harsh reality, trying to prevent me from making a sacrifice we both knew I was willing to make. I think more than anything, Kyle wanted to know where he had gotten his calculations wrong. And so I gave him a more analytical response than I had given Shreya. The story of Jack's death had nothing to do with me. I had not met Luke at the time, nor did I know anybody else connected to that night. And I wasn't involved in any decision-making to go back in time and save him. That had been all Luke. The paradox was wrapped around him. Any decision to go back in time and save his brother would have disappeared because his brother would be safe, and therefore Luke would no longer need to go back in time, causing his brother to die. Time would have looped like a scratch on the record. But when Luke chose not to make a decision, chose to let go of his brother, the paradox broke, and I was able to save Jack.

When I finished explaining, both Shreya and Kyle looked at me as if they were both getting headaches. "That doesn't make any sense," Shreya said.

"So the only way to get out of the paradox is to let go of your goal?" Kyle frowned. "Let's be extra careful not to accidentally create a paradox. I have very specific goals, and I'm not willing to give them up."

"You're welcome to enlighten me on those goals anytime," I said. But the sound of cheery greetings on deck filtered through the walls to us, interrupting the conversation.

Ricky and Zetta were back, hopefully with enough rations to last a while. We all walked upstairs to see how we could help. Kyle limped a bit as feeling returned to his legs. I could tell he was trying to hide it after Shreya teased him.

At least that's what I thought until he reached the stairs and said in a pitiful voice, "I could use a little help." And he glanced pointedly at Shreya.

She chuckled. "Nice try. You'll find I'm not easily manipulated." Then she sidestepped him and started walking up the stairs.

Kyle watched her for a moment before giving me a hopeless shrug. "Well, it was worth a shot." And he bounded up the stairs after her.

I groaned inwardly, embarrassed to have witnessed that attempt at flirting, and frankly a little peeved because that would've been the perfect moment for Luke to smile at me and take my hand. We would have walked up the steps together and teased everyone else at how easy our relationship was. But instead, I walked up the stairs alone, keenly aware that this was the path I had chosen.

Ricky and Zetta Noble were an unusual couple. Ricky stood tall and wide like a pirate Santa in his early years, with a thick beard and wide shoulders. He had an earthly, solid aura, which always gave the impression of great big bear hugs. He had been born in Shakespearean times but spent most of his years growing up in a post-apocalyptic ghost town. Zetta, his wife and meditation guru had a rainbow aura of bright, fresh colors. She wore her hair in a pixie cut and no-nonsense dresses, which flowed with her steps with a feminine strength. She'd been born in said ghost town and learned it took creativity to survive from an early age. But she never let that stop her from creating the life she wanted. She and Ricky met, fell in love, and created a life of freedom on their ship full of adopted kids — until I came along and The Shadow followed. It attacked their ship to send me a message, and in an act of desperation, Kyle and I traveled the whole family to the only place we thought would be safe — the petrified wood forest in Arizona. Unfortunately, we accidentally landed them right smack in the middle of the Wild West era. But I wasn't worried about them holding the chaos of my life against me. Ricky himself invited me to stay, knowing one day I would have to leave the home where I no longer belonged.

But I was still shocked to see the giant smile of relief spread across Ricky Noble's face when he saw me. "Penny!" The giant rushed toward me with open arms, picked me up, and swung me in a hug like a kid. I laughed and hugged him back, grateful to feel so welcome. It was so rare a feeling. Lately, I treasured every second. Ricky and his family didn't feel like home. I knew that immediately. But this makeshift family did feel like visiting an uncle's house. I belonged here, even just as a guest. "You came back!" Ricky set me down and held me by the shoulders as if to take inventory that I was healthy and strong. "How?"

I pointed above him, where a door hovered alone over thirty feet in the air. "I had to get away from the sand," I explained.

He frowned. "That's quite the fall."

"Handy new healing powers," I reminded him. "But I'm afraid I can't jump that high, and unless we can reach the door somehow, I won't be able to make any portals."

He nodded. "There's a small town not too far from here. We should be able to make do until a staircase can be built. So," he clapped his hands, excitedly, "which one are you?"

I knew what he was asking. As we were both time travelers — me through tearing holes through reality via my new inner dark energy, and Ricky because I left one of those tears open in the form of a door — we never met in the same order. "I just came from Luke's house," I said. "We saved Jack."

Ricky's humor faded when I said Luke instead of Stranger. "Oh," he said. "You just left him."

My chest tightened. Ricky was there that day, told me I always had a home here and walked up the stairs to distract the others as I slipped away. At least, that's how it was supposed to go. But Luke caught on to Ricky's little distraction, ran downstairs to stop me, and we argued our goodbyes. When I ran away, Ricky stayed to clean up the mess.

"How long ago was that day for you?" I asked.

"A few years," he admitted. "Wondered if this version of you would ever show up or if you'd ran away from us too. I'm glad to see you came back. You always have a bed here." He reminded me of the promise he'd made that night.

"How did they take it?"

Ricky gave me a sympathetic pat on the shoulder. "Let's just say your sister can get quite creative with her threats. Poor Jack was confused and, as an officer, concerned that a minor had run away. I tried my best to explain your...situation is different than most."

I almost didn't want to ask, but.... "And Luke?"

Ricky tried to give me a smile, but it had no comfort to it as if he were thinking *That poor girl.* "I think your Stranger understood."

"So he's okay?"

"Quiet. He was quiet."

"He'll forget me soon enough," I said it as if to comfort myself that I hadn't hurt the boy I loved, but instead, it only made me feel worse.

Ricky frowned at that. "Penny, you know that's not how any of this works. Those of us who accept the darkness as a part of our realities remember you completely. Yes, to the oblivious, you may pass by unnoticed, but to us who have felt the darkness, who have stared eye-to-eye against the consequences of its existence, to us, you are a hero, friend, family, and treasure. Luke Hendricks will never forget you."

"He'll move on, though," I said.

"Perhaps." Ricky shrugged and straightened up but then gave me a pointed glance through the corner of his eye. "Because he moved on so gracefully after the loss of his brother. He didn't obsessively investigate theories on time travel and trigger a chain of events ultimately ending in the convoluted timeline we now exist in."

"I'm not family. It's not the same thing."

Ricky snorted. "Listen, I might not read energies as well as you, but I can read enough to understand the type of love he holds for you." He glanced at his wife. "It's not the kind of love one merely shrugs off after a breakup. Or any kind of separation."

"Stranger doesn't love me." I'd spoken the words to him once, back in that basement, but he never said a word back.

He cocked an eyebrow at that. "I see you're in the denial stage of this breakup. Warn me before you hit anger, will you? After seeing your sister ticked, I'd hate to see what you and your powers could do."

"Ha ha." I laughed dryly as he teased me. "My powers are useless here."

"Yes, I noticed that. You do look a little pale as well." He frowned at me in concern.

"Not feeling great, to be honest," I admitted. The petrified wood was a great place to hide away from The hateful Shadow, but it also attacked the darkness within me. It not only stifled my powers but my body. My muscles began to shake with exhaustion the longer I stayed in the open air, where dry wind blew up the sediment.

While Ricky and I caught up, Kyle spoke with Zetta and Shreya. One of them must have heard our change in conversation because they all stepped closer. Kyle looked as bad as I felt. Color drained from his face, and he held his arms firmly across his chest but couldn't hide the twitch of his fingers. "As welcoming as you all have been," Kyle said, "I'm afraid this is not a place we can stay." He looked at me when he spoke, and mouthed *I'm sorry* as the realization hit.

He was right. We couldn't stay there. Not because we had too much to do or because we were being chased, but because the land itself hated me and wanted me gone. It attacked my soul and weakened my body. This could not be a home base for me, which left me with nothing.

"We would have to walk through the desert to get away from the petrified wood. I made the trek once, but it wasn't pleasant," I said.

"Maybe we can figure out another way you two can come and go." Ricky looked to his wife. "What do you think?"

She frowned like she knew exactly what he was thinking. "They won't work together."

"Oh, sure they would for a time traveling door back," Ricky argued.

Kyle and I shared a confused look as Shreya groaned in realization. "What are you two talking about?" I asked.

"Two of my siblings." Shreya shook her head. "Both lost their families about six years ago, so Mom and Dad took them in. Steve is seventeen, and Dana…." Shreya pursed her lips out in thought. "She turns eighteen tomorrow. Anyway, they both have a natural engineering brain. Problem is they came from what you would see as futuristic Washington. Post the Cheyenne Circles and consequent drought. Washington had a lot of glaciers for a while, which meant the people had water there, but the limited resources caused tension between the people. The state split in two and, throughout the generations, began warring. Rumors of demonic descendants, animalistic manners," Shreya rolled her eyes. "The two cultures went all the way with their hatred of each other."

"The kids are great," Zetta defended them. "They both chose to live here with the blessing of the towns who couldn't feed them, and they treat the rest of the ship as family."

"But not each other," Ricky finished. "Hatred is a tough instinct to meditate away, especially when one excuses it as self defense. They both grew up being told that the other was evil and dangerous. But if we could get them to work together, perhaps we could makeshift a ladder or staircase to that floating door of Penny's, and get them a way in and out without touching the ground."

"That would be preferable," Kyle admitted with a leery glance at the sand and stones below us.

Zetta nodded to her husband in agreement and clapped her hands once, as if ready to get down to serious work. "That means I'm off to play supervisor. Davey," she called out to one of the smaller boys running around the deck, "come help Mommy. I need your puppy eyed expression to convince your siblings to help out."

"Meanwhile," Ricky gave Kyle an accusatory look as if Kyle were his kid and had come home past curfew. "I think it's time you brought us up to speed on a few things, young man."

I had to agree with him. Kyle left a lot unspoken, and the time of trusting blindly was over. We needed answers, and we were safe enough here to demand them. Yet, I knew I was more in the loop than Ricky. As I understood it, Ricky spent some of his teenage years with Kyle as one of his best friends. The two boys and teenage Zetta had gotten into a lot of mischief together. Now, decades later, Ricky found out his high school buddy was The Void. The Shadow had attacked the ship moments after that realization, so I doubted anyone here had much time to process. Now Kyle would have to answer for all the lies he'd spread.

Chapter 4

I have to admit I expected Kyle to protest—telling the truth didn't seem to be a natural instinct for him—but he nodded and sat down in one of the plastic beach chairs on the deck. We took his cue and sat down as well. I was glad to have the seat as my legs were getting shaky. Technically I would've preferred to go downstairs away from the open air and the constantly changing shift in the wind, which spurred up sediment and the conflicting energies of petrified wood and my own darkness. But there was no way I would ask everyone to move this meeting downstairs. I wanted to feel like I belonged. So I sat down, folded my legs underneath myself, and leaned into the back of the chair to conserve energy as Kyle began to speak.

"I think it's important that you all know I never intended for anything to get this complicated," Kyle said. "The plan was much more simple than reality turned out to be. I'm not the one who figured out how to travel between the worlds. That was my...I guess you humans would use the word friend. Penny met it. She called it Expert. The Expert is the one who snuck behind The Shadow's back, who opened a crack between the worlds and let me slip through. Only we couldn't do it alone. We needed somebody on the other side to complete the connection. That's when we found Luke Hendricks. His refusal to grieve his brother and determination to somehow get him back was the perfect opportunity. All The Expert had to do was nudge him along the way, little thoughts and ideas planted in his head to create the machine we needed. Of course, Luke didn't know we were there nudging him along—how could he? Few of you humans could see or hear us. So once he got his experiment working, it was a breeze to slip through unnoticed. Only I knew The Shadow would feel my absence the moment I left. And I was right. The Expert kept him off my trail as long as it could, but if I wanted to escape, to truly leave that world, I needed a fall guy." Kyle glanced at me and gave an apologetic shrug. "I needed to find somebody with strong natural psychic powers, who saw the world like us enough that The Shadow would believe that person was me. In my world, we exist only as thoughts. Once you convince us we are something, then we truly become that thing, whether it is scared, bored, clever, weak, or all powerful. So I thought that if I convinced Penny that she was from the other world, that she was the traitor, The Shadow would read her energies and be convinced too.

"But I underestimated her. Since my world only exists of darkness and thoughts, I had no idea of the power of memories. Of physical evidence. Penny knew she was human because she had a sister because she had a body. Although, I think I did manage to make her doubt herself a little."

Kyle was right. After growing up with natural empathic abilities, I never felt like I belonged. Always the freak. Always the girl who knew too much. It wasn't too much of a stretch to think maybe I never did belong there. Ironically, it turned out to be true in a way, since any hope of the home there had since faded away. But I didn't speak up—better to keep quiet and keep him talking.

"I started by teaching her how to control the darkness."

Kyle stood up and started to pace as he talked. His fingers still shook, and his face was still pale, but I had a confident guess that the accusatory gazes that Shreya and Ricky bore down on him were what gave him anxiety. This wasn't easy for him to admit, and I found myself relieved to see that this was hard on him. If Kyle was as heartless as I at first assumed him to be, he would have bragged about this plan. Watching him nervously confess made me feel sympathetic.

He brushed his hair back with his fingers as he continued. "I guessed correctly that Penny would be powerful and would catch on to controlling the darkness easily. Our energies are not so different than yours. It's all about intention, no matter the world. But I don't think even The Expert could've guessed how stubborn Penny would be. She didn't just learn how to control the darkness. She used it. She traveled through time, and she saved people, changing the natural timeline. Not that any of us cared. I sure didn't. Time to us really isn't anything important.

"I'm not sure when The Shadow caught on to our scheme. Long before I became human. I think it better understands human relationships, the power of love and hate and desperation. I admit I didn't understand it. I didn't understand why Penny insisted on going home to a town where she didn't feel like she belonged, where everyone treated her like she was a freak. Seemed to me that she would want to leave like maybe she would want to go back to my world where the locals would better understand her and her abilities. So while I was busy trying to manipulate you, Penny, The Shadow slipped into the past and changed your very DNA. Made you fifty percent human and fifty percent darkness. It was a power move and a good one. Because while I was thinking there was no reason you would want to stay, The Shadow believed there was no reason you would want to leave. That you would do anything to go back home. Even let Jack die, betray Luke, and help The Shadow close the portal The Expert and I had worked so painstakingly to create. But you did neither. You saved Jack, and you defied The Shadow." Kyle stopped pacing and looked at me. "The longer I've had a human body and experienced reality the way you humans do, the more I understand your interpretation of what I did. It was unforgivable. I can acknowledge that."

I didn't say anything and swallowed hard against the tightness in my throat. Because the more Kyle seemed to understand my side of things, the more I seemed to understand his.

"Wait," Shreya said. "You said after you got your human body. How did you even do that? Is that something everyone from your world can do?"

"No. As far as I know, just me. Although I got the idea from local myths shared in my world," Kyle said. "After I realized what The Shadow had done to Penny in her childhood, combining the two worlds, I...studied her DNA, her unique combination of energies. Then I replicated it."

Shreya and Ricky both looked between us, perhaps for the first time noticing the similarities in skin tone and eyes. "Whoa," Shreya said, then looked at me. "So he's your what? Clone?"

The Expert's offhand comment back in the dark world popped into my head. Brother. The Expert had called Kyle my brother. Perhaps genetically, but clone was as close as I could process right now. "Pretty much."

Ricky frowned in confusion. "So what about the Cheyenne Circles? The holes between the worlds? Was that because of you and your Expert trying to get out?"

Kyle shook his head. "The Expert's first portal was solid—100%. And though Luke's side of the experiment might have seemed unstable at the time, seeing as his calls for help caused Penny and Dinah to run into his house, I can assure you that the entire experiment was a success and controlled. That being said, I always assumed the Cheyenne Circles were my fault because I stayed on this side. I wanted to belong to this world so badly, and I had been told that that was wrong. So I assumed the two worlds ending was my punishment—some divine wrath.

"Turns out it was a scare tactic. The Shadow is opening the portals on purpose. I found out when I went back to my world to help Penny. The Expert found me and covered me as the Shadow searched. It told me what it could. The Shadow fears losing control, fears what might happen to its quiet, and mostly bland, world if thoughts got out that I had escaped. That it is possible to move, to change. It wouldn't be enough for me to surrender myself because I got to experience this world. The only way to close the portals is to undo everything we've done. To go back in time and stop me from coming through in the first place."

Well, obviously, that wasn't going to happen. Too much good had come out of it, even if it was unintentional on Kyle's part. Jack was alive. Ricky was able to grow up, find a home, meet his wife, and create this wonderful makeshift family. Not even including the random rescues Luke and I had successfully pulled off as we traveled from time to time.

"There is another way," I said. Everybody looked at me, waiting. "We overpower The Shadow."

Ricky's mouth dropped. Shreya cocked an eyebrow in shock, and Kyle laughed as if I had told a joke.

"You can't overpower The Shadow. None of us can. Have you forgotten how big that thing is?" Kyle asked. "We're lucky it prefers to play mind games because if it had wanted us dead, we would've died long ago. We wouldn't even be born."

"You said it yourself. It's just a thought," I argued. "The Shadow isn't all-powerful. It just thinks it is."

"Therefore, it is," Kyle spoke slowly as if I didn't understand.

"Right now," I agreed. "But thoughts change. If this Shadow loves mind games so much, let's give it one. Turn the tables. Start fighting back."

"How are we supposed to do that?" Ricky asked.

"I'm not sure yet," I admitted, but that flash of The Shadow when I fought it in darkness kept coming up in my head. Behind that all-powerful, manipulative being was a terrified soul fighting the monster of its childhood. "We could wrap a paradox around it and trap it, or maybe make some kind of weapon that'll keep it from our world. The Shadow is more powerful than us, but no way can it outmuscle a paradox. It's just an idea, but every plan has to start with one. I think we can do this. We can't give up. I've spent too much of my life exceeding expectations, doing the impossible, to give up based on a little intimidation."

I looked to Kyle, hoping that he had my back. But Kyle had a tendency to go even more cynical than me. His plans usually consisted of run and hide.

But to my surprise, he nodded. "Okay," he said. "We'll have to be careful — one mistake, and it's over — but you're right. We've come too far to just give up now."

Kyle's support meant more than I expected. I had been ready for a fight, to have to defend my choices each step of the way. But when I looked around, everyone shared my determined expression, albeit with varying degrees of apprehension. It occurred to me that my days of having to prove myself might be over. Better yet, maybe I wasn't as alone as I thought.

Chapter 5

Our conversation was interrupted by arguing coming from the stairs. Zetta led a group of kids of varying ages, most of whom wore exasperated expressions as the two in the front snapped at each other. The girl, Dana, kept calling the boy "grey water," while the boy, Steve most likely, claimed her volumized hair hid devil's horns. Zetta scolded them, and they both apologized to her before glaring at each other.

Dana only stopped glaring once the hating duo reached the door hovering directly above them. She looked up and squinted. "That's quite the climb."

Steve stood next to her and mirrored her squint. "We have rope in the storage."

"Not thirty feet."

"Our tallest ladder is what, six feet? We need a higher, sturdy base."

Just like that, the glares were forgotten. Dana and Steve bounced ideas off each other, some of which Zetta immediately nixed for being too dangerous. They continued to call each other names, but it lost the hatred, almost becoming sibling banter. It reminded me of when I was little. Dinah and I convinced Mom it was okay to play mutiny in the living room. The game consisted of foam swords, a ball for keepaway, and Dinah's kindergarten spelling bee award. The owner of the trophy was in charge until the other rebelled and successfully stole it. It was usually an outdoor game, but a long stretch of spring snowstorms made us antsy and, now that I thought back, extremely annoying. We convinced Mom it was fine to play indoors, and we'd be careful. Long story short, I broke Mom's favorite lamp, but we'd been in sync when it came to convincing her to let us play indoors in the first place. We could finish each other's sentences back then. Ugh, I missed those days so much it hurt. The days when I belonged and life was normal. Bantering with Dinah. Eating dinner with Mom and Dad. Maybe I wasn't as over my past life as I thought.

"Penny, you okay?" Shreya asked.

"Huh? Oh, sorry." I gave her a smile and returned my mind to the present. The past was over. No good dwelling on it. Better busy than mopey. "How can I help?" I stood up too fast, and a wave of nausea made me sway on the spot. I swallowed hard and could feel the blood rush out of my face with dizzying speed.

Ricky frowned at me. "I think you should take it easy."

"No, I want to help."

"They've got plenty of hands if they need them." Shreya waved at the siblings running below deck to retrieve whatever Dana and Steve mentioned might be useful.

Kyle looked as pale as I felt, and he glared at the blaring sun as he spoke. "If you help, I have to get up and help. No one wants me to be in their way."

"You should go downstairs," I suggested. "Get away from the petrified wood. You're more connected to the darkness than me. I can handle this." Their doubt fueled my willpower and, though I didn't feel even a touch better, I would have run across the deck to prove I was fine if another person doubted me.

Shreya jumped to her feet with a sudden urgency. "Emergency meeting downstairs. Right now."

"What?" We all chorused, but she grabbed my arm and half-dragged me down the stairs. As weak and sick to my stomach as I was, it took all my effort just to stay upright. She gestured at Kyle, who looked relieved as he followed us off deck. She didn't stop until we were downstairs and back in her bedroom. The distance from the open air relieved some of the pain, and my stomach started to calm down.

"What was that all about?" I asked.

"You had a stubborn face." She let go of my arm and knelt down to grab something from under her bed.

"I did not. And I could have helped," I persisted.

Kyle snorted at my words as he sat down on the corner of Shreya's bed, and she gave me a *who are you kidding* look I didn't appreciate but agreed I probably deserved.

"You'd help or die trying. Not everything has to be so dire, you know," she said. "This stupid bag's stuck—"

She gave a hard tug, and a bag of candy appeared. She dumped it on the bed and gestured for us to take our pick as she plopped down on the pillows. I grabbed a Snickers and took a seat in a vintage style rocking chair which swung precariously far back before moving forward again.

"So," Kyle said as he sucked on his teeth after chewing on a caramel. "The plan is to play mind tricks on The Shadow, huh? Any ideas where to start?"

I shrugged. "What do you know about it?"

"Just what I've told you."

"You know what would really mess with it?" Shreya asked as she crunched on Nerd candies. "If we knew what its biggest fear was and played off that. And I'm not talking about fear of spiders or something. Real deep, subconscious stuff. Like what Mom talks about with her meditations. A core fear that's part of our identity, something we think is true but negative about ourselves. Something that holds us back makes us think in limitations."

My mind flashed to when I faced The Shadow back in the dark world. How, just for a moment, it shifted from an imposing dictator to a scared kid looking up at a monster. Was that how The Shadow saw humans? What was that all about?

"A core fear. Like what?" Kyle asked. He stuck his pinky in his mouth and started picking at the caramel between his teeth.

She sighed. "Like…I guess for me, it would be my fear that I'm not supposed to exist. I'll never fit in anywhere outside of this ship because I wasn't supposed to be…anywhere."

"That's not true," I said instantly. "You exist, so you're supposed to exist."

"I didn't say any of that for a pity party." Shreya held up her hands to stop me. "And goodness knows I get plenty of affirmations from my mom. But one, nothing anyone else says can convince a person to give up on a core fear like this unless the person themself chooses to let go of it, and two, I was just giving an example. Everyone has one."

I thought for only a moment before recalling mine. One Kyle used to his advantage in the past. "I'm forgettable. Even before all this, I was forgettable." I reached out and grabbed another candy.

Shreya looked to Kyle. "What's yours?"

He scuffed. "We're not like you humans."

She rose an eyebrow. "What's. Yours?"

Kyle opened his mouth to give another snarky response, but something in the way Shreya looked at him must have made him change his mind. He sighed, and his shoulders caved in a bit. "I don't know if this is what you're looking for, but I always had this thought in the back of my mind. That I'll never change. I'll always be what I am."

"Which is?" I asked.

Kyle tapped his thumb against his knee. "Desperate. The Shadow is like our leader. Although tyrant might be a better word. There's no life or death in our world. No time. Everything simply is. Shadow says it's the purest way to be. To wish to change is to go against the natural order of the dark world. Which works great for The Shadow because it loves control and orders. And I'm realizing how good it is as manipulation, convincing souls to blame themselves. The Expert has always been smart, cocky, and quick to lie for the masses—a cushion between us and The Shadow, who has been in control as long as I remember.

"But me?" Kyle stood up and started absentmindedly studying the posters plastered along Shreya's bedroom wall as he spoke like he needed a distraction. "I've *always* been *wrong*. My thoughts and reactions were just a little different than everyone else's. And while all the other sounds there are content to simply exist, I got bored. Actually, humans and I have a similar reaction to boredom. When you're bored, you search for something to do. Music, a book, calling a friend. But when that's not an option, which was the case with me, humans become anxious. And then desperate. Humans have gone insane from it before. The world around me was still, and I was going crazy from the stress of it all. The never changing silence. I became desperate, and then desperation became me."

"Fresh start," I whispered. Those were the words I heard—gosh, it felt like so long ago. Shreya looked at me in confusion, but Kyle gave me a look I'd never seen before. Gratitude because I *saw* him. In that second, I knew exactly who Kyle was. "The first thing you said when you entered our world and stole Luke's memories. You said '*I'm sorry. I need a fresh start.*'"

"Did you get it?" Shreya asked. "Does being human fix your desperation?" The way she spoke told us she knew the answer was no.

"I'm not bored, but no, it didn't work. I'm still desperate."

"Maybe it's less about being bored and more about feeling trapped," Shreya guessed.

He considered it a moment as he picked through the candy but eventually shook his head. "Not really either. What if The

Shadow is right and our kind aren't capable of change? What if I can never be happy because I *am* desperation?"

Holy crap. Shreya and I shared a wide-eyed look before staring at him. He continued to sift through the candy, still sucking on a caramel-covered tooth in annoyance as he searched for a sweet good enough to eat. One, perhaps, that might satisfy him.

"That's one extremely depressing thought." Shreya finally broke the silence.

To my surprise, Kyle laughed. He dismissed all the candies and leaned against the wall. "Tell me about it." He sighed and stared at the ceiling for a moment as if reclaiming his thoughts. "You're unto something, Shreya. I'd do anything for proof my kind can change. That I can change. If we learned The Shadow's fear, we could use that."

"Think The Expert would know?" I asked.

"If it did, it would have told us by now."

"Well, I can't read The Shadow's mind, and if time doesn't technically exist in the dark world, then we can't travel through it. How else could we get the information?"

Kyle smiled as, I hoped, an idea formed. "Now there's a thought," he said. "I knew about this world all my existence. Everyone did. It was a part of us like the universe is to you. You know that beyond the blue, there's galaxies, even if you've never been there. But there were these myths about the Old Ones, souls like us but who traveled to Earth, who aged with the time spent there. They grew to be extremely powerful and even interacted with humans, experienced the worlds as humans did. The Shadow would tell us it's the only Old One left. That the rest came here and died. The Expert and I always thought it was just a story, to make The Shadow seem older and different, more powerful than us. But what if it's true? What if The Shadow really did come to Earth before? With others?"

"We'd know about it, right?" Shreya asked. "I mean, wouldn't a human have written it down?"

But I shook my head. "There's lots of ancient stories about meeting mystical creatures out there. If it did happen, it might have been lost or saturated amongst other myths."

"Hmmm…." Shreya furrowed her eyebrows in thought. "You know, for most humans, that core fear becomes ingrained in our minds between the ages of birth through eight. You said that in the dark world, there is no time, not really. Everything just stays the same, right?" Kyle nodded. "So if The Shadow and the Old Ones came to Earth, one might say they started aging as soon as they crossed to this side. Perhaps their minds became open to new fears. Maybe something happened to The Shadow which made it return to the dark world a complete control freak and tyrant."

I started to catch on. "And if we found that time period where The Shadow first experienced Earth, maybe we could get an idea of how it thinks."

"And how to control it," Kyle agreed. "I like this plan."

Chapter 6

It took the rest of the day and deep into the night before a temporary ladder system reached the hovering door. Ricky came down to tell Shreya, Kyle, and me. "It's too late to do anything tonight," he said. "Let's wait until morning. Have some breakfast and make a plan. Then we'll go from there."

"He's delaying," Shreya muttered under her breath once her dad left. "Dad doesn't want you to leave."

"We can wait until morning," I justified. "Sleep might be a good idea." Although, to be honest, I didn't feel sleepy. My body ached, and my soul felt small, hiding from the petrified wood. But I didn't want to disappoint Ricky. Even when he was angry at me, the door was always open. I was always welcome, and I didn't want to do anything to risk losing that.

Kyle didn't feel as concerned. "I'm not staying in this hateful desert one more second."

He stood up to leave, but I grabbed his arm.

"The plan is to wait until morning."

"Ricky's plan. He's not my boss."

Shreya clicked her tongue in thought. "We could wait until they fall asleep and then sneak out."

I rose an eyebrow at that. "We?"

She grinned wickedly. "Yeah. Come on, you two need someone to keep you from going overboard. Kyle, no offense, but you tend to lean toward chaotic neutral at best. And Penny, you have a strong self-sacrifice personality. Besides, I'm going stir crazy. I've been time traveling my whole life, and it's been *ages*."

"It's been a week, right?" Kyle asked.

"Yeah. Exactly." She waved at Kyle as if he'd proven her point.

"I don't know...." I let my voice trail off. Leaving in the middle of the night would offend Ricky enough, but taking his daughter with me? That might be hard to forgive. On the other hand, she and I rarely got a chance to hang out. I was always zooming from one time to the other, always on a mission. Our paths rarely crossed, but we got along, and I had the sneaking suspicion she could be a forever kind of friend. It would be nice to travel with a friend. Not a boyfriend or an estranged sister, or a clone/void who had limited bothers about humanity.

"How about this?" Shreya rose her hands up and jumped off the bed with a bounce of energy. "We sneak out tonight, go to the door, and say if future me walks through the door and says it's a bad idea, then I'll stay."

"Wait, what?" Kyle asked the same time I said, "That's possible?"

"Of course, it is. Don't worry. Steve and I did it all the time back when we had a door. That way, we know it's fine to travel."

Kyle looked at me and gave a shrug. "What do you think? I'm down."

I sighed. "All right."

So we waited until everyone went to bed. Kyle mentally scanned the ship for any auras out of bed before giving the all clear and, just like that, the three of us snuck out up the stairs.

The second Shreya opened the door to the deck, the fresh petrified wood saturated air slammed against me. I faltered and almost lost my step but caught it in time. "Geez," I mumbled. Kyle grunted in agreement next to me, his hand a little tighter around the stair rail. But we made it to the deck and took in the makeshift stairs.

Makeshift was the key word. A table stood at the base, adding a few feet before a weighted down ladder led to....

"That's just rope," Kyle gasped.

"It's a rope elevator," Shreya sighed in amazement. I admit I probably would have been more amazed if it wasn't for the fact that we'd be trying it in a few minutes. Ropes interweaved together along the distance between the top of the ladder to the floating door. A hanging bathtub took the place of the elevator, which touched the tip of the ladder. Gadgets and gears hung off both sides with a lever for, I assumed, moving up and down. "This is practically art." Shreya walked around it.

"But will it work?" Kyle asked. "Looks like that door itself will be holding the weight."

"Did Ricky say they tried it already and it was all clear?" I asked. I tried to remember Ricky's exact words but couldn't trust what my fearful brain came up with.

"It works. Dad said they tested it." Shreya started up the stairs. "Ready?"

Kyle and I exchanged a nervous look. On the one hand, we had quick healing, which would help if this whole thing collapsed on us, but Shreya didn't. On the other hand, Kyle's fingers shook from being in the open air too long, and I was starting to get woozy. If anything, it felt worse than before. How long could we last in this forest?

"We're as ready as we'll ever be," I said, and Kyle nodded. So we jumped onto the table and looked straight up. I'd never had vertigo before, but looking up at the long distance between us and the door, thinking all the ways this could go wrong, made me dizzy.

"I'll go first," Shreya said and started climbing up the ladder with no hesitation. Kyle and I both held onto the ladder just in case it wobbled. There were a few moments where the weight shifted, but it seemed to hold firm. So far. Finally, she made it to the top of the ladder and climbed into the tub. "It'll be a tight fit," she said as she looked around. "But we can make it. No dancing when you're up here, you two."

"I think we'll be safe from that happening," Kyle groaned.

"Although a tub would make for good tap dancing sounds," Shreya admitted and started tapping against the porcelain. Kyle and I both cringed in fear, and she laughed. "You two are too easy. Get up here before we get caught."

I went next because Kyle looked a little frozen in place. Each step seemed to take forever, but I was not going to trip and fall on this thing because I was rushing it. The worst part was stepping from the ladder to the tub. The tub swung a bit from the added movement, but Shreya grabbed my hand and tugged me in.

"That wasn't so hard, right?" She teased.

"Shut up," I playfully moaned as my hands gripped the edge of the tub for dear life. "Okay Kyle, your turn."

"I changed my mind. I'm just going to waste away here where The Shadow can't find me, and I can't fall to a painful demise."

Shreya raised an eyebrow. "Wow. You're dramatic. But okay." She shrugged and reached for the lever.

"Wait." He grumbled to himself and started up the ladder. Shreya and I made room, and he squeezed in between us. "Now what?"

Shreya started winding up the lever on her end, and I did the same on mine. There was a bit of resistance, but considering the weight we were moving, I was impressed by the ease and functionality. It was, if anything, too easy.

We'd gotten about a foot away from the ladder when Shreya's speed went quicker than mine. The tub went uneven, and everyone slipped into my side of the tub. Shreya was quick to react, though, and unwound the difference before anyone fell off. After that, we moved in careful unison. Kyle counted us off, keeping a steady beat. The ship became smaller and smaller as the vast expanse of the Wild West desert took over the dark horizon.

"Wow," Kyle said. "It's gorgeous."

He looked better, the higher we got, more color to his cheeks, and I felt my stomach starting to settle. The less pain I was in, the more I could appreciate the natural beauty around us. Funny how something which made me so sick could be so pretty.

The tub hit the bottom frame of the door, and we jolted to a stop. "All right, let's get out of here." Kyle steadied the tub by the door with his hand. "Where should we go?"

I thought back to the myths he'd told of the Old Ones from his world. "Do you think you could find where The Shadow first came to our world?"

Kyle gulped. "Those are myths, Penny. I don't know if they're real. And if they aren't, then we'll be running straight toward The Shadow, who wants us dead."

"But what if we could find out why The Shadow hates my world and change so much? We can use that against it."

He sighed as if annoyingly getting the point. "When he spoke of the myths, there was always water nearby. The land split into water, and water from the sky, some falling from cliffs. And there were islands — it called them pockets of land. Lots of greenery. The Shadow spoke most often about a circle of rocks, five circles growing out. That's one of the places they came through. Right in the middle of the circle. Oh, and sheep. The Shadow definitely talked about sheep."

"Sheep?" Shreya squinted in thought.

Kyle grabbed the doorknob and closed his eyes. "Let me see if I can find it. I've never thought to go there. Mostly because there's a high chance of running into the one being who wants us dead —"

"You've said that already," I pointed out.

"You didn't seem appropriately concerned the last time." He

paused and gave a deep frown.

"What?" Shreya and I chorused.

"I think I found it."

Chapter 7

Kyle swung open the floating door, and we all gasped as cold air rushed through. The view was enchanting. Moss and wildflowers blanketed the ground. Large cliffs marked the horizons, and birds sang from the distance. If magic were a land, it would be there. Salt flavored wind filled my lungs, seasoned with a mossy freshness. Naturally carved rocks were set in five perfect circles set inside each other, and we were in the middle.

Kyle stepped through first and turned to help Shreya and me through. The second my body crossed the threshold, an overpowering connection to the spiritual world took over my physical senses. The rocks were a natural, balanced red, and dots of yellow auras marked where birds hid within the bushes. Shreya's aura sighed with a peaceful, curious blue as she looked around. And there was the blackness, the darkness which was Kyle and me. Only two dark auras. By the time my physical sight returned, I knew we were the only sources of darkness there. The Shadow and the Old Ones weren't there. Either we were in the wrong place or at the wrong time. But fresh air invigorated my tired soul, and I felt the severe release from the petrified wood.

"It's breathtaking." I slowly turned around, taking in every changing view around us.

"This is the fairy glen." Shreya spoke with as much awe as me, though she obviously knew more.

"The what?" Kyle asked.

"It's in the Isle of Skye, Scotland. They say the veil between the human and fairy realms is thin here. See that?" She pointed at what looked like the ruins of a castle, jutting through the periwinkle blue sky. "It looks like ruins, but it's natural stone, nothing manmade. So the legends ask what if it belonged to the fairies?" She smiled. "This place is on my bucket list. I've always wanted to go, but it's not exactly rich in supplies. Dad likes to kill two birds with one stone and stock up wherever we travel, so we never came here. I can't believe this." She closed her eyes and opened her arms to fully feel the power of the sea wind. Then, with a "Don't leave without me" mumble over her shoulder, she went to explore.

The view was magical enough. I understood why people might think fairies would live there. But as beautiful as it was, the longer we were away from the desert, the more likely The Shadow would find us. So we needed to get a move on and find the actual spot The Shadow traveled to before it became a tyrant, or we wouldn't have anything to use when it did show up.

But then Kyle nudged me and said, "I bet I can make a portal to the top of that cliff before you."

Maybe I needed to blow off some steam after leaving my old life because I said, "You're on." I closed my eyes and imagined a connection between where I was now and the most level spot of the top of the cliff. I stepped through, and the grassy, soft ground turned to hard stone. Again the physical sight faded to the spiritual, but I could see Kyle's darkness pop into place just above me. It teetered on the spot, and I snorted. "You're going to fall."

"I said the top of the cliff," he responded. His aura leaned precariously to the side and then blinked out of sight, only to pop back into view right next to me. "Technically, I won."

"No, I got here first."

"But you cheated because no one said go."

"Fine." I blinked away the remaining spiritual sight and pointed at some hills in the nearby distance. Shreya was already over there, squatting at some wildflowers. "Last one to make it to the other side has to say the winner is the best."

"Oh, I'm so ready to hear you say that," Kyle smirked. "Ready?"

"Set."

"Go!" We chorused.

I would have won if I hadn't heard the voices chattering. At first, I thought it was disembodied, that perhaps the Old Ones truly were there. But then humans stepped into view from behind a cliff with spears, swords, and armor from the days of the Romans, or maybe earlier. I didn't know enough about history, but I knew an army when I saw one. I connected to where Kyle had already portaled, near Shreya, and jumped to them.

"You can't just portal behind me and freak me ou— Aah!" Shreya's aura jumped as I appeared next to her. "Ugh, why can't you two go through doors like every other time traveler?"

"Army over there," I said, quick to get to the point. Shreya's eyes widened, and Kyle groaned as if to say *just our luck.* "We should go—" I started, but then yelling interrupted my reasonable reaction.

We all ducked in surprise and hid behind the safety of the cliffs. But I risked a peek around the corner. The small army had gathered in a circle, and one man in decorated armor, most likely the leader, shouted into the wide, perfect circle they'd created. "We've come to make a deal!"

The dark tendrils appeared dead center of the circle. The men didn't appear to see it because no one ducked in fear. The leader repeated his demand, but the darkness was already there, escaping in controlled measures, never touching the ground as it grew and grew. A portal. And then —

"The Shadow," Kyle whispered as the familiar energies settled in the air, measured, analytic, and so heartless, I wanted to shiver from the coldness of it. But this wasn't the same Shadow Kyle and I knew. There were no undertones of rage and revenge, none of the toxic stubbornness which created our mutual enemy. This was The Shadow back in the beginning. And it wasn't alone.

Five beings stepped out of the portal, of various heights and widths, but it was clear The Shadow was the youngest of the group. It watched their steps before moving, unsure and following the lead of others. They mirrored the circle around them, face to face with the humans, and only once everyone was in place did the portal close, and each stepped onto the ground. The humans reacted to the searing of darkness on moss, sudden footprints of charcoal in a perfect circle. Only one human remained still, the leader who, now that I looked closer was not a military leader, but a religious one. A priest, perhaps? Protective symbols hung off rope around his neck. He wore sigils instead of armor and held no weapons. While the rest of the army stared at the seared proof of the darkness nearby, he looked eye level with the shadows. He saw them. Why? How? My only guess was that his occupation as a religious leader meant many hours of meditation and prayer, which connected him to the energies, much like Zetta and her family were aware of the darkness even if they didn't see them like Kyle and me.

We are here, the tallest of the dark figures said directly to the religious leader.

The priest shivered and grimaced. "We need to make a deal. Our people are under attack, and we need aid."

What are you willing to give for it?

"We have gold —"

Gold is meaningless.

The priest cringed. "We then offer our souls for the protection of our people."

Kyle groaned next to my ear. "Shreya, you're killing my arm. Wanna loosen up?"

I turned to see her face had gone pale, and her fingers dug into Kyle's skin. "This is a demon's deal," she whispered.

But before Kyle and I could react, the priest continued. "But I warn you, I plan on getting my men back. I will find a way to your hell and destroy you with swords that do not melt."

The shadows laughed, and it was an eerie sound—five creatures of darkness with an empty confidence echoing against the cliffs of Skye.

I do not fear your threats. The deal is made. We will help you in your war.

The priest's face went deathly pale. The shadows disappeared. "They're gone," the priest said, sounding sick. "It is done."

No one celebrated. They stared at the scalded footprints in the ground, the only evidence of the moment, and with solemn reverence, they found large rocks and placed them over the burns, as if hiding their deal from the world. Then they picked up their weapons and continued on their march. All that was left were five rocks in a perfect circle.

And three teenagers from another time.

"I don't understand," Kyle said. Shreya had let go of his arm, and he absentmindedly rubbed feeling back into the red area. "What was that?"

"A demon's deal," Shreya repeated as she stared at the circle. "I always thought it was some kind of religious myth, a tall tale to teach the consequence of giving in to one's temptation. Almost every religion or mythology has some story of a dark, evil being making deals to help people in exchange for their souls. A moment's happiness and an eternity of torture in hell. When those men die, their souls are torn from their bodies, and they're tortured for eternity unless they beg their God for forgiveness."

"No." Kyle shook his head. "There's no human souls in the dark world. Whatever deal they made, that wasn't it."

"He's right," I said. "There's no human souls there. Although…." I frowned. "Would we know?"

Kyle blinked at me like I couldn't see the obvious. "I mean, the colors are kind of a giveaway." He gestured at Shreya, whose aura tensed in a light flash of red at being in the spotlight.

"Right, but I'm human," I said. "And look at me. The Shadow knew exactly what to do to turn my soul dark. What if that's what it did back in the past with the old ones? What if they took souls?"

"Why?" Kyle asked. "What's the point of that?" He seemed defensive.

"I don't know," I admitted. "Did you recognize any of the others?"

Kyle shook his head. "No. Just The Shadow, but the others were all gone before I came to existence."

"How does that work?" Shreya said. "I thought your people were immortal. But how can one be born and not die?"

"We weren't born, and we always existed, but my conscious, the version of me that had thoughts, developed over time. Just like my desperation grew over time, I first had to grow awareness."

Thinking about how that might work made my head hurt. "Okay, well, what happened to the rest of the Old Ones?"

Kyle glanced at the rocks. "The Shadow said this world was evil, full of traitors and pain. It claimed to be protecting us from the horrors of change that happen here."

"You found this place because you were looking for the history of The Shadow's hate for this world," Shreya reminded him. "So maybe we need to find out how that battle went."

Battles were never my favorite places to travel. Last time I stepped into the middle of a war, I'd gotten shot. But Shreya was right. We needed answers. "Let's stick to the outer edges of it," I reminded everyone. "We're there for research, not to interfere."

Kyle nodded. "I'll find it," he said and closed his eyes. Shreya and I shared an awkward expression as we waited. Nervous energy made me want to bounce on the balls of my feet, but I didn't want to interrupt his meditation by squirming around. Still, just knowing we were going to a battle next made me hyper aware. Dark energy I could see and fight, but I had few fighting skills.

Kyle didn't warn us he'd made the connection before wrapping a portal around us, so I had no time to prep before we were jolted through.

Chapter 8

Screams and a watery confusion churned through my conscious as we traveled through the portal to the battle. Then my feet hit solid ground, and it all caught up with me. "Oh, geez." I leaned over, hands on my knees, as a dizzying wave spilled over me. Overwhelming colors burned my eyes as a red-hot fear screamed in front of me. "A little warning next time."

"Sorry," Kyle said, and he half sounded like he meant it, which would have been a big deal if I wasn't too busy trying not to hurl. "I forgot you get like that."

"Is it always that bad?" Shreya asked, somewhere to my left.

"You do seem more pale than usual," Kyle admitted.

"Did you feel that? When we traveled?" I loosened my grip on my knees and, when the ground remained steady, risked straightening up. "All those souls."

"It's getting bad," he agreed. "If we don't act soon, there won't be any souls left to save."

"What did I miss?" Shreya asked.

"The dark world is...." I shook my head. "The screams are getting louder. Whole place feels unsteady." I blinked and stared wide eyed around me, waiting for the physical world to return.

And wow, what a view.

The enchanting grasslands and cliffs were a breathtaking background, and there at the base, sandwiched between the sea and a forest, was a village. The houses were small and modest but also designed in intricately skilled patterns and symbols. Gold jewelry and carved wood. The people wore animal skins and fabric in practical yet flattering styles. I wanted to place us around Roman times but had to admit I had no idea. They didn't seem Roman. Celtic?

The elders gathered the kids and pulled them into the houses. The adults, men and women, grabbed spears and swords in a frantic race. Near the shore, the army who made the demon's deal with the Old Ones lined up, weapons ready and armor tight. One look at the sea, and I understood the fear.

Roman fleets surged through the currents, way more than needed to take this small village. This wouldn't be a battle—it would be a massacre.

Shreya shifted next to me. "Are the Old Ones here?" she asked. "When are they going to interfere?"

I shook my head. The skies were clear of darkness. No Old Ones, no dark energy to give this small town a fighting chance. Not even a cloud in the sky. The bright sun beamed down at them as if to shout, "Here they are! Straight ahead!"

"What do you know about the Old Ones?" I asked Kyle. "Were they tricksters? Reliable? Are they coming?"

Kyle stared at the scene before us. He had to see the impending doom, the hopeless way the army stood with their weapons, not ready to save but to go down defending their people. "I don't know," he whispered. "I don't.... I don't think they understand death, so maybe they wouldn't take it seriously?"

"But they made a deal. They can't take souls if the humans die."

"Like I said, they wouldn't understand death."

From one of the houses, a kid escaped the arms of her

grandma and raced out. A woman from the front line with the same blonde hair and heart-shaped face turned and dropped her weapon. She picked up the kid and raced back to the house as the kid cried.

"We're helping, right?" Shreya asked.

Kyle sighed. "That's usually the plan." He spoke reluctantly as if this was some annoying human trait he'd rather we got over. But I caught how his eyes followed the kid, the tightness around his mouth as he held back emotion. The indifference was an act. He didn't need colors in his soul for me to see the concern there.

I took the first step toward the village. Without a word, they kept up. Our speed increased until we were at a full run toward them. The woman saw us first. She pushed her kid toward the safety of the house and reached for a knife at her belt but didn't pull it out. Her eyes went to our clothes and any threats we might pose. "We can help," I said and held up my hands to show we were weaponless. She didn't release her knife, but she didn't aim it at us either, so, given the circumstances, I figured that was as good as we could get.

"Who are you?" the woman asked.

"We're just passing through and saw the ships." I waved at the dotted horizon.

"We refuse to join the Romans," she said, and her chin rose. Her defensive aura deepened with a stone colored strength. The land around us was such a part of her home that as she searched for strength within, her soul mimicked the power of the cliffs.

"Why don't you run?" Shreya asked.

But the answer came when an older lady limped to the front of the shelter and grabbed the kid to take back inside, to hide because they couldn't run—not the old, sick, and too young. The able fought, and the rest hid, but the community all stayed together.

A fresh wave of determination slammed against my chest. I would help these people. No one in this village would die. I could scare the Romans. If Kyle and I worked together, we could disarm every single one of them and use the darkness to create a supernatural, theatrical bluff which would have them turning their ships around without any bloodshed.

"Come on." I grabbed Kyle's arm, and half dragged him to the front of the line.

"Hey, watch it," he said, and stumbled after me. "And just so you know, blowing up the ships would be ten times more efficient than a whole big act."

"We don't kill people," I reminded him.

He tossed his head from side to side as if to say *we could, though.*

"What are you doing?" The woman chased after us and asked, just as Shreya asked, "What's the plan?"

"We're getting rid of the Romans." I reached the line of soldiers. They all turned and measured my apparent threat levels.

A few asked the woman who we were, but she waved them aside and asked me, "Can you do that?"

"I can try," I promised. Then, grinding my heels into the rocky shoreline for a steady stance, I took a deep breath and raised my hands, ready to connect to the darkness and put on a show.

"Wait." Kyle put an arm out over mine. "They're here."

A second later, I saw them, large darkened masses in the sky. Like clouds of black holes, they hovered above the ships. Huge, thick tendrils streaked down like silent lightning and slammed against the water. Waves splashed, the ships swayed, and then....

The splintering cracks were so forceful the sound of it reached the shore. Like a knife through butter, the tendrils sliced through the Roman ships. They were too far away for us to hear the screams, but I'd been on a sinking ship before.

We have to help them.

Don't you dare. Kyle slammed his warning into my head. *The last thing we need is for the Old Ones to see us. I don't know them, Penny. If they're anything like The Shadow, we can't let them know we exist or that we're here. We need to go.*

"Penny, put down your arms," Shreya whispered.

"What?" I asked, dazed. But the soldiers were starting to look from the sinking ships to my still outreached hands. "That wasn't me," I said. "Obviously. There's no way...."

No one put their weapons down. In fact, a couple of the soldiers tightened their grip. A few of their faces looked familiar from the demon's deal. Arguing the logical impossibility of me single handedly taking out those ships just became a useless tactic.

And yet, no one attacked. A few of the soldiers gulped and looked from one to the other, wondering what to do. Their souls ached with a new doomed red, a deep dark color—no more fevered last fight. The deal had been kept. Now it was their turn. Except it wasn't. I wasn't there to collect for the Old Ones.

"We'll go," I half whispered. The fight had been punched out of my system. First from the sinking ships along the horizon, and now here, having to stand there as an entire village's army stared at me like I was a hellhound coming to collect. "We're going." I turned and started walking, half racing actually because their eyes never left me, and the dark, blood red in their souls was all aimed at me.

"Slow down, you two," Shreya gasped once we were clear of the small village.

I slowed and realized I'd been doing a full run. Kyle slowed down a tad more reluctantly and made more distance. His jaw was tense and hard, his expression as knotted as his shoulders. Shreya, however, leaned over and put her hands on her knees, gasping for air.

"Geez," she managed to get out. "You two booked it. Just give me a second." She sighed and sucked in a deep inhale before straightening up. "I'm guessing the Old Ones kept their end of the bargain. Those ships just...." She motioned an explosion.

"Yeah." I confirmed her theory but couldn't shake the way

those soldiers had looked at me. It made me feel…low, dark, and gross to even be thought of that way. Demonic or something, I didn't know, but they were so scared of me when we'd gone down there to help. People had been afraid of my powers before, but this *doomed* look was a whole other level. These soldiers were willing to lay down their souls for their people, and they thought I was someone willing to enforce the deal.

"The way they looked at us." I almost didn't hear Kyle's words as the Scottish winds picked up. He hadn't moved toward us, his head still straight ahead as if his mind was still running away. "They're so terrified of the Old Ones."

"Who wouldn't be?" Shreya asked.

I wasn't sure, but I thought I saw Kyle flinch at that answer. Then he cleared his throat and turned to us. "We came here for answers, so let's just get this over with." He closed his eyes, and a moment later, I could feel the connection between moments snap into place at his control. I braced myself for another whirlwind travel, squeezing my eyes closed, and tensed up. But a second later, when nothing happened, I opened my eyes again, just in time to catch Kyle look at me and say, "Ready?"

One word. Two syllables, but it meant Kyle cared enough to check. I smiled and nodded, then there was the rush of energetic connection before we passed through the portal and landed back in the same spot. The only sign we'd traveled through time was the dark clouds swallowing the sky. Drops of heavy rain slammed against my skin as rushing winds shocked the air out of me. I blinked ferociously to get the energetic world back in the background so I could see the physical storm around me. My physical vision came too slowly, and I didn't know where to turn to hide from the elements. But when my vision balanced, no shelter came into view. The cliffs were too steep and the hills too low to do us any good.

The rocks still stood in exactly the same spot, but nature had healed what the Old Ones had burnt. Wildflowers and moss grew under the rocks, and it looked as if nothing had happened, as if those rocks had magically settled there. In the middle, five shadows lurked in waiting, their backs to us as they watched the bottom of the cliffs.

"They must be waiting for the army," Kyle said.

"To collect their souls?" Shreya asked. "I'm not sure—"

"We're not demons," Kyle whispered, more sharply than he must have intended because his tense features instantly relaxed. "Our kind never wanted anything to do with this world. The Shadow—"

"Probably lied to you from the beginning," I pointed out. "It's not above deceit, and I don't see it sharing details which might risk its control over your kind's narrative."

"I know," he said, and there was a touch of an apologetic grin. "But you have to understand that human souls aren't as valuable as you humans like to think they are. All those stories about exchanging miracles for souls. How pretentious can a species be?"

"Shut up." Shreya laughed and lightly punched his arm. He chuckled, and it seemed the tension was over, although his defensiveness of the Old Ones didn't go unnoticed by me. This affected him differently than us, and I had no idea what was going on in his head, but there was no time left to discuss it as the army returned to the scene of their deal. The priest stopped as soon as he saw the five waiting dark beings, and the rest of the army soon stopped too, searching with wide eyes for what only he saw. Whatever these Old Ones really wanted from the humans, we were about to find out.

I spotted The Shadow lurking in the back, letting the four other Old Ones take the lead, watching and learning from how they dealt with situations. A kid really, still learning the rules of reality.

It is time, the tallest of the Old Ones said.

"No—," the priest started, but the Old Ones either didn't hear or care because tendrils wrapped around three of the soldiers. They screamed in pain and fell to their knees, but the tendrils never even touched their skin. Blackness wrapped around their auras and slipped through the color, leaking through like ink in water. The darker the human souls became, the more solid the Old Ones became.

"What are they doing?" Shreya gasped. Her voice shook, and I looked at her, half scared she would jump to save the soldiers. She didn't see how outnumbered we were against the Old Ones. This wasn't a moment to fix. But her skin was pale, and her leg stepped back. She was ready to run. "I can see them," she whispered.

Kyle jerked his head away from the scene, jaw twitching as he stared too forcefully at the ground. His body radiated horror at the scene in front of us, and I could have sworn I saw a flash of red through his darkness, but it was just my imagination.

I returned my attention to the exchange. We had come here for a reason, and I needed answers. The Old Ones weren't stealing souls, not like the demonic myths and legends. They were studying the souls, mimicking them, exactly like what The Void had done to me. It hurt like hell, and I sympathized with the soldiers, but the Old Ones weren't taking anything. The soldiers would live and maybe even have super healing after this, while the Old Ones would get to experience Earth as humans, with bodies and all five senses. It made sense, and my jaw dropped as I realized that, to The Old Ones, this was no traumatizing event. They didn't understand pain. They thought this was a fair deal. The Old Ones became more solid, more earthy, and the soldiers' eyes met their demons for the first time, necks craned up to see their faces.

"Now!" The priest screamed. "We refuse to deal with you anymore, devils!"

The remaining soldiers raised their shields and weapons, ready to attack in unison. They were going to get themselves killed. I braced myself for the horrible end until the shift in energy reached my skin as the soldiers lifted their weapons and caused a dizzying push against my soul. Like the opposite of an attraction, as if I was a magnet and those swords were the opposing end, impossible to touch, those swords and my life force refused to exist together.

Kyle shuddered, and I knew he felt it too. "Swords that don't melt," I said, remembering the priest's warning. "Petrified wood."

The army attacked, and the Old Ones tried to defend themselves, but it was no good. They were too human. Sharp blades glinted in deep wooden reds and browns as it punctured their souls, tearing them apart. The Old Ones tried to reconnect with the broken parts of themselves, but the humanity they'd taken would be their downfall. The cuts didn't heal, and before the Old Ones could react, it was too late. The young Shadow saw it all happen, and I recognized a dark horror radiating from its energy. They weren't supposed to die. And yet its elders fell around it.

But then the terror turned to rage. The Shadow grew larger and larger in uncontrollable emotions, and I remembered how hard it was for Kyle to fight against his thoughts back in the dark world. Desperate to understand The Shadow, I mentally reached out and connected with it.

The rage was more than I'd ever felt before. It wasn't just grief. It was betrayal. The humans made a deal, and instead of keeping their end of the bargain, they called the Old Ones names and tore down its leaders. But these humans were petty traitors, ants pretending to be giants. The Shadow knew it was better than them. Honorable. Reliable. Its kind were not made to suffer by the hands of disgusting, ever changing humans. This world needed a lesson. The calm decision which darkened The Shadow's emotional storm made me shudder in fear. *Traitors. Changers!*

A pull against my arms pulled me back to the physical world. Kyle had grabbed one arm the same time Shreya grabbed the other, and they both pulled me to move. The Shadow had grown larger than the cliffs and stared down at the army like the ants it believed them to be. But it kept growing, and any second, it would reach the hillside where we hid. I scrambled to my feet, and we hurried out of the way. The swords swung in the air as the army attacked the last Old One, but The Shadow was too big now, and it hadn't connected to their humanity. Unkillable.

Priest! The Shadow yelled for the only one in the army who could hear it. *Run.*

And he did, dropping his weapons, hiking up his ropes, and screaming "Run!" over his shoulders as he beelined for their only exit. The army tried to get away, but they were too close, and The Shadow already knew exactly what it would do.

It happened at once. One sweep of The Shadow's giant arms and the rocks from the cliffs lost their footing. The heavy rainfall around us turned the unsteady rockfall into a devastating mudslide. The soldiers didn't have a chance as the waves of rocks and mud and debris overtook them. The mudslide didn't stop but rolled on, bulldozing everything in its path, and headed our way.

Outrunning it was out of the question. Shreya held back the impulse to scream by the barest of threads, but Kyle and I just looked at each other and nodded. There was only one thing we could do. We didn't have to consciously read each other's minds to agree on a plan. He took the left, and I took the right. Using the darkness from my soul, I wrapped a protective wall around me and connected it to Kyle's wall. Shreya stood between us, holding her breath.

The mudslide hit us with the force of a freight train. I stumbled but held strong, with the intention to be stronger. The rainwater sizzled, and the mud dried to a stop. Around us, what seemed like a never-ending stream of mud swirled as the screams of the soldiers continued. My natural impulse was to intervene and save as many as I could, but Kyle couldn't hold back this onslaught alone. It was a horrible choice, but one I didn't regret as I gritted my teeth and focused on staying under this new, angry Shadow's radar.

The Shadow waited until the last of the screams faded before it portaled back to its world. As soon as it left, Kyle gave me a nod. Trusting him, I broke my wall, and he portaled us to the top of a steady cliff, far enough away from the mudslides to be safe, but high enough to see the devastation. The cliffs were permanently scarred, half fallen in jagged edges. In one spot, a narrow, high beam of natural stone still stood. We stared at it in silence.

I didn't know what to think, let alone say. Didn't know how to feel. The soldiers had tried to defend themselves from a fate universally believed to be worse than death, but was it? The dark energies weren't evil, just different. They didn't understand each other, but I understood both. The Old Ones never intended a torture like I'd learned about in Sunday school. These weren't devils. And they had made a deal. The exchange would have given the soldiers ten times the power they'd had before, even after. They would have been able to control the darkness themselves — travel through time, heal with superspeed, protect those they loved from future attacks. And even if they never learned how to control the darkness within their souls, they would have all gone back home. The Old Ones never intended to kill. The humans did, though.

But I also understood false deals. I'd made them before, always desperate for the happy ending, willing to take back my word to make it possible. I lied to The Shadow as a distraction while I saved Jack. I lied to Kyle back when he was The Void I feared so much. Made deals I fully intended on betraying because I figured they were doing the same. The Void did betray me. The Shadow took back its word too. If I had learned anything from my time against and working with the dark energies, they weren't so different from me, which didn't necessarily make me feel better. Only one survived this attack on both sides.

The priest escaped through The Shadow's warning, but it wasn't a mercy. It said it wanted the humans to be taught a lesson, and who better to tell it than the one human there who fully saw everything. The Shadow only lived because of its rage. Which side was right? Who was the bad guy here? I couldn't unscramble the mess of confusion and fear.

"The needle," Shreya whispered as if realizing something. I jumped at the sound. Kyle and I both looked at her in confusion. "In the book, I read about the Legends of Skye. There was this place called the Needle." She gestured at the lone standing beam. "That's what people call it. And the.... It's one of the few places on the Isle that doesn't have some magical story attached to it. According to her book, this place is filled to the brim with negative energy. Even centuries from now, in the 1800s, they say something so bad happened here that no one wanted to remember, and the story died with the generation, but the land remembered, and if you hiked to this spot, you'd feel it. The horribleness of what must have happened."

Kyle looked like he wanted to say something, but a dark glower took over, and he just stared at the needle.

"Is everyone okay?" I asked.

Kyle didn't meet my eyes but nodded.

Shreya took a moment to respond, but after a moment of stunned silence, she shook her head. "I'm sorry. I...I've never seen anyone die before." She sank down to the grass.

I stepped forward to comfort her, but Kyle was already there.

He knelt down next to her and squeezed her hand lightly for her attention. "Hey, let's get you home."

"Yeah," she said. "That'll be good." She forced a smile. The colors of her soul were muted, still, afraid to move, to process everything we just saw. Guilt gripped my gut for bringing her here. "They can't get us in the desert," Shreya added, more to herself as she got to her feet.

Kyle tensed, but he quickly made a door and opened it for her. "Be careful stepping down," he said, and helped her onto the steps. He didn't close the door until she reached the deck of the ship, but when he finally did, the click of the knob felt too loud against the eerie silence.

"They," he said as he looked at the door.

"What?" I asked.

"She said *they* can't get her in the desert." He waved his hand dismissively, and the door faded away. "I'm one of them."

I opened my mouth to argue, but any argument felt shallow. Everything the Old Ones had planned to do to the soldiers, Kyle had done to me. Maybe I was starting to understand his point of view, but I also understood the terror the humans felt. "They never meant harm to the humans."

"The Old Ones practically tortured the soldiers." Kyle ran his hands through his hair, and it was clear he was barely keeping it together.

"You said it yourself. The Old Ones couldn't possibly have understood death. Do you really think they understood pain? It doesn't exist there. There's no nervous system, no bodies. There's no way the Old Ones could have understood what they were asking. This mess was all because of miscommunication because no one understood the other's point of view." I would have continued, but nothing I said seemed to have an effect on Kyle. He just continued to stare at where we'd run, where it all happened, and still hadn't looked me in the eye. "Kyle?" I asked. "Where did you learn how to mimic souls, how to exchange a bit of your darkness for a body like mine?"

There it was. He flinched and bowed his head. "We have our own legends of the Old Ones. Not stories of demons and deals, but ways to experience wind and watery currents without losing yourself. I'd never met anyone who'd done it before, but I knew the stories. Everything the Old Ones did to those soldiers, everything they planned to do, I did to you." He turned then and finally looked me in the eye as he spoke the last few words. "And ever since that day, I have experienced pain and air and—" His voice cracked. "The soldiers had every right to defend themselves from that." Kyle held my gaze and waited. His body was tense, and it was like he was bracing for an impact.

"I'm not going to pull out a sword and attack you, Kyle," I pointed out.

"Why not?"

I raised an eyebrow at that one. "For starters, I've known what you did to me for a while now. It's not like this was an epiphany. To me," I added, because he was obviously going through something.

"You hate me, though." He shrugged, but the tension stayed in his shoulders, and the thick darkness crowded close to his skin, the way a self conscious human aura might.

"I haven't hated you for a while. At most, I've been confused because the longer we hang out, the more my instinct leans toward trusting you. And it's weird for me, but I guess that's what happens when you forgive someone."

His lips tugged almost like a grin. "You forgive me?"

I rolled my eyes teasingly. "Sure, might as well." Kyle's grin widened, and some of the tension eased from his shoulders. I waved at the Scottish land around us. "You know, there's a lot of stories from here. Fairies and magical beings who travel from realm to realm, more in tune with nature than humans naturally could be, and connected to something else too. If the Old Ones kept deals in the past, maybe that's where the happier legends come from. I bet people talk about us too from where we've traveled. Bet we're the stars of some legends. Hey…." I nudged his shoulder. "Stories don't have to be sad just because there's darkness in them."

He scuffed. "You really think fighting The Shadow is going to end well for us? All that rage, Penny. I don't know how we can fight that."

"I don't know. There are things out there stronger than rage."

"Maybe," he said, and I got the impression he was humoring me. "I'm just not sure it's something we've got."

Chapter 9

We needed space and time to think, but standing there in the middle of history made Kyle and me sitting ducks for The Shadow's hungry vengeance. I searched space and time for a place of refuge, a safe haven as we collected our thoughts, rested, and made a new plan with everything we'd learned. There were a few places which lightly called back, but one popped up in my mind with a blinding strength. I made a connection to the place and portaled us there.

The second I stepped into the new space, my spiritual eye went haywire. The energetic colors blurred with a strange heaviness I'd never experienced before. It wasn't the dark world, but as if earthly energies were thicker here. The slight grounding reds of the plants who strained for sunlight had a tilt to their color as if some strange magnets pulled the energies one way while the physical world pulled another. The tilted tension made it difficult to read the energies, which hopefully meant The Shadow couldn't read us.

I blinked the physical world back into view and looked around. We were in the middle of a circular grassland lined by trees that curved and twisted in strange ways.

"Where are we?" Kyle asked.

"No idea," I said, and turned around to take in the thick trees and strange atmosphere. "This reminds me of one of those creepy haunted forests from horror movies."

"Haunted?" Kyle made a disbelieving face.

I cocked an eyebrow at him, like *really*? "Says the otherworldly soul which snuck into our world and created a body to habitate."

"Fair point," he allowed. "Still, have you ever seen a ghost before?"

"No," I admitted, but then the dusk colored sky above us became particularly ominous. Something about how the air touched the back of my neck, how my hairs stood up on edge, made me feel like I was being watched. "Not sure I'm in the mood for that right now."

"You found this place because you were looking for a safe space, right?" Kyle shrugged. "I'm sure it's fine."

"Yeah...." I bit my lip. "I might have focused on being safe from The Shadow."

Kyle blinked twice at me without changing his expression. "Huh. Well, we're here now, right? Besides, we're two powerful souls. I highly doubt anything here could mess with us — What was that?"

Kyle instantly tensed at the same time sticks snapped in the woods. He had jumped a bit, and I would have teased him, but wanted to make sure we were safe first.

I squinted toward the trees and tried to focus on the energies for a soul of a human or an animal, but everything was so blurry I soon gave up and nudged Kyle. "Go check it out."

"Nah, I'm not going down that way." He shook his head, adamantly. "Let's just stay in this clearing where things have to show themselves before they can attack."

"I'll be right behind you. Just go check it out," I repeated, and nudged him again.

He grumbled under his breath and started walking toward

the trees. I kept my word and stayed right behind him. Well, maybe a few steps behind, because the place was creepy. Even the air seemed to crawl around my skin. I didn't really want to see what kind of creatures had settled down in a place like this but knew I wouldn't be able to focus on anything else until I found out.

We reached the trees. Kyle motioned for me to stay put and stepped between some trees. "Hello?"

Silence. Maybe it was just a bird or our imagination.

Crack.

Nope, definitely real. And big. The sound came from our left, and I would have jumped only the adrenaline kicked in, and my senses went on high alert. I was still, tensed, and ready to defend myself against…whatever lived here.

"Stay here," Kyle whispered, and stepped deeper into the woods. "Anyone there?"

There was a scream, and light flooded around Kyle, a stream of artificial light which blinded us. The light rushed to the ground to reveal three hikers weighed down by supplies, their flashlights aimed at the ground at our feet. They appeared in their late twenties, a guy and two girls. The guy had overnight stubble across his face, and each of the girls' long hair was up in sweaty ponytails. They jumped the same time we did, and the guy released a string of cuss words that would have been funny if I hadn't been expecting some deformed, bloodthirsty wildlife instead.

"We thought you were ghosts," the girl with the flashlight said with a British accent. She sighed and leaned over like she was lightheaded.

"Sorry, we scared you." The guy moved a small handheld device from one hand to the other and reached out to shake Kyle's hand. Kyle took it, and I stepped forward to do the same. "Name's Qasim. These are my coworkers, Stephanie and Jami. We're investigating the area."

"Kyle, and this is Penny. What are you investigating?"

Qasim chuckled at Kyle's question until he realized it was genuine. "Oh, sorry, you don't know?"

Kyle immediately gave me a tense look as if to say *where did you take us?* But Qasim thankfully continued without waiting for a reply.

"Ghosts, man. We're investigating the ghost reports."

Oh. I'd never seen a ghost before and wasn't one hundred percent sure I believed in them, but the energies here were *really* weird. Something was going on. "What kind of reports?" I asked.

"You really don't know?" The girl with the flashlight, Stephanie, I think, said. "Why are you here if not to investigate the area?"

"We're just…camping," I said.

"You sound American. You came all this way to camp in one of the world's most haunted forests, and you didn't know it's haunted?"

"We threw a dart at a map," I said, and waved aside their questions. "Let's go back to the question of what kind of reports?"

The other girl, Jami, brought up her hands and started to check the reports off her fingers as she spoke. "Let's see, there's the floating white lights, ghost sightings, campers have reported singing while they were trying to sleep, and there are multiple disappearances from this area."

"Disappearances." Kyle nodded like no big deal, but turned and widened his eyes at me like *safe, huh?*

"People disappear in the wilderness all the time," I countered. "That's not exactly paranormal."

"True, but we have video of a previous investigator literally disappearing on camera, and reappearing fifty feet away."

"Oh." I frowned. My brain went blank because I didn't know how to process that. As strange as this forest felt, it was distinctly earth energies, and that's not how energies from my world were supposed to work.

"Don't worry," Qasim said. "We're in the forest, so I'm expecting the most we'll experience are weird shadows and maybe some floating lights. The real action happens in the circle."

Kyle and I exchanged an uneasy look. "You mean the circular clearing five steps that way?" Kyle pointed.

Jami grabbed Qasim's arm, and all three of them grinned like Kyle had just told them where to find cotton candy land. "Ready to set up camp?" Jami asked her coworkers. "You two kids okay, or do you want to join us?"

Did we want to join a ghost hunting investigation? I wanted a good night's sleep and a moment of peace to recollect my thoughts after so much had happened, but Kyle mirrored their eager grins and said, "What can we do to help?"

Chapter 10

Kyle and I followed three ghost investigators out of the forest and back into the clearing shaped in a strangely perfect circle. As creeped out as I had been when we first got there, it was tripled now. I liked energies to act a certain way. Even the dark energy which seeped into our world and burned or created portals to other times and space maintained a consistent list of rules, and figuring out those rules were fine. I had no problem doing that, and this forest held all the earthbound auras I had grown up seeing. Yet none of them acted like they should, like I was familiar with. The glow to the grassy red, the soft pale blues of the birds on the edge of the forest all contained a fuzzy filter like there was something between my eyes and the energy, something that distorted the truth. I'd never experienced anything like it, and somehow, perhaps because of the familiarity of the simple forest, the grass and birds and trees, it became creepier to me than battlefields and other worlds. This was truly unreadable, and I couldn't quite place my finger on why.

The investigators moved to the middle of the clearing and set their packs down. Kyle sat down on the grass and brushed his fingers through it as if enjoying the weird buzz of the energy.

"Let's set up camp and then get a base read of the place," Jami said as she pulled out a blanket from her bag.

"Wait, you're spending the night here?" I asked. "After all those stories?"

"Of course. We're here to test the stories." She chuckled like I had asked a silly rather than completely logical question and shook out the blanket before spreading it out on the ground.

"I don't know about this," I mumbled to Kyle.

He gave me a curious look but must have read something in my expression because he sobered up. "Hey, it's fine. The energy is off here, sure, but it's not actively trying to destroy us in a fate worse than death, which is better than literally anywhere else. Look at this." He stretched his arm out, and the blackness of his soul came into view. The lines of his aura were as fuzzy as the rest of the place. He almost blended right in. "The Shadow can't find us here. You wanted a place to rest, right? Recharge? What better haven than a forest where even the air hides us? This forest isn't scary. It's...." He looked around and smiled. It was a wistful smile I'd never seen on him before like we'd just stepped to the doors of heaven.

"What?" I asked. "How are you going to finish that sentence, because all I can think is this is creepy."

"This is unknown." He grinned and shrugged like he knew I didn't get it, which was a correct assumption. "There's so much to learn on your earth. And outside of it is all this space and other planets. The list of things we don't know infinitely outnumbers the things we do. Doesn't that make you excited? My legs get jittery just at the thought, and if I think about it too much, I get frustrated because I want to get started on that list, you know? I want to check something off. Learn something no one else has ever learned before. Understand what's never been understood. Because I get that feeling of not being understood, and I wonder if the energies of all those undiscovered things are waiting to be found. Like me." He looked away from the trees and chuckled when he caught my face. "Weird, right?"

But it wasn't weird. It was beautiful, and it helped me understand Kyle more. This wasn't a soul of desperation at all. The need for adventure and discovery pulsed through him like blood. No wonder being stuck in that darkness of sameness for centuries had driven him to desperation. I had the crazy urge to hand him an Indiana Jones hat.

"Not weird," I managed to say through my surprise, and it wasn't. It made sense. "It's a very *you* thing to say."

The words settled on him with a visual response. Kyle's shoulders unconsciously settled straighter. His chin went higher, and the tug of a smile against his lips was for him, not me. His posture corrected itself, and before then, I'd never noticed the tense, defensive way he carried himself. It had been just how Kyle stood for as long as I'd ever seen him, but now? *This* was Kyle, comfortable in his own skin. A wave of satisfaction coursed through me, knowing that I had something to do with that. My words, unintentional though they were, had helped him understand himself.

In that moment, I realized what I wanted to do for the rest of my life—help people figure out their truth. With all I saw in people's souls, how I could tell if someone was lying to me or themselves…it was something I could do. Once all this was over, and we were free from The Shadow, I could graduate from high school, go to business school, maybe get certified as a life coach, and then open up a psychic shop. It could be cute and cozy like a cottage, so clients would feel like they were just stopping by a friend's house. The inside would be warm and bright with flowers and wistful, dreamlike paintings. There'd be cushions and chairs—oh, and a little tea station so people could make their favorite comfort drink—and we'd sit and chat. The clients would walk away more confident in who they were, more ready to embrace the challenges in their lives, while I would close up shop, go meet my Stranger for dinner, and tell him all about how happy I'd be. I could help people. I could do good in the world.

Kyle sighed and leaned back on his elbows to look at the sky as clouds rolled by. "That would be a nice life, I think, chasing the unknown."

I spread out on the grass and leaned on my side. The moisture from the dirt seeped into my shirt and cooled my elbow in a pleasant way as I held my head up with my hand. "Is that what you'll do? Once we're free from The Shadow?"

He snorted and kept his gaze firmly directed at the sky. "Sure, Penny." He sarcastically played along. "Once we're free from The Shadow."

Yeah, I thought, good point. I turned to my back and fully laid down on the cold grass—chances of that happening made thoughts of a life after it a waste of time. Tears tickled the edges of my eyes, but I blinked them back. Bitter regret stifled the dream I'd foolishly made of a future. Never should have envisioned that psychic shop.

We were quiet for a moment, watching the clouds roll through and listening to the chatter as the ghost investigators set up. The sun started to set, but neither Kyle nor I made any effort to get up. Exhaustion started to set in my bones as the on-the-run lifestyle I'd developed hit hard. As strange as this forest energy was, it wasn't aggressive against me like the Petrified Forest where Ricky's family lived. In fact, once I got used to the ever-present feeling of being watched, it was kind of peaceful. Maybe I just liked the forest more after hearing how Kyle saw it. The mystery of it didn't have to be frightening.

I must have fallen asleep because I closed my eyes for a moment, and then my own snore woke me up. A loud snort came from Kyle as I opened my eyes. The sky had darkened completely, and it was hard to see, but the moonlight silhouetted Kyle's shaking shoulders next to me as he struggled to keep in a laugh.

"Shut up," I grumbled. I hadn't slept that deeply in a long

time. My muscles had relaxed too much, and an overwhelming yawn silenced my next retort to Kyle. Grogginess slowed my brain, but I managed to glare at him. He buried his head in his shoulder to control his laughing, but it did little good.

"Did you get a good sleep?" He teased.

"Shut up," I repeated and stretched. "Where are the ghost investigators?"

He nodded to my left. "They're doing a perimeter check, I think. I don't know. They said something about getting base EMF readings."

"EMF?" I tried to talk over another yawn. Gosh, the sleepiness settled into my bones, and I could totally have gone back to sleep, but Kyle was clearly awake and ready to do more than make fun of my snoring.

"Electromagnetic field." Kyle pushed himself off the ground to a cross-legged, sitting position and brushed the grass from his clothes. "When the EMF reader spikes, there's a ghost nearby."

"Mmm," I said as I forced myself to sit up, not sure what to make of the team and the whole ghost thing. "I wonder what the science is behind that."

"Apparently, the human body creates and uses electricity to work properly. Their theory is that all that electricity is actually connected to the spirit, so when a spirit is disconnected from the body, it creates — or maybe it collects — electricity to communicate with the physical world." He shrugged. "I asked. We chatted quite a bit while you snored away."

"I only snored once," I said, but couldn't be sure that was true. He gave me a pointed look, which significantly increased my doubt. "Anyway," I continued, quick to change the subject, "are they finding anything?"

"Nah. They thought they caught some strange sounds earlier, but it turns out it was just you sleeping."

"Okay," I sarcastically warned and ripped some dirt from the ground to toss at him. He flinched and laughed.

And then something else laughed. Not Kyle or me or the three ghost investigators, who all stood up straight with wide eyes. The giggle echoed through the clearing like a breeze. Kyle and I looked at each other, jaws dropping. The ghosts were awake.

Chapter 11

"Did you hear that?" Jami asked.

Kyle and I nodded. Stephanie and Qasim both said yeah at the same time, and then we all listened. I seemed to be the only one hoping we didn't hear more giggling to follow because the team picked up their devices and started spreading out, swaying the EMF readers like metal detectors. Kyle's eyes were wide but slightly unfocused. He must have been trying to see the energies.

"Where did it come from?" he asked.

I tried to remember. "I wanna say everywhere. It felt so close, but—"

"From nowhere at the same time," Kyle nodded. "Yeah."

My heart was racing far more than my pride liked. I wanted to be strong and calm. I felt like I should have been—after all, I had gone through far more life threatening scenarios—and yet something about this felt different. I was more exposed here, and the longer I looked without finding a hint of where that giggle had come from, the more frightened I became.

If Luke were here, he'd grab my hand and give me a grin. He'd make me want to jump into the adventure. Those pale blue eyes, short dusty blond curls, and that sunshine aura would make even this terrifying forest manageable. What were ghosts and murderous monsters when we were together? I ached for my Stranger to squeeze my hand and say we were in this together. Kyle was a great companion, as unlikely as that seemed, but I could be surrounded by people I trusted, people whose company I enjoyed, and I'd still miss Stranger so much it hurt. Especially in moments like this, when I felt exposed, confused, and needed him to anchor me back to reality.

"There!" Kyle grabbed my arm and pointed. Between the trees, just for a second, a floating light hovered and then vanished. Jami, Stephanie, and Qasim grabbed their bags and chased after it. Kyle stepped forward, but I couldn't bring myself to move. He stopped and turned back. "Don't you want to see what it is?"

The hairs on the back of my neck prickled. Something was watching me. I'd felt that way ever since we stepped into this forest, but it had just tripled — no, more than that. Something was studying me so intently I could feel the pressure of its gaze between my shoulder blades. "Kyle, I don't think it's in the forest."

"No," he whispered, and glanced over my shoulder with a steeled expression as the muscles around his eyes and mouth tensed to conceal a reaction. "I don't think it is."

I whipped around and looked, half expecting a monstrous ghost to jump out at me. When I didn't see anything in the physical side, I let my eyes refocus to the energetic fuzz around me — still nothing. Confused, I turned to ask Kyle what he saw.

Only to catch his steeled expression break into laughter.

It had been a prank, and I wanted to punch his arm for making me so scared. "I can't believe you just did that." My hands were shaking from the adrenaline, but I could already feel some of the fear easing from my muscles. I had gotten in my own head about the dangers of the unknown environment, but nothing really had happened. A giggle and a bit of a light. I saw energies all the time. A little white ball shouldn't have tripped me up that much.

Feeling in danger without Stranger by my side was a whole new world, and not one I enjoyed.

The fact that Kyle now felt comfortable enough to laugh at my snores and tease my fear did not escape my attention. He had a good laugh, and I wasn't sure I'd ever heard a sincere one from him before now. Something about this place seemed to wake him up. He apologized for teasing me, but there was no sincerity in it. Only, since the joke had successfully knocked me out of my spiraling fear, I had to forgive him anyway. He smiled and nudged at me to join him as he went after the investigators, and I found myself accepting, not because I wanted to know what was going on here, but because Kyle was smiling with his whole face. True, genuine excitement brightened his expression.

The way he'd been teasing me ever since we got here had a distinct brotherly feel to it. And, if I was going to be honest, it had started before then. Back at the Scottish cliffs when he dared me to race him. The Expert had called him my brother, and my first instinct had been to correct him, to which Kyle had been offended. No, not offended, hurt.

Just as my mind had jumped to create a painfully vivid future of a psychic shop, it now forced me to imagine a family dinner table. Mom, on one end, still in her business clothes from working at the museum. Dad, on the other end in a wrinkled suit, just home from a business trip. My twin sister Dinah opposite me, chatting away about her friends or her latest venture into a historical memoir. And then—Kyle, next to me, soaking it all in.

What did he want? To go explore the unknown or to be a part of a family? Or maybe one didn't negate the other. Perhaps Kyle wanted to explore, knowing he had someone somewhere in the world who cared about him, who would ask about his adventures when he came home. He'd been so shocked when I came to rescue him from the dark world. As peaceful as that place was, in the few spots untouched by the chaos and drowning fears, there was no love there. Just...sameness. Were there mothers or fathers?

Siblings who kept you humble with teasing jokes? Had anyone ever loved Kyle before?

And what made someone family anyway? Was it just about the blood and genes? Couldn't be, because there were adoptions and makeshift families full of love. So then, what was it? The choice? Was that all that separated one's family from the masses? Was the only reason Kyle wasn't my brother because I chose not to claim him?

I frowned at my own inner thoughts. Kyle was relaxed, and he felt safe. I was looking too much into things. He never said he wanted to be a part of my family. In fact, back when he was the terrifying Void, he tried to convince me my family held me back. So many times, he questioned my loyalty to people who could so easily forget me. He never once wanted to be a part of it. To Kyle, my family was a weakness. Right?

The ghost investigators, Kyle, and I walked deeper into the woods. Every once in a while, someone would shout they saw or heard something, and we would all shift directions. I didn't see or hear anything personally and quickly began to doubt the reliability of their claims. We could have been chasing squirrels for all I knew. No more evidence of the paranormal popped up.

Singing whispered in my ear and flushed all my spiraling thoughts from my mind. The ghosts. Was it ghosts? Were there other campers nearby? I stopped and turned toward the sound, but everyone else kept walking.

"Whoa!" Jami jumped and aimed her flashlight at the high tree branches. "Did you see that? It was like a flash."

The others chorused they hadn't seen it.

"Anyone hear that?" I asked.

"Hear what?" Kyle replied, but he seemed distracted.

"The singing." I stepped closer to the sounds and listened as hard as I could, slowing my breath so it wouldn't get in the way.

"No singing," he said, and pointed the opposite direction from where I heard the voices. "But I think we should go this way."

"There's something conscious this way." I nodded toward the music. Was it just singing, or were there instruments? Humming? I couldn't quite place it. What language were they speaking? "Where are we?"

"What do you mean?" Kyle asked.

"What country?"

He frowned. "I have no idea. Hey, Qasim, what country are we in?"

The three investigators turned and openly gaped at us as if the mysterious lights and sounds were nothing compared to two lost teenagers in a forest. Granted, usually, one could at least place what country they were lost in.

"Romania," Qasim finally choked out. "Did you not know that?"

Holy crap, I'd never been to Romania. I racked my brain to recall their language compared to the singing. "Could be Romanian...," I mumbled to myself. The singing got louder. I took another step toward it. "Seriously, none of you hear that?"

"Now I do," Kyle said, but he couldn't because he was looking the wrong way. "They're whispering."

"No, they're singing."

"Is that a scream?" Stephanie jerked toward a sound only she heard. Away from the rest of the group.

They were separating us. "Don't chase the sounds," I whispered.

"That's why we're here," Stephanie pointed out.

But Qasim looked from me to Kyle to Stephanie, and he must have realized the same thing I did. We were all being called in different directions. "Go in pairs. Jami, go with Stephanie and keep your walkie on. I'll go with the kids." He came toward us.

"Go with Penny," Kyle said. "I think I hear something over there, and I'd like to check it out."

"Uhm, no." I spoke louder than I intended. "Buddy system."

He winked at me. "I'm not scared. I'll check it out and come find you." And then he left through the trees and got lost to the darkness.

Qasim laughed. "Your brother would make a fantastic ghost hunter."

Brother. "He's not my—," I started, but couldn't get it out. I'd left my sister and my parents. Might be nice to have a brother.

"Oh, sorry," Qasim said. "I assumed. You two look identical."

"Right. True...." My voice trailed off. "So, the singing was this way."

Separating didn't seem like a good idea to me. Stranger and I would never willingly separate, but I guess that was because Stranger couldn't time travel. If something happened, I didn't want him to get left behind or lost to time. But Kyle could handle himself. Logically, there was no reason why we should stick together, but I still didn't like it. I didn't want to be the only one who knew me when going into danger. Something about even walking in the woods with someone I didn't know made me feel exposed, alone.

That's when it hit me. I was alone. Stranger would never have left—yes, that's why I loved him. Dinah never would have let us get separated either. Kyle wasn't nearly as horrible a companion as I expected—he might even be fun and loveable sometimes—but it wasn't the same. He was a loner, and I *really* wasn't. As much experience as I had, I could never quite get used to loneliness.

Qasim motioned for me to lead the way, and I started after the music. It was like a lullaby, very calm and sweet, and the longer we walked toward the sound, the more relaxed I began to feel. Nothing that sang this sweetly could be dangerous. If anything, it sounded like mothers singing their babies to sleep. The subtle hole in my heart where I missed Stranger and my family had been tucked away to an almost endurable ache, but the closer we got to the music, the more raw that wound seemed to get.

Mom never sang us to sleep as kids—that was just not her style—but somehow, the song made me think of her. She used to tuck my hair back behind my ear when she was worried about me. And whenever we had our family nights, where we'd pop popcorn and watch a newly released movie, Dad's job was always to get everyone's drinks. He used to make fun of me because I preferred sparkling water over soda. It was a running joke between us. The past tense of that really hurt.

Qasim stumbled. It pulled me out of my thoughts and back to the present. "You okay?" I asked as I rushed to him.

He caught himself on a tree trunk and groaned as he straightened himself up. "I'm fine. Just some scratches. I tripped on a tree root." He brushed off his shoulder and forearm. "Don't know what came over me. Just started thinking about my wife and got distracted."

"I was thinking about my family too," I admitted. "I think it's the song."

He nodded. "I almost hear the music in the whispering every now and then. It's mesmerizing."

"Full of longing, I think." I picked up one of the bags he'd dropped when he tripped and handed it back to him. "Is that something ghosts can do? Hypnotize a person? Or mesmerize us into a false sense of security? Make us think about specific things?"

"There's reports of that happening, but it's never been proven."

"Has anything to do with ghosts been proven?"

He laughed. "Good point." Then he stretched his ankle and cursed.

"You sure you're okay?"

"Let's just hope the injury is the walk-it-off kind." He gave me a teasing smile and tested his weight on it. "Okay, I think it's fine."

"You're so convincing." I let the sarcasm drip off my tone.

"You remind me of my little sister. She's a teenager too. Keeps me humble." He laughed. The singing got louder, and his eyes widened. "Oh, I heard that," he whispered to me. He tested his weight on the ankle, nodded more to himself than to me, and we continued walking.

Five steps later, we squeezed through a curtain of trees and stepped right back into the clearing. "Wait, how did that work?" I narrowed my eyes at the scene. "I thought we were walking parallel to the circle."

"It's easy to get lost in unfamiliar forests," Qasim was quick to reply, but he didn't seem too certain. "But I thought the same."

We both went quiet again when the branches about twenty feet from us started rustling. Qasim stepped forward until he was in front of me, whether to better capture the data on his logger or protect me, I wasn't sure. We were both tense, ready to be confronted with the unknown, when—

Jami and Stephanie stepped into view. I huffed a harsh exhale of relief at the familiar faces. They saw us and gave open armed shrugs. "Lights led us here," Jami said. "Anything?"

"No," Qasim sighed. "Although we might have experienced something similar to the stories about messing with people's emotions. Both of us got homesick."

"How long did it last?" Stephanie asked.

Qasim gave me a look as if to confirm. "We'll let you know," he said, and rubbed my shoulder comfortingly. Was it that obvious? The raw hole in my chest hadn't softened at all, but I thought I had a thick enough mask on.

"Did either of you see Kyle?" I asked, ready to change the subject before anyone else acknowledged my struggle, or else I'd lose it. Everyone shook their heads.

You okay? I tossed the thought out for him. Nothing answered. Could our telepathic connection get through this fuzzy atmosphere? Could he hear me? Did something happen?

Portaled around until I found the edges where the blurred energies end, his inner voice whispered in my ear. It was crackly like he talked through a cheap walkie talkie, but relief flooded through me that he was okay.

Answer faster, I snapped, irritated at the rush of panic that went through me.

He laughed. *You worried?*

Shut up. Find anything?

I checked the parameters of this phenomenon that takes most of the forest, which is huge, and guess what? It's an exact circle. Just like the clearing. Doesn't seem to be moving, though. I'd have to come back after some time has passed and measure it again, but I'm pretty confident it's steady. Whatever's causing the disruption isn't growing.

That's good. I hadn't thought of that and was surprised he checked. There was a new, rejuvenated energy in Kyle's inner voice, and I wanted to tease him for geeking out but didn't think he was confident enough in his new self to take the joke. *We've all gathered back in the clearing, but if you want more time, I'll tell them you'll be back when you're ready.*

Thanks.

And that was it. The connection was gone. "Bye to you too," I grumbled under my breath, too low for anyone else to hear, but then said in a louder voice, "I'm sure Kyle's fine. He'll be back when he wants."

Qasim frowned. "We might want to check to be sure. Those woods are easy to get lost in."

"Well, let's give him some time," I played along, not wanting to explain our telepathic communications. "What do you ghost investigators do next in these circumstances?"

"Well...." Jami trailed off and gave her coworkers a significant glance.

"Yeah," Qasim agreed with a sigh and a nod. "Technically, we are ghost investigating YouTubers: houses, gravesites, old abandoned buildings. We gather the data, do the experiments to test out the stories, and mesh them all together into these episodes. But to promote the episode, we always do a live stream for our viewers."

"We've never done anything this far away from civilization," Stephanie added. As she talked, she went to her bags and started pulling out a camera, a foldable stand, and some other mechanical devices. "So we brought along some of this equipment hoping to bring enough of the Internet to us to get a live stream going. This is supposedly the best portable router out there. We'll see if it works."

Jamie went over and helped her set up the stand. "Question and answer investigations tend to hold our viewers the longest, so that's what we're going to do. We'll set up the camera, put up some EVP recorders which capture sounds undetectable to the human ear, and an EMF reader. Then we'll take turns standing alone in the circle asking questions."

I raised an eyebrow. "That's brave."

They all laughed. "That's the game." Jami grinned with excitement. "All right, I think we're all set up. Who wants to go first?"

Qasim went first. He asked the air, and whatever lurked in it about their family and if they were homesick. He talked about his family and tried to make a connection with them. Jami went next and asked if they had anything specific they wanted to say or if they were playing a prank on everyone by separating the group. Everyone else who wasn't in the circle sat along the edge, straining our ears to listen. Stephanie held a cellphone, which was open on the YouTube live statistics. There were thousands of viewers watching right now. A lot of comments were on how choppy the stream was, but I was just amazed they managed to corral any Internet down here at all.

Stephanie had her turn next. She focused more on asking for name, data, stuff they could research. After she asked each question in English, she repeated it in what I assumed was Romanian, which I thought was a clever touch. But, just like when the others went through, nothing ever answered. The ghosts were done playing, apparently.

Then Qasim nudged my arm and asked, "Want a turn?"

"What?" I said in surprise, half confident he was kidding. But he raised an eyebrow at me to show his sincerity.

"Completely up to you, but it's fun. Doesn't seem like the ghosts want to play anymore, so it won't be too scary."

"I'm not scared," I was too quick to say. I looked at where Stephanie stood up, brushing grass off her jeans as she walked over. None of them saw the energies like I did. Maybe I could get some kind of intuitive response. Probably nothing they could catch on their fancy equipment, but *something*. "Okay. What do I do?"

Stephanie came over and grinned as she heard. "Nice! Qasim, go introduce our guest star while I attach the mic to Penny." She waved for me to come closer and clipped a small mic to my shirt, hiding the battery and recording tech behind my back. "So just talk normally, try to empty your mind and listen, ask questions, and pause for about thirty seconds in case anyone wants to answer." She sighed, and her aura battled between disappointment and excitement. "It's been slow ever since we lost the lights and sounds, but I'm hopeful we caught something in the EVP recorder, so don't get discouraged if you feel like you're talking to nothing. Here's a walkie so we can chat without yelling across the field." Then she patted me on the arm for the okay, and I stepped out into the dead middle of the circle.

Qasim stared into the camera with a smile and introduced me. "We've got a special treat for everyone today. Junior ghost detective Penny Grace is going to sit in next. We ran into Penny and her brother and totally interrupted their camping trip with our investigation, but they've been great and even jumped in on the action. Now Penny's going to do the last question and answer before we wrap up."

He straightened up and gave me one last nod of encouragement before jogging back to the edge of the forest. I sat down in front of the camera, keenly aware of the distance between me and the others as I opened my mouth to chat with ghosts.

Chapter 12

"So, come here often?" I said to the air and then chuckled nervously at my joke. This was dumb. I was on live stream, and literally, thousands of people were sitting on their couches, most likely laughing at me. But when I glanced at Qasim, he grinned and gave me the thumbs up. Whatever, I thought—it's not like I knew anyone. No one remembered me and wouldn't remember me once this was all over. What did I have to be afraid of? Definitely not any ghosts. There was nothing here. I even doubted the music I heard. These forests were huge. The singing was probably some campers who were too drunk or in their own little world to notice us running around. But Qasim and the team had welcomed me into their investigation, and I wanted to do this right. So I straightened up and cleared my throat.

"What's that song you were singing earlier?" I asked. "It's beautiful. I didn't understand a word of it, but the lullaby is lovely." I counted to thirty before continuing. "Are you singing to someone in particular? Any messages you want me to share?"

A static sound disrupted the silence, and I jumped, but it was the walkie talkie. "Don't be alarmed," Qasim's voice came through. "We just saw some movement over your left shoulder."

Oh, sure, no reason to be alarmed at that. My jaw tensed, and I forced myself not to whip around and look. Instead, I took a deep breath and turned in slow, calculated movements. Then I picked up the walkie and responded. "I don't see anything."

"It was just a flicker. Like a shadow."

Shadow. Fear rushed through me. It couldn't reach me here, right? I zoned out and let the energetic world sharpen into view—no dark menacing dictators in the darkness. Of course not, Qasim wouldn't have been able to see The Shadow anyway. My adrenaline was just spiked, and I jumped to conclusions.

But there was *something* – a blur of movement. I wouldn't have spotted anything except the fuzzy energies seemed more condensed in one spot. Thicker, more blended together, like something was standing there. I squinted. "Hello? Was that you singing earlier?"

And then it *moved,* distorting the soft energies of the plants and air around it. I watched it for a second or two, then I blinked and lost it. "You have a lovely voice." I decided to stick to the singing topic since it seemed to work. I pointed at one of the devices. "If you wanted to sing into this, we could record it so more people could hear you."

My walkie went off again. "Other device," Qasim corrected.

"Oops, this one." I tapped the other device. "Would you mind singing again into this?"

Silence was my only answer.

"That's okay," I said after a moment of waiting. "I get it. Sometimes you don't want to perform. I'm not really a crowd kind of person either. Actually, I get really nervous when a lot of people are looking at me." My eyes flashed to the camera. *Don't think about it.*

Qasim's voice came through the walkie again. "Looks like it's quieting down. Why don't we call it a night?"

Good enough for me. I shifted my weight to stand. "All right, thanks for your time. Oh, and thank you for your singing earlier if that was you. I've never experienced anything like it."

I'd started to stand when a soft, long note whispered through the air. And then another. A humming, one voice and then another, until it was a chorus. Or the wind. It was so soft, but I froze and listened. They were singing for me!

I whipped around and gave Qasim a strong *what-now* look. His jaw dropped, and he motioned his arm in a circle for me to keep going. Keep doing what? I didn't know a lot about music, but this song was clearly in minor key, so softly melancholy. I settled back to the ground, closed my eyes, and let the energetic colors fully take over. The blurs, if that was who was singing, were scattered throughout the circle, some keeping a strong distance and a couple much closer than I would have preferred. The closest one was six feet from me, if that. I mentally reached out and tapped on the distorted energies, hoping to get a reading.

But instead of getting a glimpse into another soul, it was like tapping a mirror. A severe sadness, an ache in their chest and a stomped down hope of belonging to a family. My family. At first, I thought this poor soul was going through almost exactly what I was going through, but there was a curiosity there I didn't recognize. It wasn't sharing its pain with me. It was reading mine.

I jumped back and opened my eyes. "What's going on?" Qasim asked through the walkie.

What was going on?! These—whatever they were—were singing a sad song because I was sad. The melody was full of longing because I wanted...I....

With a painful plop of my gut, I had to admit what I wanted. Not my old life, not watching from the outskirts, unappreciated, but I also wasn't ready to be done with my family. Not yet. I wasn't done fighting for them. Even though I had left, I hadn't let go. I didn't mean to cry, but the cold streak from the tear shocked my cheeks anyway.

"Penny, you okay?" Qasim asked.

I fumbled for the walkie and cleared my throat. "Yeah, I'm

fine. The song's getting to me."

"Some people have a sharper connection to the spiritual world than others. You might have connected to their feelings. Think you might have some psychic abilities?"

I laughed, and it came out almost hysterically. "Yeah, I might."

Maybe it was just the glint of light or the weird energy of the forest, but when I glanced toward the camera, I could have sworn I caught a glimpse of a bright, laughing sunshine.

Energies didn't care about time or space. Whenever I watched TV, I could see the souls of the actors, so it was possible I caught the energies of someone watching the show. But the song really was getting to me, and my vision was blurry. I didn't just miss my family — maybe I wanted to see my Stranger's sunshine aura. I could almost hear his guffaw at Qasim's question, then he'd nudge me and whisper *if only he knew.*

I couldn't do this anymore. I needed to get out of this forest. It was safe from The Shadow, sure, but emotionally it was tearing me apart, shoving in my face everything I missed. "I'm done now," I said and reached for the flashlight on the grass when something shifted. That blurriness only six feet from me. It was closer now.

The music stopped. It was whispering now. Female voices, every single one of them, and they arced around me. The closest blur to me stepped back further and further, and somehow it made my adrenaline spike even more into fear. It wasn't backing away — more like the water fading from the shore before a tidal wave.

I scrambled for the walkie. "Okay, this is going to sound weird," I said, "but I hear female voices. Do you hear them?"

"We don't, but the EVP recorder is going."

"I don't think...." My voice was shaking. I swallowed and tried again. "I don't want to be here anymore." *Kyle, you better get your loner butt over here right now.* I snapped the thought into the air.

The voices stopped. The blur that had been stepping back stopped, and it was like a standstill, a breath, a deadly silence before the attack. Then the blur charged.

I barely had enough time to shoot my hand up in defense before a whoosh of air slammed into me. Something pulled on my arm and yanked me back. A sharp pain like claws scraped against my skin.

And then a dark whir of void blackness wrapped around me, and I felt myself being portaled out of the clearing. The ground shifted from smooth grass to tree roots and sticks. We were in the forest, and Kyle's black soul knelt next to me. I struggled to breathe through the rush of fear and stress coursing through me, and I needed to expend the energy somewhere, so I turned toward Kyle and smacked his arm.

"Ow," he whined. "I saved you."

"The buddy system exists for a reason," I snapped and blinked the physical world back into view. Kyle rubbed his arm and seemed annoyed at my response.

"So why were you all alone in the clearing?"

"Oh, it's my fault?" I prepped to punch him even harder.

He held his hands up in surrender. "I'm sorry," he added when I didn't lower my arm. "And you're welcome," he grumbled under his breath.

I growled at him. I'd never growled before, but I was so annoyed. So *raw*. And then, "ouch." I winced as the shock wore off and a pain shot through my arm. Kyle automatically frowned and lifted my arm, tugging the sleeve from the skin. Then he gasped. "Holy crap. You've got scratches."

"No, I don't." I yanked my arm from his grip, not in the mood for one of his pranks, but the movement hurt, and I looked down. Three red marks. It didn't cut skin, not exactly, but it definitely made a mark. And then the strangest thing happened. It burned. And itched. "Oh my gosh." I shook the weird feeling out of my arm, grateful for my ultra-healing black blood, which softened the sting quickly. "This place is creepy."

"Definitely didn't expect an attack," Kyle admitted. "I'm sorry," he repeated, more genuinely this time. "I didn't get an aggressive vibe from this place."

"Me either," I reluctantly agreed. The adrenaline faded as the only vaguely fuzzy forest held significantly less risk than the middle of the clearing. "Sorry I hit you."

"Probably deserved," he said in a moment of humility I never expected. "I'm the one who wanted to stay and investigate with the team, and then I left you to do it alone." He looked down at the palms of his hands. "I know what you've sacrificed, and even if you didn't do it for me, I benefit from your choice to actively fight The Shadow. It gives me hope." He gave a big inhale and looked me in the eye. "I'm sorry I left you alone. I won't do it again. I promise."

And the crazy thing was, I believed him. So I nodded. "Deal. We should probably get back to the others before they freak."

Kyle helped me to my feet, and we started walking in silence. I watched him from the corner of my eye as we moved. He'd come to my rescue after me tossing one thought his way. No questions asked. After a few steps, I got closer and linked an arm with his, like Dinah and I used to do. He folded his arm in a link with mine and gave me a smile.

"I knew you were there for me," I said, just to clarify things. "I missed my family. No, I miss them. It'll never be past tense, and I'll always wish Stranger was around, but I never thought you weren't listening. And I was right." I lifted a chin in a bragging kind of way, which made him chuckle.

"For once," he teased. I stuck my tongue out at him.

We kept walking, and I saw the frantic red souls racing around before we heard Qasim, Jami, and Stephanie all shouting out my name. After sharing an "oops" expression, we quickened our pace. "We're over here!" I shouted and waved as we came into view.

Everyone rushed toward the sound, out of breath and wide eyed. "How did you get over there?" Qasim asked. He looked about ten shades too pale, and a rush of guilt rattled through me for scaring everyone.

"Just…got pulled," I said and gave Kyle a glance from the corner of my eye. Explaining exactly who we were wasn't an option.

"What happened?"

I explained everything as much as I could, from the voices to the rushing figure to the scratches along my skin. Of course, the marks were gone by now, but there was still a touch of red in three solid streaks. Jami took pictures with her flash camera.

"I've never seen anything like this."

"We caught your disappearance on camera." Stephanie shook her head. "It was so creepy, and the view—" Then she gasped. "Oh my gosh, the viewers! We're still live!" And she ran back into the clearing. Qasim rushed after her to help or pull her back out of the danger zone, I don't know, but Jami led us to a tree trunk, which worked as a chair and offered me some water.

"We're glad you're okay," she said, and rubbed my arm. "You're a tough one, though, right?"

"Yeah," I agreed and swallowed the words *not my first near death experience* down with my drink.

"I think we're going to call it a night," she said. "No one's going to want to go back in there tonight."

"What are you going to do?" I couldn't imagine them all hiking back to the city this late at night.

But she nodded toward some sleeping bags amongst their stuff. "We'll leave in the morning."

Not sure I was up for closing my eyes in this forest. But then again, The Shadow waited for us on the other side. "We're going to sleep here too," I said, and Kyle adamantly nodded next to me.

"Where's your supplies?" she asked.

"We like to rough it," Kyle bluffed.

She raised an eyebrow but didn't say anything. Stephanie and Qasim walked back to us, and she was speaking into the camera. "We found Penny Grace. She's shaken up, understandably, but fine. Say hi, Penny." She aimed the camera toward me, and I gave it a wave. "We're going to wrap up here. Stay tuned for the full episode of our visit to the Hoai Baciu forest. Coming later this week." Then she shut the camera off and heaved such a heavy sigh, I once again felt the power of how scared they'd been for me.

Qasim started putting their devices and recorders back into their bags to be safe from the elements as we slept. Stephanie and Jami started smoothing out the three sleeping bags while Kyle and I kicked around the sticks and fallen leaves in hopes of finding a dryish, flat spot of ground to sleep on. We'd found a reasonable place and started to lay down when Qasim pulled out a strange, new device, like an old 80s radio, and set it in the middle of the group.

"Background noise?" I asked.

He chuckled. "No, it's an experiment I'm working on. The theory is that it repels EMF signals and will protect us from any ghostly disturbances in the night." He flipped the switch on, and a soft, constant whir came from it. The energy shifted as if untensing after a rough day. The fuzzy energies didn't disappear, but the lines did sharpen a bit. Whatever had a hold on this forest lost its grip just a bit within the confines of the radio waves. Or whatever waves Qasim designed it to project.

After checking that it was working, Qasim went to his sleeping bag and settled in for the night. Jami was already snoring, which, honestly, impressed me, and Stepanie plugged in her earpods before closing her eyes. On my other side, Kyle was still, but I couldn't look away from that makeshift radio. It worked. Whatever it did to repel the weirdness in the air worked. Would it only work for EMF, or could we design the radio to project any kind of vibration?

I turned to my side and held my head up with my hand, elbow digging in the dirt, but I didn't care. "Hey, Qasim?" I asked.

"Hmmm," he answered in a sleepy tone.

"Can that radio project any vibration?"

"Radio waves, yeah."

"No, like how a person feels a certain way, they're projecting a certain energy, you know? Think that thing could mimic it?"

He hmmed again, and I was half certain he'd fallen asleep when he answered. "That's a good imagination you've got, but no." Then he rolled over and started snoring.

I narrowed my eyes at the radio. It was impossible, right? But so was I, and I was still around, so maybe this could work.

A foot nudged my leg. "What are you thinking?" Kyle asked.

I rolled over so I could look at him. "You know how the soul can mimic physical objects? Like how back when you were evil, Ricky mimicked the vibrational level of petrified wood and fought you back?"

He glared. "That's the example you're going with?"

"But do you know what I mean?"

"Yeah," he grumbled. "What of it?"

"What if we could get a device that could do the same thing? We could trap The Shadow forever in that vibration. Not even The Shadow can fight against petrified wood. It would be stuck in a makeshift prison."

Kyle's eyes furrowed in concentration as if imagining how that might go down. His eyes flicked around as he imagined the outcome, all his attention tensed and serious as he considered my idea. If his aura had color, it would have been a deep, analytical blue, and after a moment, I realized why it looked so familiar. Dinah. He looked like Dinah when he was concentrating hard enough. Geez, the family resemblance continued to catch me by surprise. His eyes flicked to the radio, and his expression deepened into an intense frown.

"What?" I asked. "What am I missing?" The theory felt solid in my head.

He didn't answer for a moment. When he did respond, his voice sounded resigned. "It could work," he all but whispered.

"What?" I asked. "Why all gloomy about it?"

"Huh?" He blinked, and the strange tension faded as he smiled. "I said it could work. It's a great idea theoretically, but we'd have to invent how to do that. You heard Qasim. He made that thing, but he didn't think mimicking a solid was viable. We'd need a scientist to help who believes in your ideas."

Oh yeah, turning the theory into a practical device. I knew I was missing something. My hope started to deflate. "You're right. I wouldn't even know where to begin."

Kyle looked at me like he wanted to say something but swallowed hard and stayed silent. After a moment of obvious inner conflict on Kyle's part, with his eyebrows tensed together and his lips pressed into a hard line like he was actively stopping himself from speaking, he turned on his back, tucked his arm behind him like a pillow, and closed his eyes. "Get some sleep, Penny. Who knows when we'll get a full night's next once we leave."

I stared at the stars peeking through the tree branches. Never had I been so wide awake. How was anyone sleeping right now? The makeshift radio force field whirred a gentle hum. Kyle and I weren't scientists. It just wasn't how our brains worked. I could keep up if someone explained it to me well enough, but there was a specific type of creativity that went into inventing new tech, and I wouldn't even know where to begin. What we needed was someone who loved doing research, who never let what they were taught stop them from seeing the possibilities. We needed someone willing to jump into danger, to break the laws of known science, someone who'd—

Oh. My stomach dropped, and my skin went cold as two

names popped into my head. Everything I needed right now felt familiar. A researcher and a scientist. My best chance of ending The Shadow's tyranny once and for all lived on the other side of a bridge I burned down completely when I left home. Only problem was, I doubted either one wanted to speak to me again.

Chapter 13

I woke up the next morning with a crick in my neck and a bad taste in my mouth. The ever present feeling of being watched in this forest made a peaceful sleep nearly impossible, but then my mind started to go through all the ways Dinah and Stranger would react if I went back home. I couldn't decide which would be worse—doors slamming in my face or them looking at me without recognition. Might be less painful just to surrender to The Shadow now. No one knew how to hurt quite like family.

Kyle groaned as he woke up and sat up to massage his side. "I think I slept on a tree root lined with glass."

"Pretty sure that's not how trees work," I teased.

"We can't confirm that in this forest." He smirked at me from the corner of his eye before stretching his neck with another groan. "I miss the pillows at Ricky's ship." He gave me a once over as he stretched his arm across his side. "I'd ask how you slept, but your sour expression gives me an idea."

I stuck out my tongue at him. "Actually, I have an idea of how we could turn that radio trap for The Shadow into a practical goal."

Kyle stiffened. "Oh yeah?" he asked, and stretched his other side, turning just enough that I could barely see the side of his face. "And how's that?"

"Dinah and Stranger. I think we need to go home."

The corner of his lip twitched, almost like a smile, but then he changed up his stretch, and I couldn't see his face. No way he smiled, though. Must have been a grimace, and I caught it at a deceiving angle.

"Going home," he said, drawing out the words as if thinking it over for the first time, which should have been more convincing, giving his rich history of successfully lying to me, but something about his tone seemed off. "There's an idea."

"Think it would work?" I asked.

He shrugged and brushed leaves off his jacket. "I can't think of anything else to try. We wouldn't be able to stay long without risking discovery, but we can't stay here either. For one thing, creepy forests don't have a drive thru, and I could eat a burger. There's burgers where you're from, right?"

"The US?" I cocked an eyebrow. "Yeah, we have hamburgers."

"In that case, I think it's a solid plan."

"Have you ever had a hamburger?" I asked, but I was only half in the conversation. A surge of fear rattled my insides. Kyle agreed to the plan. I'd been hoping he'd find some reason not to do it.

"A post-apocalyptic version of it anyway. Hey." He tossed a tiny twig at me. It hit my thigh and bounced back to the dirt. "Why's your face all doom and gloom?"

"It's not," I grumbled. The ghost investigators were starting to wake up, and I lowered my voice. "I'm just…we don't know how the paradox affected everyone there. I left almost immediately after, so they might not even remember me."

Kyle frowned. "Why would they forget you?"

I rolled my eyes. "I mean, my parents did. The whole city did. What makes Dinah and Stranger different?"

Kyle pursed his lips together as he thought. "Theoretically, since they were present during the paradox, they could exist outside of it. Although your history was erased by The Shadow and not necessarily connected to the paradox at all. Plus, Dinah already forgot you once, so she could forget about you again." He stopped when he saw my face. "Right. How about this? Knowing what I do about you, I am going to assume that since you left them yesterday, you've been obsessing about if they miss you. If we go, we get answers, not just to whether they can help us with this theoretical trap, but on if they remember you. Then we go from there. What's the worst that could happen?"

"Literally, they forgot about me," I said. "I don't know, Kyle. Maybe you should go, and I'll stay here and be backup."

"How would you be my backup if you were stuck here?"

"I could listen to the moments where The Shadow can't find me and rush in to save the day if it gets close."

He gave me an unconvinced look. "I'm not knocking on your Stranger's door. He hates me."

"He doesn't hate you."

"He punched me once. Right in the face."

I snorted at the memory. "Well, in Stranger's defense, you had kidnapped me."

"He suggested helping The Shadow capture me."

"Okay, yeah, you're not in his warmest regards. Go to Dinah first."

"Penny, imagine for a second that Dinah does remember you, and I show up without you. Because when I imagine it, my jaw starts to hurt."

I shook my head at his visual but couldn't help smiling. "All right, we'll go together. Just…. If they did forget me, let's just go. We'll think of another plan. I don't want to linger."

"Okay," he said as he stood up. Kyle stepped over and offered me a hand up. "Hey," he whispered once I was on my feet, "I know I'm not them, but you'll always have me." Kyle gave me a quick smile and walked over to say goodbye to the groggy investigators. His sincerity and comfort this morning caught me off guard, and, for a second, it would be okay if my old life forgot about me. It didn't mean I would ever be alone.

We said our goodbyes to the ghost investigators. They were going to stay for another day and see if they could duplicate last night's results — even the scratches. Ghost hunting wasn't for me, and I was glad we were leaving, but Kyle seemed a little resistant to go.

Kyle and I waited until the three adults were out of view before we closed our eyes to make a portal out of there. I tried — hand to my heart, I tried to make a connection — but the fear blocked me. Every time I tried to close my eyes and focus on home, a great big fear buzzed through my head and blurred out any connections. My heart started to race, and the only thing I could think was *run, and it'll never be true.* Going home would be like ripping off a Band-Aid. I'd rather just forget the Band-Aid was there and hope it fell off on its own.

"Got a connection?" Kyle asked.

I gulped. "Hard to focus. I might be hungry. Maybe we could see if the ghost investigators have some spare food before we go? Or fill up at Ricky's ship? They always have amazing food and —"

"Got a connection," Kyle interrupted me. "Let's go."

A string of nervous cuss words rattled my brain. Why did I say anything? We didn't need to go. This idea wouldn't work anyway. I would be going through all this pain for nothing. Then Kyle's darkness wrapped around us, and the ground fell from my feet. Like it or not, as painful as it would be, we were going home.

The first thing I noticed was the colors, the darkened layers over the blues, purples, and blues, like a grieving miasma. My first thought was that Kyle had taken us to Stranger's house first. After losing his brother last year, the Hendricks household had been weighed down with grief, but that should have gone away after I went back in time and rescued Jack. So why was the darkness still there?

Then the physical world slipped into view, and my stomach plummeted. The brick one story house with a small lawn lined with a chicken wire fence. Wide familiar windows which were usually open to let the summer sun reach the indoor plants. But today, all the curtains were drawn, like no one wanted to see the outside to acknowledge that the sun still rose. It was something I'd noticed about the grieving, even though I'd never experienced it myself. Sometimes the sun rising, the days continuing as if the loss had never happened, was like an insult, a slap in the face.

But this was my family's house. The used pale green bug car Dinah and I used to share was parked in the driveway. When I left, there was no grief attached to this house, and with a sickening jolt to my gut, I realized I had cut all ties to this place. Anything could have happened to them, and I hadn't been there to protect them. I turned my back on them because I was hurting, and now…what happened? Who died?

I raced to the front door.

"Penny, hold up—" Kyle started, but I ignored him. My hand went to the doorknob, about to twist, when I realized I would be intruding. This wasn't my house. Not anymore. So I lifted my knuckles to knock, but before I got the chance, the door swung open and there, dressed up and makeuped for an evening out, stood Dinah Grace. My sister.

Chapter 14

Dinah Grace stood eye level with me, with the same skin, face, and hair. Only instead of the messy, grimy bun of hair piled on top of my head, her thick dark hair was curled in delicate ringlets, which fell over her shoulders with a perfection only layers of hairspray could control. Half her hair was wrapped up in a pony, with a whisper of an overgrown side bang not quite long enough to tuck behind her ear. This was it. The moment I dreaded most, only it didn't matter. Not while the thick darkness twisted the household's color.

"What's wrong?" I asked. If she asked who I was, who cared? I'd push, I'd lie, but I needed to know why the house went dark.

Dinah cocked a perfectly trimmed eyebrow. Her lips were painted a deep maroon, which emphasized her cynical scowl. She looked me up and down, and I knew I'd wonder what she was thinking later, but too much fear pulsed through my veins. Her soul stiffened, the swirling colors stunned to stillness, and a thin wall of protection wrapped around her. People did that to keep psychics from reading their energies, but most of the time, people subconsciously did it when they met strangers. It was a defense mechanism, and I didn't have one care why.

"What's wrong?" She mimicked my question with a cynical laugh and a shake of her head. Then her attention went from me to Kyle, and she gave him a nod in greeting. "I see you're still alive."

Kyle gave me a confused and uncertain look before answering. "Yeah, still running around. Good to see you, Dinah."

"Doubt it." She gave him a fake smirk, and a rush of red deepened her soul. Anger. So she remembered us. That was one question down.

Dinah glanced from one side of the street to the other before gesturing for us to come in. I felt a bit like a criminal sneaking into refuge before witnesses caught sight. Without another word, Dinah guided us past the empty living room, through the hallway, and into her bedroom. The carpet was thin there, and she had a soft white rug lining the foot of her bed. Various shades of blue rested around in residual energies from studies. A writing desk was tucked in the corner with homework sprawled out on top in layers, and a laundry basket was filled with clothes.

Dinah tossed her clutch on the bed and kicked her glittered flats off as she sat down on her comforter. Two textbooks, a laptop, and multiple notebooks were open across the twin mattress, and she had to shove them aside to make room for herself. As if aware of my eyes on her books, she tossed her jacket across the titles and glared at me, like I didn't deserve to know even what subjects she was teaching herself.

I wanted to push the subject on why the house was dark, but something about Dinah's tense silence warned me to hold my tongue. After all, I had run away from her without so much as a ta-ta for now. Her silence was more terrifying than the yelling I had predicted. She unhooked her earrings and took off the sapphire ring from her index finger before undoing the half pony and wrapping all her curls in a full bun. The fun Dinah was put away. She was becoming full business to handle me.

"Where were you off to?"

"Out," she said, and stared at me. After a second too long, I got the distinct feeling that we were in a staring contest. "Hey, Kyle, why don't you watch the window in the living room and let us know if Mom and Dad arrive?" Dinah said in her sweetest voice. Made chills run down my spine, given her glare. But it held answers too. Dinah was okay, and so were Mom and Dad. Something else caused the grief in the house.

"It's safer if Penny and I stick together," Kyle said.

Dinah's jaw twitched. "Kyle, get out before I throw my lamp at you."

He gave her a look of surprise.

"It's okay," I said and smiled at him. "First sign of trouble, we'll head back to the forest." Kyle nodded at me and walked out, leaving me alone with the consequences of my actions. I shifted my weight from one leg to the other. "So—"

"What do you two need?" Dinah interrupted.

"Excuse me?"

"You're too proud to admit you were wrong to leave, and Kyle doesn't understand basic human behaviors, let alone family obligations. So if you're here, you need something."

"Kyle's starting to understand family more than you think."

Dinah gaped at me. "That's what you got from that? You know what? Never mind. Just tell me why you're here."

"Why's the house dark?" I asked.

"What do you mean? The light's on."

"Energetically. It's like grief. Did someone pass away? Uncle Herold was getting those migraines. Did something happen?"

"Did something—?" She stood up. "Yeah, Penny, something happened. My twin sister ran away, and we had no way of contacting her. Which would have been bad enough on its own, but an unworldly monster was after her, and we had no way of knowing if she was alive or dead, or worse. So if you're asking why the house is grieving, look into the freaking mirror."

Well, that was quick and to the point. "I didn't think—"

"That was clear." Dinah's glare energetically sent laser beams of maddened red at me.

I scratched the back of my neck, unsure of how to answer. "What did you expect me to do?" I asked. "Keep living in hiding? I needed to move on in my life, let go of the past, and I'm sorry, but—"

She waved a hand for me to stop. "I get it. I can't even imagine what you went through, hiding from Mom and Dad, knowing that they forgot."

"They?" I gave her a significant look.

The mad red softened in her aura as her glare slipped from her expression. "We," she owned. "We forgot. And in punishment, you cut off all ties to us."

"It wasn't punishment. It was survival."

"That's worse." Dinah sighed, and a bit of the wall around her aura crumbled as she let down her guard. "There was no way to call you, Penny. Things happened, and I wanted to share them with you, but I had to do it alone, and that stings."

"You just described my new reality." A bit of frustration had slipped to the front of my mind, and it took conscious effort to keep calm. If we wanted to count scars, I had a feeling I would win, but that would only wound both of us even more. "What happened?" I asked, instead.

She stood up and walked over to the closet, leaning in to grab something from the darkened corner. Then Dinah straightened up and threw something at me. It was long and silver and hit me right in the stomach. I caught it before it bounced away and instantly recognized the cheap foam sword. Dinah and I played with swords just like this when we were kids—back before the darkness changed my reality, and all traces of me disappeared. From my birth certificate to my clothes to my childhood toys.

"Know what that is?" Dinah asked.

"Of course, I know. I beat you up with one of these," I teased.

She snorted. "You wish."

When everything connected to me got erased, that included people's memories of me. The last time I traveled with Dinah, she had no memory of us and actually believed me to be a clone. In fact, when I left, she still felt that way. Even though she had accepted me as blood, her memories remained erased, and she'd almost killed a guy in fear that she'd lose even more.

"It's cool you still have your sword."

"Why would an only child have a foam sword?" she asked.

I sighed, not really up to playing this game. "Surely, you had friends."

"All right, I'll rephrase. Why would an only child have two?" She pulled out a second sword. The one I held was green, but hers was blue, just like when we were kids.

"Where did you get these?"

"Showed up about a week after you left." She swung the foam sword back and forth absentmindedly. "Mom found it actually, in her office. Yelled at me for going in there, thought I had put them there and forgotten about it."

"I don't understand." I stared at the foam sword with a leery eye. I had tried hard to find some way back into my old life, and it was painful to leave, not something I ever wanted to do again. This toy contained false hope, and I wasn't buying it. Not anymore. Because despite Dinah's obvious pleasure at sharing the news, she'd also reminded me that my own mother didn't remember me. A forgotten foam sword wasn't going to bring my family back. Only memories could, and those were gone.

I set the foam sword against her bed and forced my fingers to let go. A little thought popped into my brain that maybe this was cause for hope, and I shoved it down. Not going there again.

"Luke and I didn't understand either at first, but we have a theory." Dinah tossed her sword next to mine. "See, when you saved Jack, you outmaneuvered a paradox, right? You HAVE to exist in order for Jack to survive that night, and he's alive, so—"

"But I had to be forgotten for the timeline to play out the way it did," I countered. "I have to be *this.*" I gestured at the darkness within me, even though she couldn't see energies. I had accepted my new reality, and I didn't appreciate her mucking it all up.

"Yes," she agreed. "You do. That time is frozen, I think. At least, we can't risk changing it for Jack's sake. But you don't have to be forgotten now. Maybe the universe is trying to figure out a balance between all you have to be."

"Dinah." I sighed and put my hand on her shoulder. It meant a lot that she was trying to find answers. Honestly, I figured she would have been ticked, resentful, and then forgotten about me too. But her evidence was grasping at straws. "The universe already decided. I'm real and forgotten. That's the balance."

"Don't be dense. You asked why the house is grieving. Because the people inside lost you. Ever since you left, time has been writing itself, and instead of celebrating, we've been mourning because *you* gave up on us."

Of all the worst case scenarios I had imagined, this — *this* was worse. If Dinah was right, then my life and everything I longed for came back, but I was too busy being scared to notice. "Mom and Dad?" I asked.

"Don't remember everything," she began. "But they'll want to see you."

My heart started beating too fast, and I had a conflicting urge to run away or just start crying. So my fingers reached for the foam sword, and my chest tightened with quickening hope. "How long have I been gone?" I asked. "For you, I mean?"

She leaned against the closet frame. "A couple of months. You?"

"Yesterday."

"Ha." She gave one humorless laugh. "Cheating a bit, don't you think?"

And it seemed so Dinah to say something like that, I laughed. "Yeah, I guess." I glanced over the papers and books on her bed. The jacket hadn't covered them all, and from here, I could read the titles. "Why are you studying theories about time?"

"My runaway sister can time travel. Why do you think I'm studying up on it?" Her sarcastic question was meant to hit me with guilt, and she'd bullseyed her mark. "So now you know what's wrong in the Grace house. My turn to ask. What do you need?"

I wish I could have said I came home because I missed her, because I wanted to believe in everything she said, but she would have seen right through those lies, and I respected her too much to try. "The Shadow is after us, and I have a theory on how to stop it, but—"

"You need our help."

"Kyle and I think too similarly. Neither one of us are scientifically, or research inclined."

Dinah nodded unoffended. "Then it's time to catch everyone up."

I started to ask a question but paused, almost embarrassed. She had mentioned Luke's name in passing. "How is Luke?"

Dinah's serious, sober expression shifted into sisterly teasing. An evil glint brightened her eyes, and a smirk tilted her stained lips. "Checking up on your ex?"

"Maybe," I teased back, although my insides churned for the answer.

"If you want to know how Luke is, ask him."

I opened my mouth to answer, but Kyle's scared shout interrupted me. "Penny! Time to go!"

My body tensed—The Shadow. But when I mentally scanned for dark energies, I couldn't find it. I ran out to the living room, expecting to see Kyle tensed and ready to leave, but instead, he stared out the window.

A car eased into the driveway—Dad's car. They were home. Dad was tall, dark-haired, and dressed in jeans and his worn out band shirt, which meant this was the weekend. Mom wore the stretch pants I had accidentally stained with beet juice when I was a kid, only there was no stain anymore. Her hair was up in a messy bun, and she looked stressed and exhausted even as she laughed at Dad's joke. No, not Dad. He hadn't said a thing and laughed too. There was someone else in the car.

That's when Luke Hendricks stepped out of the back seat, tanner than I remembered, with sun bleached hair and a sunshine yellow aura untarnished by life's hardships. The stunning optimist. My Stranger. He hoisted a heavy looking bag over his shoulder and started for the front door. Whatever he was saying to my parents had them wheezing. They'd be at the front door in seconds.

"Penny?" Kyle asked. "Your call."

"Stay." Dinah pulled my arm, and I looked at her. "Please stay. Let's figure this out together."

But I shook my head. I'd seen Mom after The Shadow stole my past, and she hadn't recognized me even a little. That hurt more than I could describe, and I had left so I wouldn't have to go through it again. Moral of this story: I should start planning my chicken instincts into future plans.

Kyle took the hint and started to get us out of there, but then he hesitated, just for a moment, and it was too late. The door opened, and I looked my parents in the eye.

Chapter 15

Dad stopped at the threshold of the door, his hand still on the doorknob as he looked from me to Dinah and back. His usually stressed blue aura was marred with a shocking red as he stared at me, like a fear of losing something. Mom shoved past him and entered the room. Her creative purple aura seemed spastic with whirling colors of thoughts, even as her face wore a stunned expression. She stopped in front of Dinah and me. Her hand twitched like she was about to reach out, but instead, it stayed by her side—uncertain, confused, but not nearly as confused as I expected them to be.

Dad stepped into the room, but Luke didn't move to come in. He stared at me, and his energetic sunshine aura stilled with a sobering guard. Everyone was staring at me, and I knew I needed to do something—but what? Introduce myself to my parents? Run and pretend it never happened? Claim Dinah found a lookalike to play a prank? I felt unsteady and needlessly alone in the middle of this living room. There were too many people who I should have felt close to, but things changed, and I didn't know what anyone expected from me anymore.

I glanced from Luke to my parents, and my hand felt empty.

Before back when Luke was Stranger, and we traveled together, there were many moments where I felt overwhelmed, spiraling out of control, and he could ground me with a touch, a gentle reminder that he was my backup.

But then I felt him alone in his basement after he bore his heart out to me, and I understood I didn't deserve that backup anymore. So I forced my hand up and gave a pitiful wave. "Um... hi."

A slice of frustrated red ripped through Mom's aura, and she frowned. "Dinah, is this her?"

"Yeah," Dinah said.

I looked between them. "What are you talking about?"

Dinah took a deep breath as if getting courage. "Things kept popping up. Not a just foam sword, but your Hufflepuff T-shirt, some homework from classes I wasn't taking. At first, I covered it up, but then I realized, why? Why cover for your sorry butt when you ran away? Mom and Dad deserved to know, and I refused to miss you alone."

"You remember?" I asked them, but their reactions killed my hope before either of them spoke.

"We're trying," Mom whispered.

"Dinah's stories were a lot to digest," Dad said. "And I won't lie and say I believed her in the beginning, only — I'd been having these dreams for the last month or so. Nightmares really. That I'd lost something, and I didn't...." He trailed off, still staring at me.

Mom stepped closer to me. "May I?" she asked and held her hand up like she wanted to brush her fingers through my hair, like when I was a kid, and she would comfort me for being so different. She used to say so many things, kind reassurances, expectations on the world, how to protect myself from the mean things kids would say. But more than anything else, I remembered her saying *everyone has their limits.* I was very nearly reaching mine.

"Um...." Hope tangled inside me as I stood in the middle of

the room, in a spotlight of people, and hope wasn't something I could handle any more. I stepped away from Mom. She lowered her hand and looked disappointed, but not like a mom might be hurt that her daughter turned her down. Just kind of like a stranger, but feeling embarrassed for being out of place, and just a touch of something more. I turned to Dad, who frowned at me like I was an equation that should make more sense, and in the back of my mind, I remembered that I broke his tablet moments before accidentally falling through a crack in time. Was it still broken out there somewhere, or did time erase that too? To my left, Dinah looked hopeful and not at all catching my inner freak out, or maybe not caring because after everything I put her through, surely I owed it to her to see this through.

But to my right, Kyle watched me with confliction. *Just say the word, and we're out of here,* his voice spoke in my mind only. I was freaking out, but I didn't want to run either.

Then I looked at Luke, my Stranger. He had no hope or expectation in his pale blue eyes as he watched me. In fact, he looked one hundred percent guarded, which I got, even if it hurt. But then he sighed and held out his hand. "Walk with me."

Relief flooded my system. I wasn't running away, but I could still get air, wrap my mind around this.

I started toward him, but Dad's frown deepened. "I don't think anyone should go anywhere until we sort—" But something in my expression must have changed his mind. "You better come back," he warned.

I nodded numbly and walked out the front door.

The strong Cheyenne breeze whipped my hair around as I walked down the driveway. Mom and Dad didn't remember me. I'd never even considered that maybe they'd still want me anyway.

Luke matched my speed as we started down the block. He didn't say anything, which I appreciated as my mind raced, but not with conscious thoughts. Feelings. Anxiety and hope and doubt, and absolute dread at the idea that maybe I could start believing I could get my family back, only lose it all and —

"You're spiraling." Luke smirked at me from the corner of his eyes.

I sighed. "Yeah." And I was walking alone with my Stranger, which was also something I never thought I'd ever do again. It didn't feel the same, but it wasn't bad. "Dinah said it's been a couple of months since I left."

"Sixty-seven days, actually," he said. I looked at him in shock, and he just shrugged. "You?"

This time I felt extra guilty admitting, "Yesterday."

"Cheater."

That's what Dinah said too. They hadn't liked each other at all when I left, and to hear Dinah saying that she'd been talking to him was surprising. But to hear him react the same way as her was disorienting. They weren't just talking every once in a while, but hanging out enough to mimic each other without knowing. And he was what? Going out on the town with my parents now? What was him in the car with them all about? "Where were you and my parents coming back from?"

"My parents are out of town, visiting their cousin, so your parents picked me up from a seminar."

"Seminar?"

"Yeah, some scientist came to the local college to teach for a day," he said, which really didn't answer any of my questions. "How's the whole gotta-go-my-own-way life going?"

"More running than I expected," I admitted. I filled him in on saving Kyle and finding the Shadow back in the days before the worlds were separated.

"So your plan is to out-manipulate a being at least three-thousand years old." Luke nodded. "Bold, but not the first time you've done something impossible."

And just like that, I felt stronger than my problems. It was a consistent trick of my Stranger's, and with how overwhelmed I'd felt in the last twenty-four hours, one I relied on a lot more than I thought. "How's Jack?"

"Engaged."

"Cool." Oh gosh, this was getting awkward. "So you've gotten close to my family. How did that come about?" Could I be more obvious?

"Don't worry about it."

I stopped walking and frowned at him. "Why are you being secretive?"

He responded with no small amount of sarcasm. "I don't know, Penny. Maybe I don't want you to freak out and run away. Again." Here it was—the consequences. I was ready. I braced myself for his anger. "What are you doing?" he asked.

"I'm ready. Let me have it."

His shoulders relaxed, and he actually smiled. "Have what?"

"I know I left, and I'm sure you're upset." Although, maybe I was just hoping he was upset, because if he was over it, if he was okay with me leaving, then that really did mean we were over. And the way he smiled at me made me realize I'd jumped to conclusions to think he was mad. "Sorry, I guess I assumed."

"That I'm mad at you?" He tilted his head to the side. "I was, at first." He stepped closer, and his sunshine aura brushed against the darkness of mine. Even though we weren't touching, we were connected. He seemed to get the courage to say something. A flush of insistent orange melted into his aura, and he continued. "Penny, I know what I did wrong. I understand why you left."

"No, Strang— Luke, me leaving had nothing to do with you. You were the perfect boyfriend."

He made a disgusted face at the word perfect. "That right there was exactly the problem. I kept waiting for some perfect future where dating would be easy and normal. I said things like 'when things settle down' and 'once we're done fighting The Shadow, *then* I'll take you dancing.' I made you think I wanted some picture perfect future more than you." He looked down at my hand and reached out, just barely brushing the tips of his fingers against my wrist. "I don't care about the circumstances in which I spend time with you. What I intended to be romantic plans could also have been construed as demands for a normal life. Something I realize now you never believed in."

I remembered his promises with a smile. "I honestly looked forward to dancing with you."

"Until you couldn't afford to anymore." He nodded in understanding. "I get it. And I get that you left for bigger reasons than just me, but you have to admit it was why you didn't take me with you."

What could I say? He wanted life to go back to normal. That's why we traveled together in the first place, so he could go back in time, save his brother, and get that happy grief-free life back. "You seem happy, Luke. Can you honestly tell me I made the wrong call?"

His eyes flashed to mine, and I knew I'd phrased that wrong. "You're the only one who can make that decision, Penny. So if you wanted me by your side when you were fighting The Shadow, if you once missed me while you hung out at Ricky's ship, then yeah, you made the wrong call."

"I did miss you," I admitted.

Luke sighed and pulled me into a hug I didn't realize I needed. He held me tight, burrowing his face in my neck, and I realized these last sixty-seven days hadn't been easy on him at all. "No more waiting for a perfect future, Penny," he said as he leaned back just enough to look at me. "No more impossible promises."

I waited for the trapped, gotta-run-away feeling to come that I felt in the living room facing my parents, but it never showed. Luke didn't have that effect on me. The idea of barriers and lines drawn between us seemed ridiculous. "I'm not staying," I said. "Mom and Dad might have acknowledged my existence, but—"

"I know." He tucked a flyaway hair behind my ear. "It's

not the same, and maybe it's about more than just not fitting in. Maybe you love traveling, and you don't want to go back to that normal life. That's okay too."

"Is it?" I asked.

"It is to me. And I can't make you take me with you. Honestly, I enjoy time traveling and those crazy adventures we do, but I also love it here. I'm okay with the normal life. I want to travel with you, but when it's time to rest, I want to come back to Cheyenne. And by the look you were giving your parents back there, that's not an option for you."

I groaned. "That completely blindsided me."

"May I offer some advice?"

"Please."

"Your mom and dad didn't forget you. The Shadow stole their memories. There's a difference, and they're just as much victims of The Shadow as you. I know it's gotta be hard being around them right now, but they're trying, they're willing, and even though they don't remember you, they sure as hell miss you."

"It hurts," I admitted. "It hurts to hope again."

He nodded. "I get that, but you're the only one who gave up hope in the first place. And you never gave them a chance, never reached out. Dinah did and, Penny, I was there. I witnessed how quickly they accepted the truth. You may not have been around, but none of us stopped fighting for you. Not one of us stopped *loving* you." He squeezed my hand in emphasis. "I know why you never reached out to your parents before. You were scared of being rejected. But they're here, and they're not rejecting you. I felt their energies back there. Everyone's terrified you're going to run again, and that hurts too."

Despite the harsh truth of Luke's words, I smiled. When we first met, Luke didn't know anything about the energetic world around us, and now he could read the changes without going into a meditation. "Becoming quite the psychic, aren't you?"

"I learned from the best." He gently tugged my hand. "What do you say? Wanna go back and hear them out?"

I sighed. This was a level of courage way different than running into burning buildings or fighting evil monsters. It was the kind of courage that came with being vulnerable and open, tossing my emotional armor aside, and hoping no one was hiding a weapon. But my Stranger was with me, holding my hand, and I wasn't spiraling anymore. "Okay, I'll go back. I'm sorry I left."

"I'm sorry you felt like you had to. We don't want to hold you back, Penny. We just want to be a part of your life."

Luke and I walked back to Mom and Dad's house in silence, but he never let go of my hand, and the closer we got to the driveway, the tighter I held unto him. It wasn't that I was afraid of any one thing happening in particular, but of all the things I couldn't imagine. I had no idea what to expect when I walked into that room and faced my family. Would they be happy? Would I be grounded for running away? Did they want a DNA test? Did they want to travel somewhere?

Luke reached for the door handle and turned back to me, checking to make sure I was ready. I nodded—time to face my deepest fears.

Chapter 16

Polite chatter in the living room went silent the second Luke opened the door. He gestured for me to go in first, so I curled my hands into brave fists and entered. Mom and Dad were on the couch, but they stood up when they saw me. Dinah must have brought in the polished wooden chairs from the dining room table because she and Kyle were sitting in front of the couch for a better chatting scene. There were two unoccupied seats left—a place for Luke and one for me. It was the first time since all this started that I had a place here. The empty chair hit me hard and tears formed in my eyes. Ah, crap—hope had settled in, and it was here to stay. But what else should I have expected? Making me hopeful of a better life was what Luke did best.

Luke closed the door behind me, and we walked to the seats. "Hi," I said as we all sat down. "Thanks for waiting."

Dinah's eyes darted to everyone, as if anxious to get things started but wary of going too fast. "We were talking while you two were gone, and we decided that what we needed was a good old fashioned family meeting."

"We've never had a family meeting before," I said.

"No one stole our memories before," Dad pointed out.

"Things change. Significantly, apparently." His thumb beat against his knee as he spoke, and a rush of nervous reds jittered around in his aura. Then, he bolted up. "Anyone want a drink? I'll get drinks."

There was a chorus of "yes" and "thanks," and he walked into the kitchen. I'd never seen Dad nervous before. Once he had to give a presentation to the mayor, and the night before, he was up practicing for hours, but even then, he seemed calm. He was memorizing, not freaking out. This jittery energy was new to me.

But then Dad came back a moment later without a drink in his hand. The jittery red in his aura was gone, replaced by a darkly familiar black. Grief. With everything going on, I hadn't noticed the slice of grief in his energy, hovering right over his heart. But now that his aura had calmed down, it took a prominent position.

Dad cleared his throat and looked not quite at me. "I don't know what you drink."

Oh. Right. I didn't have to read his aura to know how much admitting that hurt Dad. His voice shook, and he seemed ashamed, which was crap because it wasn't his fault. Ugh, but I'd been so angry at them. I'd acted like it was their fault and left like they'd betrayed me. Luke was right. I'd never given them a chance. I stood up and crossed the room, wrapping my arms around Dad's chest. He hesitated a moment, and when he hugged me back, it was tentative, but that was okay. This wasn't familiar to him, but it was to me. Someone had to take the lead here, and I was the only one with the memories to do it.

Dad's arms tightened for a moment, and even though my eyes were closed, I could see how the grief around his heart softened and got just a little smaller.

"I like sparkling water," I said as I let go.

Dad's face was full of emotions, but he managed to grimace at my preference. "So you hate flavor, huh?"

I laughed. "That's what you always say."

He smiled at that and nodded. "Okay. Oh, but we don't have

sparkling water because, you know, everyone else has tastebuds," he teased. "Sprite, okay?"

"That'll be perfect."

Dad nodded again and went back into the kitchen. Already a heavy weight in the room seemed to be lifted. I turned and saw Mom on the point of tears, so I plopped down on the couch next to her and gave her a hug too. Her arms were shaking, and she patted my head. Dad came back with drinks for everyone. Mom and Dad both had glasses of wine, but Dinah had her usual root beer and Luke, his favorite Mountain Dew. Interesting. So not only were my parents cozy enough with Luke to pick him up from school and laugh at his jokes, but Dad knew his drink of choice? And I hardly forgot overhearing Luke and Dinah making plans to go to the theater the time I accidentally traveled to his basement. All of that was definitely a parallel universe to me.

Kyle got a Sprite like me and took it with a look of surprise. I hadn't thought how awkward this might be for him, the random stranger in a family meeting. But then again, maybe he belonged there too. I couldn't decide. Aesthetically, he fit in. He could have been a triplet to Dinah and me. What did Mom and Dad know about Kyle? And how exactly was I supposed to explain *that*?

Once Dad finished handing out drinks, he sat down on my other side on the couch. Mom and I had stopped hugging, but she'd started absently playing with my hair, and it felt nice, familiar, so I didn't move to go back to my seat. I took a sip of Sprite to wet my dry throat and then got started.

"All right, so I'm sure everyone has questions. Dinah, how much do people know already?"

"Not much," she admitted. "I told them I had a twin sister and that an evil darkness stole all evidence of her existence, and she ran away."

I rose an eyebrow and leaned back into the couch cushions so I could give both Mom and Dad incredulous looks. "And you swallowed that?"

"Like I said, it explained the nightmares," Dad said.

Mom nodded. "And why I cried every time I saw a penny. Felt so stupid for it for a whole month before she told us."

Guilt twanged my gut, and I had a feeling it wouldn't be the last time. "Okay, so full story." I spilled everything, apart from the life-endangerment bits. How I grew up being able to see auras and chakras, how that made me an outcast because I knew things about people they had never shared, how I saw this strange black silhouette outside Luke's house, Dinah and me rushing in when Luke cried for help, falling through the crack in time, learning to control the darkness. I hesitated at the parts when The Void messed with me, tried to frame me for its crimes so The Shadow would target me and it could go free. I didn't just hesitate because the guilty party was in the room, but rather because I now understood Kyle's desperation, and maybe I didn't want him to have to feel guilty anymore. But the story would have major gaps without it, so I said The Void and never used Kyle's name.

As I spoke, Kyle kept his eyes on his drink and remained too still, as if worried if he moved, someone might connect him to the crimes. But then I got to the real part that mattered. When The Shadow slipped into my crib when I was a baby and infected my soul with the darkness. I became forgettable because my very soul consisted of an energy no one on earth acknowledged to exist. I tried to rush through it, not wanting Mom and Dad to feel bad either, but their auras darkened with guilt as I spoke.

But when I explained how I outsmarted a paradox and saved Luke's brother, both parents beamed with a bright orange of pride. They smiled at me, and I was sandwiched in love and parental praise even though neither said a word. Emotion clogged my throat, and I squeezed my own hand to keep myself under control. "Anyway, so now Kyle and I are on the run from The Shadow, and we're trying to find a way to stop it before it destroys both our world and the dark world."

By the time I finished my story, Mom and Dad were both low on their glasses of wine. Dad glanced at Kyle. "Forgive me if I missed something. That was a lot to take in, and I'm not sure who you are."

Kyle stiffened. His eyes flashed to me, and I opened my mouth to say he was like me, but then his jaw twitched, and he spoke first. "I'm The Void, sir."

The room went silent. Mom's eyes widened, and Dad frowned. Dinah rose an eyebrow in surprise at his bluntness, and Luke…well, Luke clearly hadn't forgiven him yet and gave Kyle the only look he ever gave him: a cynical glare.

Dad stiffened. "You're—"

"He's a victim like us, who went about things the wrong way in the beginning," I admitted. "But he's on our side now."

Luke scuffed. Dinah tilted her head back and forth as if to say *more or less,* and my parents didn't look at all convinced.

"But," Mom said, "if you said The Void manipulated you before, how can you be sure he's not doing it now?"

"Excellent question," Luke seconded, but took a long gulp of his Mountain Dew when I glared at him.

I opened my mouth to answer, but that's the thing about trust. There's rarely any proof to back it up. It's just a leap of faith sometimes, so instead, I shrugged. "He risked his freedom to help us get to Jack. I trust him."

"Okay. And is it just coincidence that he looks almost exactly like you and your sister?" Dad pointed out.

So they noticed the few things I decided to leave out. Kyle straightened his spine and spoke for himself. "I stole some of your daughter's DNA to learn how The Shadow managed to combine the two usually opposing energies of dark energy and the human soul to exist within her. I then created my own body."

"Basically, he's a clone," Dinah summarized.

I thought about all the things Kyle said he wanted in life— happiness, change, a life without desperation or loneliness. How he watched Ricky's happy family with envy, much like I did after losing my family, only he didn't have a family to go back to. His leader was trying to destroy him and didn't mind if two worlds became casualties in the process. Kyle may have played me and tricked me, made me think I was in danger, but he also taught me how to use the darkness, which I wouldn't trade for the world. And whenever I was overwhelmed by the dangers around me, when I couldn't escape on my own, he always saved me. Even when he was The Void. So I made a decision right then and there. "He's my brother," I said.

Kyle's eyes whipped to me in shock. His mouth opened, and I wished his aura had colors because I had no idea what kind of shock radiated through him. Not until he smiled in gratitude. "Penny's always been the closest thing I ever had to family, though I know I have a lot to learn." The humility coming from the usually cocky guy was a testament to his sincerity, and I returned his smile.

Mom downed the last of her wine. "Just went from one kid to three. Honey, we're going to have to rearrange the house to make room for everyone."

Oh. No. "Mom—"

"Penny and I aren't staying," Kyle said.

The warm feeling in the room vanished into a tense atmosphere. Dad glared, and Mom froze. Dinah cringed, and Luke shook his head at Kyle's bluntness.

"What do you mean you're not staying?" Dad asked. He looked from Kyle to me. "You're home. That's it. Enough running away."

"Dad, we can't stay here. The Shadow is after us. In fact, we've probably been here too long already. It's a miracle The Shadow hasn't already shown up with how we're all thinking about the dark world right now. It's like a beacon. Thoughts are how The Shadow finds us. The longer we stay, the more in danger you all are. I'm sorry, but until Kyle and I can get ahead of this, we have to stay on the move."

"But you said petrified wood keeps it away," Mom pointed out. "What if we lined the house with the stuff?"

"No," Luke said. "It'll hurt them too. She's right. We can't stay."

"Luke," I warned. "You don't have to go with us."

"Stop, Penny. You're just being stubborn. We all know I go where you go." His aura had turned a deep, stone-like brown. Immovable. There was no changing his mind when Luke's energies turned to that, and I had to admit, relief flooded me at the thought. No more traveling without him. Good—the last day had been exhausting.

Mom shifted in her seat, like getting an idea. "Wait, what about your research?" she asked Dinah.

Dinah smirked. "Ah yes, our research." She leaned back in her chair and intertwined her fingers over her stomach. "Good thing Luke and I were proactive about all this." She cocked an eyebrow pointedly at me. "And again, I'm going to call you a cheater for jumping ahead and skipping out on all the long nights at the library."

"Accidental cheating," I rephrased, but excitement got to me. "What were you two up to?"

"Oh, nothing much." Luke leaned his forearms against his knees and smirked at me. "Just a weapon to stop The Shadow."

Chapter 17

Luke smirked at me from his chair, his half empty Mountain Dew glass in his hand as he sat in my parent's living room, explaining what he'd been up to for the last sixty-seven days, and I wanted to kiss him so much it took a conscious effort not to jump off my chair right in front of everyone.

"After you left, Dinah and I felt more than a little helpless. Unable to run after you, or even know if you were in trouble, which, once we got over the shock, ticked both of us off, if I'm going to be honest. But we also knew The Shadow would be ticked as soon as it realized you and Kyle had tricked it. And there are only two things strong enough to stop The Shadow. Petrified wood and—"

"A paradox," Dinah interrupted, too excited to let Luke do all the talking. "If we can trap The Shadow in a moment of time, it'll never escape."

Whoa. It was weird how closely their plan paralleled Kyle's and mine. Was that even possible? But when I thought up the plan, I'd gotten stuck on one vital problem. "The rest of the world would be trapped in that moment, too," I pointed out. "The only way we survived the last paradox was because I broke it. Time glitched, remember? Like a broken record, never able to get past that thirty second increment. We wouldn't be trapping The Shadow. We'd be trapping reality."

"We wouldn't have to trigger the paradox for long. Just long enough for us to take down The Shadow." Luke's eyes sparkled with a scientific challenge. "Then we'd release the paradox, and time would continue. Without the supernatural tyrant," he added for good measure.

"Take down...." I frowned. "The Shadow?" He nodded. "You figured out how to do that?"

"Well, no, not exactly, but we can figure it out," Luke hurriedly added. "I'm working on some possible leads. Mr. and Mrs. Grace just picked me up from a seminar about wave manipulation."

My mind went to the radio Qasim had used to hold off the EMF waves. "Did it say anything about mimicking a solid object?"

Luke narrowed his eyes in confusion. "No...that was never brought up."

"Because if we could create a radio which projected a wall of vibrations similar to petrified wood, it could trap The Shadow. For good."

There was a moment of silence as everyone considered my crazy idea. "Huh," Dad mumbled under his breath. "So like the meditations Luke's been training us on, but from a mechanical device. I like that idea, although I only understand it theoretically."

The meditations Luke's been training them on? I gave Luke a curious look, and he shrugged in response. "I didn't know if The Shadow would come back or not."

So that's why my family was so familiar with him, why his favorite soda was kept in our fridge. Luke had been coming here and training my family, protecting them against the darkness. I could imagine him coming over and helping Dinah sort through all the mixed memories, sitting everyone down and keeping them calm, prepared, and empowered. Cue another impulse to kiss him.

Luke gave me a smirk like maybe he knew what crossed my mind, but then cleared his throat and continued. "I truly think that if I can just speak to a few experts, we can figure it out. The problem is most experts have strong set beliefs on how energy works, which we happen to know are false, so the most difficult part would be finding someone intelligent enough to help but not too familiar with the accepted rules of the scientific community to dismiss our ideas."

"I found the perfect person." Mom sat up straighter, chin up.

"Who died in—" Dad pointed out.

"But that's not a problem if you're willing to help us out." Luke's smirk remained intact like he knew I was in before I said anything. And, of course, he was right. This plan, though riddled with logical holes, was possible and worth pursuing. Combine that with Kyle and my plan to outsmart The Shadow using its own fears and weaknesses, and this could all tie up in a nice little bow.

I looked to Kyle to gauge his reaction. *Possible?* I tossed the thought to him.

Theoretically, and more thought out than our plan, but I'm chalking that up to them having more time to think about it. We would have gotten there eventually.

I rolled my eyes at him. "We're in—," I started, but then the hairs at the back of my neck stood on edge. Darkness slipped into the room. Kyle and I tensed at the same time, but we weren't the only ones. Luke reached for the side of his belt and then cursed. That's where he used to keep the sickle made of petrified wood he'd been given during our travels. A weapon against The Shadow. He must have started leaving it at home ages ago.

Calm down. It's just me. The Expert's voice rattled through my terrified body, and I audibly exhaled in relief.

You scared me, I sighed. "It's okay. It's not the Shadow," I said to Luke.

"What's going on?" Dad asked.

"A dark being just dropped by, but it's a friend," I said. *What are you doing here?*

You're welcome for the time with your family. I distracted The Shadow when I learned where you went. Two seconds after you landed, by the way. Gotta be smarter.

Thank you, I said. *Is everything okay – ? Wait, what are you doing?*

The Expert waved at Kyle, and a rush of dark energy surrounded him. Kyle stood up, confused, and then —

Mom and Dad gasped. "Where's Kyle?"

I blinked at where Kyle had stood seconds ago, and a confusing amount of worry rattled my brain. "I...I don't know. He—"

Then a rush of dark energy returned to the room, and a blink later, Kyle was back, paler than before. He looked like he'd had a scare, and I was ready to tell The Expert off, only it never returned. The dark energy retreated as Kyle sank into his chair.

I ran to him. "Are you okay? What happened?"

He stared at the wall for a second or two, giving a delayed response when he finally looked up and blinked at me. "What? Uhm...." He frowned.

Luke stood up. "Hey, man, what's going on?"

"Nothing. Just wanted to talk."

"About what?" I asked.

"Not important." Color refused to return to his face, and it worried me. Either he had gone through pain and was trying to hide it, which wasn't Kyle's style, or he'd had the scare of a lifetime.

"Kyle, we're in this together." I touched his hand, which was cold with shock.

He pulled his hand back and gave me a fake attempt at a smile. "The Expert likes our idea. A paradox to stop The Shadow. It's the only way."

There was movement next to me. Luke had stepped closer.

"Did this expert show you anything that might be useful?"

"No. It just wanted to talk away from the humans. You're easy to read." It was true, but it was also a lie of deflection. I didn't need to read his energies to know that. But then Kyle glanced at Luke, and something passed between them. Not a psychic connection—only those connected to the darkness had that—but something else, an understanding. Luke's tight shoulders relaxed, but he avoided my eyes as he stepped back. Dinah didn't ask anything, didn't react, but her aura flushed red in anxiety. Mom and Dad frowned, exchanged a look, and their auras tightened into walls I couldn't see through. Walls, I just realized Luke must have trained them to put up in just the right way, so I couldn't read their energies. He hadn't just trained my family to defend themselves against The Shadow, but from my sight too.

Kyle caught my eye and said, "You called me your brother. Can you trust me and let this go?"

I frowned. Curiosity and concern for him made me want to push the topic. And maybe more than that. I trusted him more than I did before, but that didn't mean I trusted him blindly. The family living room held a strange new tension I didn't understand. Somewhere between our conversation and The Expert's interruption, I had lost track. There was a darkly familiar tinge to the way that set on my stomach—me on the outside, not quite on the same page as everyone else. No one else in the room wanted to pursue Kyle's bizarre absence, so I tightened my jaw. "What did The Expert tell you?"

Kyle glanced at the others pointedly. "Not here," he whispered only for me, and the look of pity he gave me confused me even more. No, not pity. Fear. A choking terror that I might put two and two together any second and realize what he didn't want to share. It radiated off him like heat from the sun in the middle of summer. Strong, overpowering, and uncomfortable. A second later, it clicked. That one little detail I hadn't considered yet.

Paradoxes were deceptively simple. Time continued like strings of moments flowing through a current. But all it took was one knot, one moment conflicting with another, to trap it all in a dam. Luke traveled back in time to save his brother, which he would only do if Jack died. Jack living meant Luke never went back, which meant Jack died and so on. Time looped, and we would all have been trapped in the whirlpool. I accidentally uncovered a loophole. Technically, I was only there through a series of random events. My decision to rescue Jack was not a direct result of Jack dying.

So if we wanted to replace a paradox, we needed someone who actively chose to disrupt that moment of time. Someone who'd run up to The Shadow, face it head on, and turn the device on *both of them.* Kyle stared at me without blinking, as if scared he'd miss something vital in my reaction if he blinked. No wonder he had been so kind to me lately. So...*brotherly.* It wasn't love. He didn't care. Kyle felt guilty because he'd already put that little detail together, and guess what? Only one of us had the guts to face The Shadow. I was the only one willing to try. I wasn't coming home after this. Fact was this paradox needed to happen, which might explain why The Expert warned Kyle and not me. If they thought I wouldn't choose the paradox, then maybe The Expert pulled Kyle aside to make sure I went through with this, and the way Kyle watched me with those eyes he stole from me, wide eyed and waiting, told me everything I needed to know.

The realization cooled any love I'd mustered for him. I called him my brother just moments ago, and he had the nerve to be flattered. Kyle opened his mouth, and the chill which had started in my chest paused. If he wanted, he could hear my thoughts, and the way he stared at me made me think he'd been listening. All he had to do was correct me. I'd believe that. But instead of erasing my fears, he whispered, "Maybe we shouldn't have come here."

My blood left my face. My core went cold, and I could have sworn I started shivering from the frozen remains of hope. Why? Ugh...*why* did I let Kyle in? Why couldn't he just...? But it was the perfect kind of manipulation. Even if it was all true and he was prepping me for a sacrificial play against The Shadow, it didn't matter. I was the only one brave enough to do it, and it needed to be done. He didn't have to make me care for him, though. That was low.

A hand touched my elbow. "Penny, you okay?" Luke asked. "You've gone pale."

"We should go." I lifted my elbow from Luke's grip and plastered a painful smile across my face. "It's been wonderful catching up, and I'm so glad we've—" I gestured between me and Mom and Dad, and then shrugged because I wasn't sure how to summarize that either. "The Expert can only hide us for so long. Time's up."

"No." Mom used her *enough, don't get yourself into more trouble* voice. She stood up and towered over me. I hadn't felt like a kid in a few months, ever since this started, but all of that fake strength threatened to crumble because my mom was there, and she was ticked. I wanted to crumble into that motherly strength and pretend I hadn't just realized how I'd end. "You are not leaving."

"Mom, I have to—"

"Fine, then you're not leaving alone." Mom looked to Dad, who nodded and downed the rest of his wine before standing up.

"What?" Dinah and I chorused.

Luke must have caught on before me because he snorted. "Works for me."

Time traveling paradox around an other-worldly dictator with my parents. I loved the idea of being a part of their lives again, of having my seat at the family table, but the thought of taking my parents on one of my adventures, which historically included battlefields and burning buildings? Not exactly on my to-do list. At the end of those adventures, once I had a working device against The Shadow, no way was I taking them to watch my last act. "I'm sorry." I shook my head. "What I do now, it's too dangerous."

"If it's not too dangerous for our child, then it's not too dangerous for us." Dad raised his eyebrow as if to warn me I'd be grounded if I argued. Too bad.

"That dark being that came by and casually stole Kyle for three seconds? That one was nice. If The Shadow finds us, we gotta run fast. I can run. Kyle can run. You all can't."

"Then there's the minor problem of The Shadow being able to read your human thoughts across space and time," Kyle pointed out. "Penny's right. But don't worry, I'll make sure she comes back home when this is all done." He lied so smoothly, I almost bought it. If only he'd argued my fears.

Luke's eyes narrowed. "I have experience fighting The Shadow. I'm going too. Just give me time to run home and grab the sickle."

"Hey," Dinah added. "I have experience fighting The Shadow too."

"You actually fought The Shadow?" Kyle asked.

She shrugged. "I was there. Didn't see anything, but I was there."

Thing was, I weirdly wanted them to come. I wanted Luke to give me hope when I got cynical and for Dinah to give me that tough love. I wanted Mom and Dad to have my back and tell me they believed in me. But I also wanted all of them safe. One look at Kyle, and I knew he was on the same page. Best to get out of there before they changed our minds.

"Thank you for this talk," I said in goodbye. "It means the world to me."

As everyone rushed to speak their arguments, I grabbed Kyle's arm and created a portal around us. Once again, there wasn't time to find a specific place. We just had to go before someone grabbed me, or else they would tag along. I searched for peace, but too many emotions slipped into the mix. *This is all too much. I can't do it.* I tried to numb my doubts, but leaving my family, everyone I loved, to trap a monster in a paradox just seemed too much for me to swallow—and I considered myself open minded.

A moment answered my call for safety, and I quickly made the connection. The physical world slipped from under my feet as home disappeared. The last thing I experienced were four screams of "No!" And outreached fingers wrapping around my wrist.

Chapter 18

We landed in a crowd of chaos. Bodies squeezed from every direction as an overexcited array of auras blindsided me. "How'd you get there?" Someone near me asked. "Don't go pushing. We all want to see."

I blinked rapidly, trying to get the spiritual senses to calm down enough for me to see where we were. People kept pushing around me, and I blindly stepped right and left, trying to keep on my feet. Two pairs of hands kept me steady. Who grabbed me at the last second? There were too many colors—blues and yellows and purples, all shifting and trying to get past each other.

"Penny, where did you take us?" Kyle's voice said from my left.

"I don't know." I squeezed my eyes shut. "It's too much. I can't see."

"Hey, it's okay." A familiar voice pulled me in. Fingers lightly brushed against my cheek and steadied me. A hand cupped my cheek and angled me to look up. It was all sunshine there. "Just breathe. We're in a crowd, but we're safe."

I complied and focused on my breathing—well, and the hands on my face. The energetic world calmed, allowing for the physical world to take the reins once more. The sunshine aura softened as Luke's concerned face came into focus. He was the one who grabbed me. He was here, traveling with me. It was dangerous and impractical, and I was so relieved to see him; I wanted to cry. I pulled him into a hug and tried to understand the overwhelmingly warm feeling in my heart that he was there — Penny and Stranger time traveling again.

Then Kyle cleared his throat pointedly, so I forced myself to let go and take a look around. We were definitely in a crowd, a seemingly endless view of heads and bodies on all sides of us. The dress style was more 1800s if I had to take a guess. The women wore dresses and petticoats, while the men wore their nicest suits. We were outside, and if I wasn't mistaken, right next to a railroad station. The huge crowd seemed to be waiting for a train to arrive.

"Why are we here?" Kyle asked.

I shook my head. "I don't know. I just thought we needed to go somewhere safe."

Kyle gave Luke a pointed glance. "Going to be more difficult now that we've got a full human and his easy-to-read soul traveling with us."

For once, I was pleased to be in an overbearing crowd. "It'll be fine. It's impossible to read any one person's soul in this crowd. We're safe."

"Besides, I can control my thoughts," Luke said. "Or have you forgotten, it wasn't me who accidentally called The Shadow to Ricky's ship last time, forcing you two to strand it in a desert?"

Kyle opened his mouth to argue but closed it again and merely scowled, which was wise since he was the guilty one in that story. Pride hit Kyle hard, as Luke and Dinah had spoken negatively one too many times about The Void, and he rushed to defend himself. Only that meant shouting his true identity to the entire ship and the ever-searching Shadow too.

"I wonder who the crowd is waiting for."

I spoke the words more to change the subject than actual curiosity. I wasn't sure how I felt about Kyle right now and didn't want to be forced to defend him. If Luke suspected what I was doing, Kyle wouldn't be casually standing next to us. He'd be on the ground, the fear of Luke's protectiveness on him, and then Luke would demand we parted ways from Kyle. Maybe that would be best. Only...I didn't know. I could still be wrong, and I didn't want to hate Kyle again.

So I ignored the conflicting impulses and focused on the immediate questions around us — namely, where and when were we, and were the excited crowds enough of a cover to keep us safe from The Shadow? But my voiced question gained the attention of a few men nearby, who turned and gave me an incredulous look.

"You don't know who's passing through town on the incoming train?" The closest man to me asked. He was older, maybe fifties, in a clean Sunday-best suit and a simple hat on his head. His skin was slightly sun-worn, and he pointed a calloused finger at me as if I was a no-good teen. "Don't you young girls read the news or anything other than those cheap novels? This is history in the making today."

"Oh right, that," I bluffed and, when Luke caught my eye, tossed him a *no idea* kind of shrug.

But the older man seemed to buy it. "Of course you know. Everyone in the United States knows. It's a proud moment for us."

My mind raced to connect what I saw with history class lessons. Okay, trains were being used for public transport, so probably the 1800s? The older man said United States, so we were in the same country as this morning. I searched my surroundings for some sign of the times, but since I found no banner screaming the year, I had nothing. Suddenly, I didn't just miss my twin sister's company, but also her extraordinary historical knowledge. Dinah probably knew exactly what moment this was. But unless

Abraham Lincoln was on his way, I had no clue. A feeling in my gut told me that guess was way off, but I had no idea why.

Then a low rumble sliced through the silent, waiting crowd. Someone on the far edge of the gathering shouted, "It's here!" and the air exploded in clapping and cheers.

Luke and I shared an excited smile, caught up in the energy, but Kyle frowned as if confused. He'd probably never been to a concert or anything before. This was all new to him, being a part of a crowd cheering like this. I couldn't help wondering how it must have felt for him. This soul who, for countless years, half-drowned in a quiet, lonely desperation, to be transported right smack in the middle of adoring fans without any context, logically or emotionally.

"Any guesses who it is?" Luke asked, low enough for only Kyle and me to hear. "Rockefeller? Edison?"

"Could be Mark Twain," I whispered back. "Or Houdini?"

But we were wrong. A train slowly eased closer, the sounds of the engines just barely cutting through the cheering crowds, until it finally came to a stop flush against the station deck. Police officers in blue uniforms with shiny buttons held the crowd back as the doors opened and out stepped…a woman.

Her brunette hair was up in pins, and short bangs framed her forehead. She wore a tough looking blue dress free of any frills or lace, only a quiet plaid pattern. Given the Wild West feel of this little town, I hadn't considered a woman to be the cause of this crowd for one moment, but the second she stepped out, the crowd doubled in shouts, each trying to speak over the others in hopes she might hear them.

"It's Nellie Bly!"

"You did it!"

"How many days left, Nellie Bly?"

"Will you make it in time?"

The crowd screamed their questions, but the woman merely smiled and waved. She seemed, if anything, a little shocked. A blush of embarrassed red slipped through a courageously strong orange aura around her as she stepped closer to the edge of the platform to see everyone.

Kyle leaned in to whisper in my ear. "All right, I give. Who is she?"

But my history books had never mentioned a woman. "I don't know," I admitted, and looked to Luke, who shook his head.

Behind us, a band I hadn't noticed started playing a song which someone in the crowd recognized as "By Nellie's Blue Eyes," and a small but pushy newsboy fought his way to the steps and handed her a large tray of nuts, fruit, and candies. She took the tray with vocal gratitude, which etched through her aura in pinks and blues as she stared at her gift with quick blinking eyes. The power of the moment, the support, and the stunned appreciation from this mysterious Nellie Bly had me entranced. She hadn't expected this when the train stopped to fill up, that much I could catch from her overwhelmed energies, but the whole town had been prepared.

"What sort of delays did you experience?" a man close to the platform asked.

"Oh, many," Nellie Bly laughed. "Storms and canceled ships—but I made it back to the States nonetheless."

"What's in your bag?" a lady shouted from the other side of the crowd.

Nellie held up a small handbag with pride. "Everything I needed for the trip. A pair of slippers, ink stand, pencils and copy paper, pins, needles and thread, a dressing gown, toilet articles, handkerchiefs, and a jar of cold cream—but I regret the cold cream. Made it impossible to close the bag!"

"How many bags did you take in total?" someone else shouted.

"Just this." She gestured to the bag again. "So much easier to travel with one."

Half the crowd murmured in agreement as if memorizing

the information for their own use, while the other half gasped in audible shock. Then Nellie's face lit up like she just got the most fantastic idea, and she smiled. "Would you like to see my monkey?"

Everyone shouted their excitement, and she ran back into the train for a moment. Luke gave me a stunned but contagious grin. "Who is this woman?"

"I don't know," I admitted again. "But I love her."

She soon returned with a small monkey on her arm, who ate the fruit she held out to it and watched the entranced crowd with complete indifference. It seemed to like Nellie, though. "Only when I was out at sea did I learn monkeys are known to be bad luck to sailors, but I wouldn't let any harm come to him, despite how dreadful the storms became. We all made it through all right, but I admit I might not take him out to sea again. I'm terribly superstitious," she laughed.

"How many days do you expect will be your total trip?"

Nellie furrowed her eyebrows together as if calculating before answering. "If we continue at the extreme speed this train has so kindly supplied me, I should make it back to New York a few days early, making my trip around the world in seventy-two days." Nellie beamed at her statement, and her chin rose just a bit in absolute pride.

"Seventy-two days! But the book said eighty!"

"The book is fiction," she pointed out. "A delightful read and well researched, but haven't we humans always exceeded expectations?"

Around the World in 80 Days. Now that tugged at my memory. A fictional book I had to read for school, but not once did anyone mention someone testing out this theory, let alone a woman who knocked eight days off the estimated feat.

"Nellie Bly, I must get up close to you!" A man from the outskirts of the crowd hopped up and down, waving his arm for her attention, and started pushing his way through.

Curiosity, more than anything, made the crowd part as he hurried to the platform. Luke took advantage of the opening and, grabbing my hand, led us closer to the platform too. Kyle, who'd been staring at the man and looked as shocked as before, hurried after us.

The rushed man reached the platform and held up his clenched fist. "You must touch my hand, Nellie Bly," he said, and held it up for Nellie. She hesitated for barely even a second before leaning over the railing and brushing her fingers over his fist.

He beamed and opened his hand to reveal a little fluff of white fur. "Now, you will be successful. I have in my hand the left hind foot of a rabbit!"

"Miss Bly, the train is ready," a man stepped out of the train and said to her. She said her thanks to the rushed man and waved at everyone in goodbye.

"Wow," Luke said as the crowd shouted their goodbyes back. "Dinah is not going to be happy she missed this."

I shuddered at the thought of the history nerd's jealous glare if she ever found out. "I'm torn between bragging about seeing Nellie Bly or not risking Dinah's anger and leaving this part out."

He grunted in agreement.

But then Kyle groaned and tugged at my arm before pointing toward the back of the train. I glanced just in time to see a flicker of dark energy sneaking in through an open window.

Chapter 19

Kyle and I shared a look of fear, just as Luke tensed up. "Hey, I think—" he started, but I interrupted him.

"It went in through a train window, but I didn't get a good look. Was it The Shadow?"

Kyle shook his head. "I don't think so. I don't feel any consciousness attached to it, which means either The Shadow is controlling the dark energy from somewhere else, or we're dealing with roque dark energy."

"Can't be from our travels. I closed the portal correctly." I double checked my memory and felt confident.

"We've dealt with roque dark energy before, right?" Luke asked.

Kyle cringed. "Ah, technically, those were all me."

Luke gave him a blank look, but his jaw switched. "Right. How could I forget?"

But Nellie Bly, her monkey, and tray of treats had all boarded the train, and the doors were closing behind them. "Wait!" I hollered and ran up the platform, only for a policeman to step in my way. "I need to get on that train," I said.

"Ticket?" But he must have quickly read my expression

because his cynical frown deepened. "You need a ticket."

Rats. We'd have to sneak onto the train then. But then Luke stepped up next to me. "Is it possible to speak with Nellie Bly before the train takes off? It's just that this girl has wanted to become a reporter for a long time, and an opportunity to get the advice of Nellie Bly herself doesn't come along every day."

"Sorry, the train's taking off," the policeman said, but Nellie Bly poked her head out one of the windows.

"Let them on, Officer. I'm sure we can make it work. Isn't that right?" She glanced behind her at who I could only assume was a train attendant, who mumbled something in return. Whatever he said made her smile, and soon another head poked out the window as the train attendant waved his okay.

The officer stepped aside and gave us the nod to continue. "Good luck with your endeavors, miss," he said as we passed.

I flushed and smiled at his sincere comment. It was strange. I had expected a man to step off the train, was prepared for cynicism from the man of the past without even realizing it, and instead, the town had been welcoming and the man supportive. I knew the past hadn't been kind to women. Nellie Bly wouldn't be allowed to vote yet. But maybe kindness always existed too. Perhaps the prejudices against each other never existed as a default, no matter the era.

We stepped onto the train. Nellie Bly stepped out of a compartment and waved for us to join her. I shared a look with the boys, and they both nodded, so I knew we were on the same page. We'd keep our cool, with an eye out for the dark energy. So we stepped into the compartment.

Luke and I took the seats to the left, and Kyle sat next to Nellie Bly, who waved at the townspeople as the train started. When the train got too far away, she leaned out the side and kept waving as long as she could. Finally, the crowd became too small, and she fell back into her seat with flushed cheeks from the wind and a huge, exhilarated smile as bright as her happy aura.

"Such a delightful surprise," she said as she smoothed her hair back. "But I'm parched from trying to speak over the shouts. Not used to public speaking. Haven't spoken to a crowd of people that big since...." She paused, and her face froze in a forgotten smile. Her aura darkened, twisted, and churned for just a split second. Then the bright, happy energies returned, and she physically shook her head as if shaking the darkness out. "But anyway, you say you want to be a reporter?"

All eyes went to me, and I opened my mouth to respond when a strong shake took the train. My hands went straight to find something steady, one hand going to the wall and the other grabbing Luke's arm. He grabbed my elbow as his other arm clutched the window frame. Nellie kept her monkey's cage steady, and Kyle hit his head against the door. This was my first time on a train, but I didn't think they'd be *that* unstable.

"That was quite the jostle," Nellie said, proving my suspicions correct.

Kyle and I shared a look. The dark energy. He stood up. "I'll go check that everything's all right."

"I'll go with you." Luke instantly went to his feet. A surge of suspicious red streaked Luke's aura as he spoke, and Kyle, who saw the colors as well as me, glared as if insulted.

I glanced at Nellie as the boys started to leave. "I'm going to.... I'll be right back," I said and rushed after them.

"I don't need a babysitter." Kyle tossed his words over his shoulder as he walked to the back of the train, where we'd seen the dark energy slip in.

"Prove it," was Luke's simple response.

"Hey." I grabbed their arms and pulled them back. "What happened to the buddy system? Time travelers don't leave each other behind, remember?"

Kyle sighed in irritation. "I'm just checking out the back. I'll be right back, or if I need help, I'll holler." He tapped his temple, reminding me of our mind reading connection. "So you can tell your boyfriend to let me do my job. Checking out the dark energy is the whole reason we're on this train."

Luke brushed his fingers against my arm and leaned in to speak only to me. "Let us handle this one."

"Why?"

He glanced behind me, and when I looked back, I caught Nellie watching us with a suspicious look as she munched on some candies. Thank goodness she was too far away to hear our conversation. Luke didn't speak again until I looked back at him. "I saw you watch her back there. She did what many people considered impossible, just like you. Then she came home and embraced the people who welcomed her. I get that I wasn't raised like you—I never experienced the same limitations. So talk to her. Get her insights. Ask her for advice on coming home."

"That's why you made all that up, me wanting to become a reporter, to get us on the train, instead of us just teleporting?"

He shrugged. "Call it hope. Let Kyle and I handle this one. It's just some roque dark energy, right? Easy. We'll be right back. You trust Kyle, right?"

Luke said the words on purpose, with no sincerity, but a note of catching my hypocrisy in the act, and maybe he was right. I glanced between him and Kyle as a lump of fear lodged in my stomach. It was one thing for me to be alone with Kyle. If he ever changed his loyalties, I knew I could handle him. My powers were equal to his own. But Luke wasn't like us, and he didn't have his sickle of petrified wood. If Kyle didn't have his back, Luke could be putting himself in danger.

Kyle shook his head at me as if guessing every thought. "Should've remembered what it means to be considered family to you. You don't trust your parents or your sister, so why trust someone you call your brother?"

It was a slap in the face, and he knew it. "Fine," I said. "First sign of trouble, say the word."

I tapped my temple, and Kyle nodded. Without another

word, he kept walking. Luke brushed a sweet kiss against my cheek in goodbye and hurried to catch up with him. Fear and guilt for being afraid battled it out in my gut as I returned to the compartment.

"Everything all right?" Nellie asked. We both sat down, and she closed the compartment sliding door behind us.

"Yeah." I gave her my best fake smile.

She raised an eyebrow, not buying it for a second. "Those two boys? Are they your chaperones? Where are you from?"

"That's Luke and Kyle. Luke's my...." Only, were we back together? What were we? Exes working together? Boyfriend and girlfriend? Friends? "Well, that's complicated. And then Kyle is my...." Brother. Just say, brother. It was easy to believe, and I'd already declared it once, right? But before I had spoken defensively. Kyle had been alone in a crowd of family, and he looked so out of place, pitiful, and my heart had gone out to him much like it had back in the dark world when I saw things from his perspective. But now? Away from judging eyes, away from his lonely scowl, I wanted to speak the truth, only I didn't know it. Kyle wasn't my enemy, but he wasn't family either. I didn't trust him, but I unfortunately still cared about him, so what did that make us? "Yeah, chaperone, I guess."

"And where are you three from?" Nellie asked. She gestured at my clothes. "I've come across many different styles in the last few months, but never this particular one."

"Oh, it's experimental. I have a designer friend. We do." I corrected myself because the boys' clothes were off for the era too.

"A designer ahead of her time. I'm guessing it's a woman. You're wearing pants. Quite the feminist statement. I've never seen anything like it."

"Yes," I said because saying any more might tip her off that I was lying—time to keep it simple and move on. My mind went to Luke and how he did all this so I could talk to someone who might understand my situation better than him. It was sweet, but whatever Nellie Bly accomplished, it wasn't the same. Still, I owed it to him to try. So I gave her a smile. "Did you interview a lot of people during your travels around the world?"

"Sometimes," she confessed. "Although I prefer to write from experience when possible."

"Must lead to some exciting stories."

"Yes." She smiled. "Like this one." She gestured around us, and her smile never faltered, but her aura dimmed once again. Not all of her adventures had been like this. Some must have been quite traumatizing for her soul to dim that much in memory. It wasn't grief, not like how Luke's aura had been marked with black after losing his brother. This was something else. Doubt, ethical cynism. Her brightness came from how she saw the world and the people in it. I could tell by the whispers of memories which attached themselves to that brightness. Laughter and celebrations and the enjoyment of meeting new friends over a delicious meal. But when the colors dimmed, the cheerful memories changed to fear and shock and screams.

I leaned against the wall and consciously disconnected myself from her energies, not wanting to read anymore. Instead, I tried to focus on my goal here. "Around the world in seventy-two days." I smiled and shook my head in disbelief. "I would never have thought it possible."

"Many didn't. You wouldn't believe how many random people from the streets felt it their duty to warn me I'd never succeed." She laughed at that, like everyone doubting her was some big joke, and she was the one to deliver the punchline.

"What if you believe them?" I asked. "What if you want to do something against all logic or evidence? Science and human error and common sense all say it's impossible."

Nellie Bly tilted her head at me. "So these plans you have for yourself seem impossible to you. That's a more difficult one to work through. Why do you want to do it?"

"Morals, to be honest. Nothing else." I could walk away and tell everyone to embrace the day, enjoy the time we had left before The Shadow caught us. But there was a tiny chance I could fix it, and I had to take that chance. Because if I didn't, I'd be haunted by what ifs.

She nodded and, to my relief, didn't ask for specifics. "A few years ago, there was this opportunity to investigate something I didn't believe needed investigating. Stories spread that insane asylums were mistreating women—horrible stories, not even half of them could be true. Or so I thought." She gave me a sad, strong smile, like a heavy tick at the corners of her lips. "Those ten days undercover…women are capable of enduring incredible amounts of pain, but that doesn't mean we should. We are strong, and doing the impossible can be as simple as packing a bag and buying a ticket. It can be as hard as biting your tongue and letting someone get hurt so you can truly save them later. Want my advice? Trust your friends. Keep them close. Yes, the impossible is an exhilarating task to complete, but I've never done it alone."

"I have friends. People I trust who want to have my back, but…." I hesitated. Here was this random woman who, yes, accomplished a lot but knew nothing of my situation, and maybe I didn't want to admit that I needed them because it came at a heavy price. The truth was rough to speak out loud. "I don't want to lose them. I made my choice, and I'm okay with the consequences of it. I want to help people, to save lives, as many as I can, and that means running into dangerous situations with low chances of coming out again. I have people who want to run with me to have my back, but the choice would be mine. The dangers would be because of me, and if anyone got hurt, it would be my fault."

"No, it wouldn't. Not if they choose to join you. Penny, isn't it?" She leaned across the small compartment and wrapped her hand over mine as she looked me seriously in the eye. "Penny, sometimes we need our friends to pull us back, so we don't go too far. Everyone needs a voice of reason by their ear. Most of the time, people take turns. Sometimes we're the voice of reason, and sometimes we're the adventurers lost in enthusiasm. The key is finding people who know the difference between holding you back and holding you steady."

Steady. The memory of Luke's fingers against my elbow whenever I got overwhelmed rushed to the forefront of my mind.

Nellie let go of my hand and leaned back against the bench as she chuckled. "Don't push people away just to play the noble hero. Embrace the help, and for mercy's sake, never turn down a cheering crowd." She gave me an excited expression and handed me some candies. I took it with a laugh. Luke was right. I needed to talk to someone without a tie to the chaos that was my life but who understood the weight of the impossible.

The second shake rattled the windows and tore that peaceful feeling from my mind.

Chapter 20

Penny, get to the back of the train. Now!

I jumped to my feet as Kyle's voice screamed in my ear. "I need to find the boys," I said as Nellie said, "I'll speak to the conductor." We raced out of the compartment and went our separate ways. People poked their heads from their seats to see what was going on, but nothing my physical eyes could see would help me, so I unfocused them and let the emotional energies take the front reins.

In the far back of the train, two souls stood against the edge, one as dark as a deep, empty cave, the other as bright as a summer's day. But it was the dark energies hovering above them that made me double my speed. That was no slip of dark energy. It wove and wrapped around them, only to release and sneak past them to swipe at the wheels of the train. This wasn't a rogue energy at all—it was too conscious. With a sick churn in my gut, I realized it was playing with them.

The Shadow.

I reached the end of the train and yanked the door open. Wind sucked my hair into my face as I stepped onto the open edge. Only a thin metal railing kept me from falling off the edge of the train barreling at rope speed. Luke had his eyes closed as he focused on his other senses to feel the darkness above us. His blond hair tossed around, and the level of severe concentration doubled my worry. Never a good thing when the optimist took things seriously. But the second I opened the door, he reached out for my hand to keep us steady, eyes never opening once. He had felt me rather than seen me, and despite the dangers of the situation, the small automatic reaction mesmerized me.

To my left, Kyle stared wide eyed above us. His face had gone pale, and fear gripped his muscles in a tense stance. He could run any second, but he didn't, and I appreciated that too.

"What's going on?" I asked.

"I don't know," Kyle admitted. "It's not The Shadow, but I think The Shadow is controlling it."

"It's toying with us." Luke's frown deepened, and his hand went to his belt, where his weapon should have been. His fingers gripped air, and the hand that held my hand tightened as if in regret.

"The Shadow has to be here somewhere." I searched the plains and the skies but only saw sage and clouds.

"It's keeping its distance. Coward!" Kyle shouted.

"Don't bait the evil monster," Luke groaned.

The churning darkness above us shot down toward the train tracks. I punched my arm out and shot a protective barrier of my own darkness. The attack bounced off and recollected above us.

Surrender. The Shadow's demand rattled my brain. Next to me, Kyle flinched. *Stop these silly games or force me to stop your hearts.*

"Don't waste our time with empty threats," I said. "If you wanted us dead, you would have just killed us. But that would seal the timeline, wouldn't it? It would finalize the past you want to change. Portals between our worlds reopening, like when you were a child. You need us alive. So you're hurting all these people, destroying both our worlds, for what? To make a point? You really think Earth is more dangerous than your rage? Because I saw what happened to your elders. And you have single-handedly killed more of your own kind than everyone who died in that massacre."

A rumble of anger surged through the air, and I questioned my confidence. Sure, killing me now would seal in the past, but rage was an unstable emotion, and The Shadow might not think its next move out properly. Then the fiery hatred pulled back, like a forced rein of control.

Things must return to how they are. My world can be great again. At no cost to you, Penny. I can take away the memories of loss. You'll go back to how things were always meant to be for you.

Kyle's eyes flickered to mine, and it occurred to me that maybe he was scared I'd take The Shadow up on the deal. What would I lose if I took it? Nothing. In fact, I'd gain my family. They'd get their memories back. Things would go back to normal, and I could have my future filled with possibilities again. Ricky would die a child on the streets of Shakespearean England, Shreya would never be born, and it would suck for about two seconds until I forgot all about them. I'd lose my memories of Luke, but we were neighbors. Surely we could find each other again. Heck of a lot easier to swallow than an endless future trapped in a paradox with The Shadow. And if this had ever been about self preservation, I might have considered the deal. But it stopped being about me a long time ago. The Shadow wanted to hurt countless innocent souls to maintain a status quo, and I wasn't going to turn a blind eye to that.

"You can't hurt people to make a point. Kyle doesn't belong in your world, and he's not hurting anyone by choosing a different life."

Then deal with the consequences of your choices.

The voice went quiet, and I knew The Shadow had left even before the churning darkness above reacted to the loss of control. It dropped like an anvil toward the passenger train. My hands shot up in a defensive cross, and it slowed but refused to stop. It was too heavy, too much, and I needed help. "Kyle! Anytime!"

But relief never came. I opened my eyes, half worried The Shadow had stolen him. But there he stood against the train door, staring straight at me. A sickening look of regret distorted his face. He shook his head, and just…stood there as the darkness pooled over the edges of my weakening barrier. Shock and confusion shook my nerve, and the darkness slammed against my walls. The jolt of it was too much. My knees hit the shaking train floor hard, but I focused my strength on the barrier just in time.

By my side, Luke cursed loudly. "I can stop it from hitting the train, but Penny, it might hurt. Brace yourself."

"What?" I asked, but a second later, I understood. Luke's aura changed. Rays of sunshine swirled and darkened into amber ringlets. His energies stretched and strengthened. The colors and patterns were so familiar — petrified wood.

I'd only ever seen a person do this once. Months ago, back when we were fighting The Void, Ricky created a barrier of petrified wood to protect us using only his aura. Years of training had given him the ability to mimic the vibrational level of petrified wood strong enough to repel the darkness. And here my Stranger stood, accomplishing the same feat with mere months of training under his belt. And yet, his aura was strong. It would work. And it would hurt like hell.

I scrambled to the edge of the opposite railing, but it would do little good. He'd need to get his energies further than that to help me stop the darkness. One foot away. Six inches. I clenched my jaw and steeled my nerves.

It covered it, surrounded me, and I should have been shaking in agony, but instead, it felt like a hug. Like Luke's delicious "everything will be okay" kisses. I looked down at my hand and nearly started crying in relief and more. Where his aura met mine, a protective pale pink layered my own energies. Just a thin layer, but impenetrable. I stood surrounded by dangers from the impending darkness, the unsteady train, and petrified wood, but the only thing I felt was safe and strong and steady. I should be used to this by now, all these random moments in the middle of chaos where he made me redefine love.

His aura reached above us and took some of the darkness's weight. Together we shoved it away from the train. I jumped to my feet and leaned over the edge of the railing, expecting it to fall and hit the ground with a searing explosion since the darkness and our world rarely mixed well, but instead, it hovered above the plains, as if being pulled back. Then it streaked toward us.

"It's coming back!" I yelled, and grabbed Luke's arm. "Get ready to—" But then it streaked past us.

Kyle leaned over the side toward the front of the train. "It's going after the bridge!"

I peeked over the side, hoping for everything merciful in the world that we had enough time to stop it, but the front of the train was already touching the bridge. No, on the bridge now. The tendrils of darkness wrapped around the base of the bridge and squeezed.

Luke and I reached out toward the darkness at the same time. My own dark energies and his golden amber streaked out against the threat. We pulled it back, twisted and loosened the burning tendrils, but it was too late. Some of the wood seared to ash. The bridge shook against the weight as the train raced to cross. As I yanked the tendrils back from destroying even more, Luke kept those tendrils from coming back. We were *almost* across the bridge when it fell.

Chapter 21

Wood cracked under our feet. The bridge was falling. Luke yanked me to him as the back of the train leaned down. Broken wood and twisted metal fell hundreds of feet below the canyon. I clung to him as my stomach lurched. Then the train whipped back onto the tracks. We stood there, terrified, and too scared to move. Where was the darkness? I waited wide eyed and braced, but it was as if The Shadow backed off to make a life-threatening point another day.

Luke's arms were still around my waist, and he set his forehead against my shoulder with a sigh as we both seemed to realize the darkness had retreated at the same time.

"That was close." Kyle's voice chilled my relief. Yeah, it had been too close. Because of him. Luke and I looked at him and, though I couldn't see his face, I could imagine Luke's expression of enraged disbelief.

I wanted to yell at Kyle, and yet I couldn't. The vivid memory of him refusing to help had burned itself in my mind and combined with my suspicions that he didn't actually care about me. He was just using me. Nothing had changed — but I couldn't think about this right now. I needed to make sure everyone on the train was okay.

"I'm going to find Nellie," I told Luke. He nodded, and I headed back into the train.

"Penny—," Kyle started, but I shot him a warning glare. I couldn't even think of a decent retort. No words could hurt him the way his cowardness had hurt me, and I refused to show him how stupid I'd been to trust him. My pride refused to let my voice shake with emotion. So I couldn't talk yet. Personally, I'd expected Luke to stomp off with me, and we'd leave Kyle standing there alone and friendless like he deserved, but Luke stayed behind. Maybe it was for the best. Luke would yell at him, maybe send him on his way, and this time, I wouldn't stop it. Kyle didn't belong with us.

Nellie found me near our compartment. She gasped and rushed to me. "Are you all right? The bridge fell just as we passed. To think, I almost didn't touch that rabbit's foot."

Her amazed relief made me laugh, half hysterical. The train gave everyone free tea to stabilize their nerves, and Nellie told me her side of the story. She'd been speaking to the driver, so she saw when the bridge started to crack. She mentioned the rabbit's foot more than a few times with a superstitious reverence, and I found myself a bit relieved she'd done it too. The mixture of bad luck and miracles of the last few minutes was unbelievable.

Not long after, Luke knocked on the compartment door before opening it. To my disappointment, Kyle stood behind him. No matter, I'd tell the guy where he could go. Luke listened to Nellie's story of the rabbit's foot and smiled, his eyebrow cocked up a bit in entertainment. When he looked at me, that pale pink protective barrier popped back into my memory, and I felt all warm inside. It was so strange to go from hating Kyle to loving Luke so quickly. I was filled to the brim with romantic urges and a numbing rage. I wanted to grab Luke's hand and run away. Never look back.

"Penny, can I speak to you a moment?" Luke asked. "Alone?"

He gave Kyle a pointed glance.

I stood up and took his hand. We slipped past Kyle without a glance, and I found myself alone in a compartment with my Luke. He closed the compartment door, and it was only then that I realized something had changed. Something was different. A bucket of ice water-to-the-face kind of different. His aura had returned to his natural sunshine, but the colors were dimmed.

"You okay?" I asked. Fear gripped me. "Were you hurt?"

He shook his head. "The question is, are you okay?"

"Yeah, I'm fine." I brushed the question aside. "Why didn't you tell me you could do that? Luke, I wish you could have seen how powerful you are. I know you can feel it, but...." I shook my head at a loss for words. Then it clicked why he was acting weird. "You didn't hurt me. If that's what you're worried about."

He nodded, but the weird, standoffish energy between us didn't soften. "I tried to make sure it didn't touch you. When you're in pain from the petrified wood, your hands shake. I watched for that."

"Actually felt kind of amazing." Seemed vulnerable to say it out loud like that, like it was some kind of confession.

He gave me the softest of smiles, and it made my heart flutter. "Good. I'm glad." Gosh, this moment would have been so nice if he was all the way in the room with me, but his mind was somewhere else.

"Okay, then what's wrong? Is it Kyle? Because I'm convinced. He's out. In fact, we could just leave right now. He doesn't deserve a goodbye. I'm so sorry I put us in that position and that I trusted him, but it'll never happen again...." But my voice trailed off as Luke's energies reacted to my rant. Instead of relief, a thick protective wall lined his aura. I couldn't read anything from him anymore. It was a cheap trick but an effective one, and stronger than I'd ever seen before. He really had been training while I was away. "Why did you do that?" I asked.

His thumb tapped against his thigh for a moment, as if

thinking, and then he stepped closer and grabbed my hands, holding them together against his chest as he stared into my eyes with a determined look. My hands rose and fell with his breaths, and I relished the warmth of him, which slipped through the thin T-shirt. "Penny, remember all those times you kept secrets from me, and it sucked, but you had a good reason, and in the long run, it was a good thing you kept those secrets?"

Well, that's never a reassuring start to a conversation. I squirmed. "I remember you being very bitter about those secrets, and me learning that keeping secrets between us is never a good idea."

He hesitated. "In that case, I'll start over. Penny, I'm going to ask you to do something, and you can't ask why. You just have to trust me."

"Trusting you is never a question."

"Good." And his soft smile was back. "Because Kyle stays with us."

I withdrew my hands from his grip and stepped back. "I know I didn't just hear that," I said, giving him a chance to see reason on his own. But Luke just gave me a complicated look as his walled up aura held no hints to an explanation. "You hate him. You don't trust him, and you were right." But Luke didn't offer any argument. "Wait, you were alone with Kyle. Did he say something? Is he blackmailing you? He's done that before. We can't—"

"Penny." Luke closed the distance and held me by my shoulders. "Just trust me."

I almost said no, but stopped myself in time. "You were there, right? When Kyle flat out refused to help us?"

"I was there."

"Then why—?"

"I've trusted you before." He played the one card I couldn't argue. "I've trusted you blindly multiple times, across space and time. I'm just asking you to do the same."

I opened my mouth to argue but was disappointed when no quick response popped into my head. "I can't believe he didn't help. I don't understand."

"I know." He pulled me into a hug. "And you don't ever have to talk to him again if you want. Just...let's keep him in eyesight. Keep your enemies closer and all that."

But the streak of a lie etched through the walls of his aura. Luke didn't see Kyle as an enemy. Not anymore. So what had changed? But I couldn't ask, and I knew he wouldn't answer. So this was what it felt like to be out of the loop. I'd made my Stranger trust me blindly so many times, but I'd never been on this side of the situation before. Didn't love it, to be honest, but I also promised him no more secrets. "Luke?"

"Hmm?" he answered, his cheek against the crown of my head.

"You wrapped me in this pale pink love. That's why your petrified wood aura didn't hurt me. Did you mean to do that?"

"You know the deal. You protect the world. I protect you. That's not something I have to think about to do."

I imagined for a moment growing up with that feeling, going through college, maybe opening that psychic shop, and waking up every morning to that kind of love. That was a painful daydream which tore up my insides with longing. I was destined for a paradox, but I wouldn't trick Luke into a false hope. Not again. He was right. I really had held more than a lifetime's share of secrets from him, and I was done. Being open with him felt right, even if he wouldn't understand, even if he fought it.

"Luke, you know that to create a paradox, someone has to get close enough to trigger the device. Someone has to be trapped with The Shadow. Someone stubborn, who's willing to make that choice and never regret it."

His shoulders tensed for a moment, but he remained steady, unsurprised. "Yeah. I know," he whispered, and it was like some terrible secret spoken to the wind. I barely heard it over the churning of the train tracks below us. So he'd put it all together too.

"I would rather live the rest of my life going on adventures with you, but I have to—"

"Hey." He pulled back and looked me in the eye with a forced smile. "It's not happening yet, right? Let's not think about it. I want to live in the now with you. No more wasting time thinking about the future. I want as many nows with you as possible, so we can't waste time worrying. Okay?"

I nodded. Yes, that would be best. Fill me up with happy memories to get me through a trapped eternity. "What are we? During the rest of our todays?"

"All I know is that I'm yours."

The smile on my lips strained my cheeks, I was so bursting with happiness from those words. "I'm yours too. 'Til eternity and after."

"I can work with that."

He leaned down and pressed his lips against mine, and it felt like the sealing of a promise, the start of something new. We had changed, Luke and I, and done so apart. I thought we'd never be able to go back to what we once were during the days of Stranger and Penny. Foolishly, I'd mourned the loss. But this…I'd never felt this before. It was different, *more*, and I realized I could change. I could become whoever I wanted, and then change my mind and become someone else completely, knowing that whoever I was at any given time, Luke would wrap me in that intoxicating pink love. I could make mistakes.

We lingered in our kiss for a moment, cherishing the new truth that was us. Then we held each other in a tight hug, my head on his chest and his cheek against the crown of my head.

"What do we do now?" he asked.

I thought about fighting The Shadow's half hearted threat, which nearly killed an entire train of people. Luke and I had been lucky. If Kyle had helped…. But as it was, Luke and I wouldn't be strong enough if The Shadow decided to come at us at full strength. And if Luke said he'd trained my family as well, and if we could get that paradox trap theory working, then I'd need all the help I could get to stop The Shadow's reign of terror once and for all. Nellie Bly was right. The impossible wasn't so hard to overcome, but it couldn't be done alone.

"We go home. Get ready to fight."

Luke's arms tightened around me. He pulled me back just enough to look him in the eye. "You won't regret this, Penny. I promise. Maybe we can figure something out where no one has to...." His voice trailed off. "No matter what happens, they'll want to be a part of it. Thing is, I think we can get more. If we're going to take the fight to The Shadow, then let's use all the help we can get."

"What do you mean?"

"Ricky and his family. The ones that are old enough anyway. My brother Jack will want in."

"We don't need to—"

"Penny." His eyebrows rose slightly as if warning me I was putting up stubborn distance. "It might be outside of your comfort to accept this, but you have an army of support. Use it."

He might have hit it on the nail there because a nervous squirming feeling worked its way in my gut at the thought of going home and being surrounded by so many people. People who had asked so much of me in the past, people who at times hated me or forgot about me and made me doubt my own existence. The thought that they were the exact same people who'd go to battle for me rattled me with confusion. Worse was the idea that they'd get hurt, and it would be my fault. But if I didn't stop The Shadow, more than the people I loved would hurt. Worlds would end. Ours would dry up as another drowned. If I fought The Shadow alone, I'd fail. There was no doubting that, which meant that the only way to save the world was to risk my family and friends. And Kyle, but I was warming up to *that* idea.

A rattle against the compartment door disturbed the tiny haven Luke and I had created. He reached over and tugged the door open, his other arm still around my waist. Kyle stood there, looking annoyed at having to wait so long. I must have thought his name too many times and summoned him.

Chapter 22

"The train is about to stop," Kyle said as he stood in the doorway. "I suggest we leave now before we get caught up in another of Nellie Bly's adoring crowds. We should find another busy city next. I think all the different souls made it harder for The Shadow to find us. It took a while to—"

"We're going home," I said. "Luke and I need backup if we're going to fight The Shadow. You can do whatever you want." Luke's arm tightened around me with a warning. I wasn't keeping to my promise. With a loud sigh to show this wasn't my idea, I added, "Of course, you're welcome to join."

"How big of you," Kyle said dryly, which grated on my nerves. Seriously? He was going to be all sarcastic? I gave Luke a *you see?* look, and he shrugged like *you promised.* So I couldn't do anything but glare at Kyle. "Going home will be dangerous. We won't be able to stay long."

"We won't," Luke agreed. Luke and Kyle agreeing. I was in a strange, parallel universe, and I didn't like it one bit. "We're going to grab everyone who wants to help Penny, the tech and research I need to make that trap, and then we're out. After that, you're right. A big city would give us time."

"The Shadow didn't show up until the crowd started to leave," I reluctantly agreed. "It's a solid theory."

"Thank you for agreeing with my *theory* on how my own kind think."

"Are you serious right now?" I snapped.

"Let's leave," Luke suggested as he stepped between us.

I glared at Kyle. *Traitor.* I slammed the thought into his mind.

He smirked. *Ah, don't go breaking your promise to your boyfriend now.*

I tensed up. How did he know Luke asked me to keep him along? Was he listening at the door? Did he read it in Luke's aura? Or had they made a deal those few minutes they were alone? What if Kyle had something over Luke, something to blackmail, to force Luke under his will? But as the suspicions crossed my mind, Kyle's expression turned from smug to resentful. *You really don't think I've grown at all. Joke's on you then. Luke and I have no deal. Your perfect Stranger is working entirely on his own with that promise. Careful now, don't break his trust.*

"I know you two are talking." Luke waved at both of us. "No one does staring contests that long. Now, what's it going to be? Are we going home or not?" They both looked at me for the final say.

I didn't respond but went straight to work. Closing my eyes to block out the waiting expressions, I summoned enough of my own inner darkness together into a portal. It only took a moment to find the right time. The same day we'd left, but later. Evening maybe. The energies of the home were tense. Frustrated reds, analytic blues, and a recurring question spoken aloud and echoed many times within their souls. *What if Penny doesn't come back?*

Guilt itched my core. If I'd been the one left behind, it would have hurt, and yet I couldn't seem to stop running away and hurting the people I cared about. When did running away become so easy for me? I'd felt the anxious impulse to run before, many times really, but to actually do it, to escape for the sole purpose of not wanting to deal with the mess of life, it wasn't something I wanted to be known for. And if I only had a few more days with my family, I didn't want them to doubt I loved them. Even if I never got the time to convince them to love me back.

I made the connection and wrapped the portal around Luke and me. With a dismissive flick, I grabbed Kyle at the last minute and could only hope he caught the hesitation. The physical world whooshed out of sight as we traveled. Luke tugged me against his side as the hard tile floor of the train compartment turned to soft carpet, and the colors of the wood and benches morphed to the sharp, energetic world. It warmed me all over to know he felt how my whole system went haywire during travels, how my sight changed, and I always got a bit dizzy.

Dinah's familiar blue aura spiraled with anxiety as it bent over as if she was squinting over the dining room table in research mode. There were two auras near her. No, three. A deep purple, which was Mom, and a striped blue and red, which seemed to be Dad lately. The third was a deep, rock strong brown, and more familiar to me than my parents lately. Jack. Luke's older brother.

We landed in the living room. I could see my own deeply dark aura and Luke's sweet sunshine right by my side. A few steps away from us, Kyle's own dark soul settled into the room. That void-like emptiness with a desperate undertone, which was the way he always was. A whisper of red pulsed through the black fog of his soul, like blood and life hiding under a fog of black.

I mentally reached out in impulse and tapped the shadowy streaks of red. A rush of desperation overcame me. No, not just desperation. Longing. A deep endless longing for…but that was the problem. He didn't know what could satiate the hunger. It was like there was something deeply off in the core of his soul, some life experience he knew he deserved, knew he'd love, and he had no idea what it was or how to find it. All he knew was that he would never have it. Centuries old, an eternity ahead of him, and no way to stop the pangs of yearning from rippling through him. It was torture, and it was worse now that he was a human with a body. He could feel, and the longing physically hurt.

The energetic world faded, and our family living room slipped back into view. The faded couch, the historical artworks Mom got through work, Dad's travel mugs, and Dinah's extracurricular schedule marked in blue on the family calendar.

The family was in the dining room, glaring over a splay of paperwork across the table and a strange makeshift device on the table. Parts of a radio and a large, sturdy looking battery had been combined with some other mechanical parts I didn't recognize.

Dinah must have seen me first. She stood straight up and gave me a *you're busted* glare. "Well, look who finally decided to come back."

Mom and Dad turned around. Mom put her hand to her heart, and Dad sighed as if in relief. He looked like he wanted to hug me but never made the gesture.

Jack, on the other hand, had no hesitation. Tall, with a wrestler's body, Jack worked for the police station a few cities over. If time had gone its natural path, he would have died in college protecting others, but I intervened, tricked a paradox, and now he was in my family's living room, pulling me into a tight hug. "Penny, so good to see you!" He lifted me up a bit when he hugged, and I squealed in surprise, laughing as he let go.

"What are you doing here?"

"Dinah called and said you were back. I hopped in my truck and drove straight here. Hey, bro." Jack and Luke fist bumped in greeting. "So, time traveling again. Where did you two go?"

"We shared a train ride with Nellie Bly."

Jack scrunched up his eyebrows in confusion. "Who?"

"Famous reporter from the late 1800s." Mom stepped into the room. "Did you have fun?"

This was weird. Conflicting emotions battled it out in splashing colors within people's auras, but everyone stood there, unsure what and how much they could share. My parents were angry I'd left. Dinah resented that I didn't take her with me, and Jack, though genuinely pleased to see me, hid fear that his younger brother had once again left for another century. Unresolved issues lurked behind placid expressions and polite smiles. Even I stood there, pretending I didn't hate Kyle for refusing to help me fight The Shadow, or that I was fine that my parents had forgotten about me, only to be ticked that I did something about it.

I waved at the device on the dining room table, ready to change the subject before one of those lurking emotions jumped out in the open. "Any progress on a way to trap a paradox?"

"Maybe," Dinah called, her attention going back to the nearby books. "Problem is Luke's the closest thing we have to a scientist in this group. No offense, Dad."

"None taken," he said. "I'm a coder, not a builder."

Luke went to the table and frowned as he picked up the device. "Any luck on collaborating it?"

"No." Dinah shook her head. "I don't even know how to begin."

I walked over to the table and glanced at the blueprints. Different hand drawn versions of the device covered the papers, proof of all the research, time, and effort my family had put into creating this last hope. In the blueprint, most like the actual device, waves of energy had been scribbled along the sides, like polar magnetic energies shooting out the top and bottom and wrapping around the device in a circle. "What's this supposed to do, anyway?"

"Remember what I did when The Shadow attacked the train?" Luke asked me.

Jack rushed back into the dining room and shared a worried look with Mom and Dad. "I'm sorry," Jack said. "You did what when?"

I ignored them and nodded, eager for Luke to continue. "You mimicked petrified wood to…. Oh." The blueprint in my hands seemed suddenly ten times more ominous. The magnetic energies drawn on the page. Petrified wood on all sides. Eternity in that trap would be worse than empty. Pain would radiate from all corners.

Chapter 23

Fear shivered down my back, but I swallowed it down. "This would definitely hold The Shadow back. If we can get it strong enough."

"That's the problem," Dinah said. "We can do it through meditation, but I don't know the actual numbers. How can we recalibrate a machine to the exact frequency?"

"If we get it just a little off, the whole device becomes useless," Dad added. "We need a scientist to look at this. Someone who understands frequencies and signals."

"But also someone who's not set in the confirmed laws of science," Mom joined in. "If we gave this to a studied scientist, I worry most would turn us away."

"So an expert in frequencies and transmitted signals, but not someone who's an expert in frequencies and transmitted signals?" Kyle lingered against the wall where the living room turned into the dining room, not quite in, not exactly out, and watched our conversation with a cynical expression, one eyebrow arched, the other narrowed. "This is a solid plan, everyone."

"There's a sweet spot there which might hold the answer," Dinah responded, undaunted by his disbelieving tone, but it grated on my nerves. Everyone in this room was working hard to fix his mistakes, and he just stood there and judged? Was he capable of helping at all?

"We've got one chance at this," Kyle continued. "It needs to work on a practical level, not a theoretical. This plan is too complicated, too wishy washy. Maybe we need something more simple."

"We're open to suggestions," Dad said, and tilted his head. "Got any?"

"That's not my job," Kyle responded.

Excuse me? I opened my mouth, but Luke nudged me and shook his head. I gave him a questioning look. Why exactly should I let Kyle stand there and be rude to my family? Sorry, Luke, Kyle crossed a line. "And what is your job exactly? Hmm? Stand there and judge people? Because you're not doing anything else useful."

"Penny —," Luke started, but Kyle interrupted him.

"Actually, Penny, can I talk to you in private for a moment?" Kyle asked. He stepped back as if to get into the study where a door could be closed behind him. He waited for me to follow before taking another step.

Luke frowned. "I don't think —"

"I'd love to talk privately," I sneered at Kyle. If anyone thought it would be a pleasant conversation, the bitterness in my tone would correct that. I promised Luke that I wouldn't kick Kyle out of the team after what he did, and I intended to keep that promise, but that didn't mean I had to bite my tongue and pretend we were all frolicking in a field of daisies here. Grumbling under my breath, I passed Kyle and walked into the study. He followed close behind and shut the door behind us.

A desk caught the evening sun through the window. The walls had been painted a soft bluish white, and a professional work chair on wheels made it possible to go from desk to filing cabinet in a hurry — Mom's study. Once upon a time, it was my room. The desk was where my bed once stood, and instead of blue-white walls, mine had been a pastel purple. Clothes used to litter my floor because I hated folding even more than I hated doing homework. Now the only clothes I had were the ones on my back, charity from Shreya. And yet, my childhood foam sword had come back. Would my clothes one day reappear? Would Mom come home from work, eager to get a little more of her project done before dinner, only to find a bed on top of her desk? Or would time reach a standstill once I triggered that device? Would I forever both exist and not exist? Be a part of reality and yet forgotten?

How badly would it hurt to be stuck in that trap with my enemy?

I sniffed and took a deep breath to toss those questions from my mind. Then I turned and gave Kyle an unfiltered glare. "How dare you talk to my family like that."

"I want to go back to the forest," Kyle said abruptly. "Let's stay there until we figure out what those blurs are."

"No." I shook my head at his incredibility. "Why would I go anywhere with you? Why are you still a part of this team?"

"Because you need me."

"I think your actions on that train proved we don't need you, and you're a liability. What did you say to Luke? He's never taken your side, and he hates you, so what did you do to make him change his mind?"

"Don't worry. He still hates me." Kyle sounded bitter. "Everyone does. It's one of the rare consistencies amongst humans."

I stepped closer to him and pointed at myself. "I didn't. I gave you a chance. You're the one who threw it in my face."

"Didn't you hear what they're making out there?" Kyle waved at the door. "That's going to be a whole new level of pain, Penny. You have no idea. Either it doesn't work, and The Shadow tears our souls apart, or it works, and one of us is going to have to—"

"Don't worry. No one expects you to follow through," I sneered. "I'll be the one activating the device. You can go back to the forest after, free from The Shadow. You'll get your happy ending, Kyle."

There it was again—a rush of red through his blackened soul. Before, I'd thought I'd just seen it wrong. Beings like him never had color. And yet, it was so strong in this moment I could see it even without closing my eyes on the physical world. It radiated from him like an ominous red sun through thick storming clouds.

My anger dissipated as curiosity took over. "How are you doing that?"

"What?" Kyle asked.

I grabbed his hand and held it out in front of him to put his aura in his sight. He frowned and lifted his arms, turning his palms inward and outward. "Huh." He flexed his fist and then stretched out his fingers. "That's new."

"The human half of you has reached your soul," I guessed. "You're in color."

"Almost," he agreed. "Weird, I always hoped I'd have more orange. Color of willpower and strength. Instead, I'm painted in fear."

"Welcome to humanity," I said, and I kept my tone cynical, but a touch of pity slipped its way in against my own better judgement.

"I thought I'd be happy once I escaped the dark world. And then I thought it would happen after I got a body. Or when we were goofing around back in Scotland."

"I thought I'd be happier when my family accepted me, remembered me even if it was just a little. But I'm not," I admitted. "Maybe happiness isn't something you chase. It's something you choose. And if you can't choose it on your own, then you get help."

"And if you're alone?" he asked.

Personally, I was a little ticked that he'd managed to soften my anger. Somewhere between him wimping out on helping me fight the Shadow and here, I'd forgiven him. "Oh, come on, Kyle. I'm angry at you, but I'm here. And Luke was there for you, even though I still don't get why. You're not alone."

"I will be," he said. "When you're gone, I will be alone. Not one of those people out there would spare me a second's thought once this is over. I'm a means to an end, and what do I do when I'm not useful? I'm terrified of what's going to happen to me the second your family figures out how to make that device work. Everything is going to change, and I know I want to change with it. I escaped the dark world because I was going insane without it, but nothing's changing for the better. It's slowly getting worse and worse, and I'm scared one day it'll be too much for me to handle, and I'll break. Penny, I'm not used to this humanity thing. I don't like it. I care about people, and it hurts. I made promises to you and broke them, and it meant nothing before, but now I'm riddled with guilt because you're disappointed in me, because I'm a coward. I know what's going to happen if we continue this plan, and it might just destroy me, so…so let's go. We can run and hide, and things don't have to change."

"Kyle…," I sighed. "This is happening."

"You'll regret it," he promised.

"Probably at times," I admitted. "But then I'll think of all the people we'll save in both our worlds and I'll feel good about this decision. I know what you're going through. I've run before. I've tried to escape a hard truth, but you can't run from it. Eventually, you'll just end up in the exact same spot. I tried to run from you, remember? I tried to run from the sacrifice of saving Jack, but I always had to deal with it eventually. And I'm done hiding or running away. I know I'm strong enough to handle it this time, so better just get it done. Of course, I'm scared, but I'm not afraid of the unknown anymore. You don't have to be scared either. It'll change, yes, but good things will come out of it. You'll be free.

And even if there is no longer a place for you in this group, the world is filled with communities of different people. You'll find like-minded souls somewhere. Your own community of people and support."

"What if I don't?" he asked.

"Yeah, but what if you do?" I countered with a shrug. "It's all theory until it's not, so why default to the worst case scenario? What if this works and the pain's not so bad? What if everyone moves on and is happy and safe? What if everything we worked so hard for happens? The people I love are safe, and you experience happiness. It's all about what you put after the *what if*."

He didn't look convinced, but he nodded. Hopefully, the words would settle in with time and comfort him because once this was over, I wouldn't be around to help out. And once I was gone, he needed to step up.

"Kyle, I do have something to ask you. Something only you can do, so you have to follow through on this."

He frowned. "What?"

"After I stop The Shadow, the tears in reality will still be open. Water will still get trapped in your world, destroying both realities. You need to close them and return the water to Earth. Stop the devastating drought in the future, and save all those souls from your world trapped in unfamiliar currents. I need you to promise me. You're the only one who can do it."

To my surprise, he actually smiled. "I have no doubt in my mind those tears in reality will close. It'll happen. I swear."

He didn't say he'd do it. I caught that. Maybe The Expert already planned to take the lead, although why Kyle would be shady about it, I didn't understand. Unless...unless Kyle didn't want to admit he wouldn't do it. Maybe he wanted me to think he had, deep down, a strong orange soul instead of the coward's truth radiating from him. As long as it happened, I guess I didn't care who did it. It was disappointing, but it was Kyle, so I should have been used to it by now.

"Okay." I nodded. "Thanks." Without another word, I left the depressing study and returned to the dining room.

Everyone cast curious looks at each other as I stepped up to the table, but no one asked what Kyle and I had discussed. "So...." I clapped my hands together, eager to get moving and get this over with. "Any leads on a scientist we can take this device to?"

"Actually, I think I found someone." Mom straightened her back as she talked, and her chin lifted up a bit. "A scientist before her time, extremely intelligent, although she never received a formal scientific education."

"Sounds perfect," I said. "I can make a portal to her as soon as you give me the details. Luke, Kyle, and I will hop over and get her help, and then—"

"Actually, there's been a change of plans." Dinah folded her arms and gave me her signature stubborn glare. "We'll give you the information as soon as you promise to take us with you."

That request was so ridiculous it actually made me laugh—not in humor, but surprise. There were seven of us squished around this dining room table meant for four. Two or three people might be able to slip into a moment in time unnoticed, but seven bodies popping into view would turn heads. Besides, with the level of danger that went along with time traveling, no way was I sticking my family into that.

"I appreciate the gesture," I said. There was an underlying tension in the room, only some of which stemmed from Kyle's earlier rudeness. The rest, I had to admit, came from me ditching them earlier today. I needed to make my point without causing more frustration. "But time travel is difficult, and the more people I'm responsible for, the more dangerous it is for everyone. I can't guarantee people's safety. Luke, back me up here."

"Ah, well—" Luke visibly cringed and gave me an apologetic shrug. "I would argue that it's safer to bring everyone." I blinked at him, waiting for him to realize how absurd this idea was, but he just stared back with a stubborn expression. "Penny," he continued, "I told you I trained them to meditate too. I think they could help. I'm not saying they should run into battle—no offense everyone—but they wouldn't be helpless."

"You have to realize you've been gone for months," Dad said. "And maybe your mother and I have been struggling to understand, to catch up in all this, but Dinah and Luke have been actively preparing for your return." Dad straightened up and gave his strongest, no argument, dad-tone. "We're going with you, young lady, and that's final."

In my experience, continuing to argue against that tone meant getting grounded and even, after one particularly ugly fight a few years ago over whether or not I could go to a party, I lost dessert privileges for a week. He couldn't ground me anymore, and if I wanted dessert, I could get it myself. I didn't rely on him for anything anymore. So why did I want to cave? Could be that years of mental programming took over instinctively to prevent punishment. Or maybe, just maybe, I missed my parents.

"Fine," I said with an irritated sigh, but a small flutter of happiness warmed my heart. This might be my last adventure, and I got to share it with the people I loved most. I cleared my throat as a wad of emotion threatened to choke me up. "So, where are we going anyway?"

"1942," Dinah said. "Look for a big party, lots of people dressed in their best, expensive foods. Think Hollywood, really. The crowd of the party should help us slip in."

"Plus, the crowd will give us time before The Shadow can find us," Luke added.

"We're looking for this woman." Dinah handed me her phone, where a screenshot of a gorgeous, glammed up woman smiled in black and white. "Her name is Hedwig Eva Maria Kiesler, but everyone really knew her by her stage name, Hedy Lamarr. She's incredibly smart, and we technically owe our WiFi and cellphone tech to her ideas."

"But," Mom lifted her chin and gave me a proud look, "she was never formally educated in the sciences. Her first husband sold weapons to the Nazis. She listened in on their conversations and learned how a lot of stuff was made before making her escape to America. She and the composer George Antheil developed an idea to stop torpedoes from being sabotaged by the enemy, but the tech for her idea hadn't been invented yet."

"We're hoping," Dad continued, "and emphasize on hope, that when we show her our device, she'll be able to tinker with it and get it working the way we need."

Kyle frowned. "How would we know if it does? If it's a mechanical frequency, I can't see those."

I walked over and patted Kyle on the shoulder with a fake smile. "Well, for it to work, it'll have to hurt, so that should clue us in."

He paled. "Oh, right."

But Dad frowned. "We do have a plan for keeping you two out of the danger zone when we confront this shadowy person, right?"

"Yes," Luke said before I could answer. He rushed to speak, and the one syllable lingered like a shout in the room. Everyone gave him a weird look, but he looked only at me. We knew what would happen—only Luke, Kyle, and me. No one else could know. Last time my life was on the line, Dinah pulled a gun out on Luke and threatened to shoot if we didn't stop. This time, no one could have any suspicions. It had to go according to plan.

"Let's get this party started," I said without any emotion as I rubbed my hands together and closed my eyes to focus. Crowded party…Hollywood. Hedy Lamarr.

"What's she doing?" Mom whispered.

"Meditating to find the right spot," Dinah answered.

"Do we need to be touching her to go with her?" Dad added, his voice barely even quiet.

"No, she can take us from here."

"Will the portal take the furniture too?"

"Will people please be quiet?" I groaned.

The room went silent, although Dad mumbled, "It was a valid question," under his breath before Mom whacked his arm in warning. I closed my eyes and tried again, but the humor and familiarity of Dad's grumbles and Mom's playful whacks warmed my heart. I couldn't stop the smile.

There. One moment shined bright in the vast space of moments behind my eyes. I grabbed every soul in the room as promised—Mom, Dad, Dinah, Jack, Luke, and Kyle. Then I tapped that shining light and created a portal between the times. With a whoosh and dizzying rush of energy, we traveled.

Chapter 24

Seven souls of so many different colors surrounded me as I waited to get my bearings back from the travel. Luke's warm sunshine was always by my side, and there was Dinah's blue, Mom's creative purple, Dad's strong red, and Kyle's strange silhouette, not quite a void black but not quite color either.

"I can't believe that worked," Dad said from somewhere to my left. "We're not in the living room anymore."

"Not exactly a glamorous party either," Mom said. "Where are we, a janitor's closet?"

"Storage room, yeah," I said as the physical world slowly slipped into view. "Seven people literally popping into a party might be noticeable. I figured we'd walk in."

"We aren't going to blend in looking like this anyway." Mom gestured at her paint-stained sweatpants.

"I thought about that," I said, and started looking around. There were boxes lining the walls filled with spare silverware, table cloths, and—ah ha! "And I tried to find a moment with uniformed staff. Hopefully, everyone will see these aprons and coats and just think we work here."

Dad took the apron with a cynical look. "This isn't going to convince anyone."

"It will," Jack spoke with a wistful tone as he wiggled into a tight black suit jacket. "If you act like you belong, no one will question it. Played a prank on my friend in college once. Walked right past security after a short chat about my dog and an oh-shoot-I-forgot-my-pass."

Dad shrugged and tied his apron behind him. He looked kind of hilarious in his casual business khaki pants, pastel blue button up shirt, and a frilly apron, but I didn't laugh until he caught me looking and gave me a goofy little twirl. Ugh, parents are so embarrassing, and I loved every second of it.

Everyone put on their aprons and waiter jackets. Kyle's was too big for him, and he practically swam in the sleeves. Mom and Dinah managed to look stylish somehow. If I plopped Dinah right smack in the middle of school looking exactly like that, apron over jeans would become the new trend. And then there was Luke. He made everything look attractive.

"One of these days, I'm gonna need to see you in a proper suit," I teased, and gave him a flirty grin. But then I remembered. There were no more one-of-these-days—just this party, and then my trap.

He must have thought the same thing, because he struggled to smile. "This'll have to do for now." The room got weirdly quiet. Everyone finished shuffling their clothes around and gave us a nervous glance. Music from a live band slipped in through the doors. Luke offered me his hand. "Let's get a closer look at that band."

I took his hand, and together we led the way out of the storage room. The hallway alone had a softened golden glow, whether from the paint on the walls or the delicate lighting, or maybe it was just the feel of the place—rich and expensive, and it wanted everyone to know. We followed the music to some swinging doors and then....

Flashing jewelry and swinging silk. Mouth watering aromas

and thick perfumes. A live band played as a blonde woman in a silk dress and white gloves sang softly into a mic. Polished couples danced to the beat or sipped from crystal champagne glasses, and laughed with their table. The energies of the place were a stark contrast to the visual glamour. As women laughed and joked, their souls were nervous twitches of fear that their jokes would land wrong and cost them getting cast or their dresses weren't right, and it would cost them a job. Men danced and laughed while their insides were a matted mess of anxiety, fearing their charm wouldn't give them the lead role they needed to feed their family. And hovering behind everyone's smile was the unshakeable truth that the world was long at war. WWII. Everyone had someone in danger, but they smiled and tried to forget, tried to hold on to the normal.

"There she is." Mom gasped and grabbed Dad's arm. She nodded once toward the piano, where a woman leaned against the side, listening to the music, her toe tapping along. The black silk of her dress shimmered as she swayed, smiling at the piano player as if they were in on some secret, and the power of her charisma made everyone want in on the secret too. Her dark hair was up in tight ring curls pinned back from her face, and her deep red lipstick remained in place, as only the highest quality of makeup could do. People stopped by her to chat and compliment her. Men flirted, and women asked where she got that dress or who her stylist was. As they asked about her looks, whirling thoughts zoomed around her head, ideas and plans and theories that needed to be tested. As a couple spoke to her about her latest film, a twinge of frustration tinted the colors of her thoughts as she forced a smile and took their compliments.

We lingered in the background and tried not to look out of place as the couple chatted with Hedy Lamarr. Mom and Dad apparently knew the song and quietly sang along, swaying on the spot with Dad's arms wrapped around Mom. Dinah picked up a tray of tiny puddings and held them out for guests walking by, while Kyle joked with a tween girl who looked suspiciously like Shirley Temple.

There was a movement to my left, and then Luke was there. He offered me his hand. "Dance with me." He smiled, but it was sad. The ticking clock was an ever present weight between us. I took his hand, and he led me to the middle of the dance floor before pulling me close. The weight of his hand on the small of my back was a comfort, and I sighed into the embrace as we started to move. He knew the steps, which, personally, I found incredibly attractive. But the dance was formal, the same as everyone else who slowly spun around us with so much modest space between them, and this was the last time I'd get to dance with him, so I pulled him closer and put my head on his shoulder.

"A scandalous dance for the era," Luke whispered, but he tightened his grip around me, holding me close, and I could feel his relief at the loss of distance same as me.

"I distinctly recall an old song called 'Put Your Head on My Shoulder,'" I pointed out, whispering because we were so close.

He chuckled, a low throaty sound. "Pretty sure that doesn't come out for close to another twenty years."

We danced in silence for a full song, just enjoying each other, and I realized Luke once promised he'd take me dancing. This was him fulfilling that promise. So I closed my eyes and pretended there were no plans, no devices to trap darkness, no paradoxes to trigger, and no futures to sacrifice. Just Luke, me, and how much we loved each other.

Another song passed, and I didn't want the peace to end, but with my eyes closed, I could vividly see the power to Luke's soul, that hope and logic-defying determination to do the impossible, curse the odds, and there was so much potential there I ached to know what it would become. What would my Stranger do once life returned to normal? Who would he grow up to become?

"Luke?" I asked, not quite ready to open my eyes yet. He hummed in answer. "I know we said no more talk of the future, but I want to know. What will you do after all this?"

He gave a deep inhalation, and it lifted my head. "I think I want to become an engineer. All these ideas we've had, all the things science thinks we can't do, I want to delve into that. Push the limits. Maybe I'll get my PhD."

"I wish I could see that happen." I didn't mean to say it, but the words slipped out.

Luke stopped leading the dance, and I lifted my head to look at him. He studied me with a conflicted expression. Finally, as if forcing down whatever thoughts or emotions he wrestled with, he managed to respond. "You'll always be with me, Penny. A part of every decision I make."

Then he kissed me. It wasn't a desperate kiss, but soft and reassuring. His fingers tangled in my hair as his other hand held my hips closer. This was the kind of kiss that had become home to me. The desperation I felt softened in his calmness. We were making the right choice. I trusted my reason over my fear, and his support validated it. I loved that he wasn't scared, wasn't stealing kisses or touches as if we were running out of time. This *felt* like a casual dance, and that meant everything to me.

But the lyrics to the singer's crooning slipped through the illusion and hit my heart with a sharp accuracy. *Now I find that I don't want to walk without the sunshine.*

Luke broke the kiss first and leaned back just enough to smile at me. He brushed back some stray hairs from my face and looked at me with such an unfiltered expression of love that it actually got me teary eyed. "What would you do if you survived all this?" he asked.

"I had a thought—," I started, but longing choked the words in my chest. "I would start a psychic healing shop—protective crystals, healing energy readings, go all out. Think I could help people, and it would be fun." It was surprisingly nice to share that dream with someone. No one else knew. Now, even if I faded from the world, someone would know.

He smiled. "I can see that. Hey, I want to tell you something." He whispered with a gentle excitement like we were just teens on a date, and he wanted to share something fun with me. "I was researching meditation techniques, and there were these scientists who studied the brainwaves of monks as they meditated on different things, like want and love and peace and healing. And guess what mindset reached the highest brainwaves?"

"What?" I asked, thoroughly enjoying this. All of it. The sad but beautiful music, lyrics of heartbreak and longing, the feel of his hands on me as we chatted out over science and meditation. "What thoughts reach the highest vibration?"

"Forgiveness." He held me tighter like maybe this wasn't just a passing conversation. Maybe he was trying to tell me something. "Every time they forgave, their brainwaves spiked, and their new base reading also became higher."

"That's cool." I played along, highly aware that I was ten steps behind him in this conversation. "You saying you'll forgive me?" I teased with a smile.

Luke tried to smile back, but his lips shook with emotions, and it faltered half a second later. The easy, everyday tone was gone. Reality came crashing in between us. His sunshine soul darkened not with grief but regret—a sickly blue, like a storm. When he spoke, his voice shook with so much emotion, it broke my heart. "I'll need you to forgive me."

"Oh, geez, Luke." I wrapped him in the tightest hug I could muster, and he buried his head in my neck. He was shaking. All those times he promised to protect me, and now there was no possible chance. I'd never thought how that might sit on his soul. "There's nothing to forgive."

"I don't want to lose you."

I didn't want to be lost, but wasn't that where all this was heading? From the very beginning, it all made sense to end with me stopping The Shadow. To finally be lost. "Luke, I trust you. No matter what happens, I love your warmth and your support."

He groaned, and there was so much unsaid in that groan that it filled me with confusion. As much as he opened up, there was something huge he hadn't shared yet. I was willing to hold him until he was ready, and he didn't seem inclined to let go. "I don't support this, though. You can't possibly think I'm okay with this ending. Penny, you're the first girl I've ever loved. And it's not like anything I've ever seen on TV or read in books. I want to know how long we can last. I want that future, and I'm going to do everything I can to make sure you come home with me." He leaned back, and his warm hands caressed my jaw, angling my head to look him in the eye. "I might need you to forgive me."

"Hey!" Dinah hissed in our direction.

The sharpness of her tone made me jump, and the little haven Luke and I had created was shattered. She gave us both a what-are-you-two-doing shrug before pointing at Hedy Lamarr. The passing admirers had said their goodbyes, and she swayed alone by the piano, listening to the music. Time was up.

Chapter 25

Luke and I walked to the piano, and I tried my best to push the heavy conversation we'd just shared to the back so we could focus. "Excuse me, you're Hedy Lamarr, right?" I asked.

She flashed me her stage smile, red lips posing. "That's me. Great party, don't you think?"

"Definitely charming," I agreed. "We were wondering if we could pick your brain for a moment over some of your work?"

"Of course. Any movie in particular?"

"No, we actually wanted to ask you about your expertise in frequency waves and disrupting torpedo signals."

The piano player fumbled his keys and looked up sharply at us. Hedy froze in place, a breathing painting if not for the rush of tensed confusion discoloring her soul. The loss of piano music caused a ripple effect within the party. The cellist stopped playing to see what was off. The singer paused with the loss of her melody, and the dancers stopped mid waltz, which made the chatting tables look over to us.

Hedy straightened up and used the height she had against me. "What do you know about that?"

I looked to Luke, confused about what I'd said wrong, but

he shrugged. Hurried steps came to a stop next to me, and Mom smiled over quickened breath. She put her hand on my shoulder in a motherly, *don't kids say the darnest things* way. "Hi, forgive my daughter. She's blunt to a fault and even more inquisitive." She smiled, and Hedy gave a nervous but unconvinced chuckle. At her wave to continue, the piano player resumed playing, and the party slowly moved away from its frozen state. Mom leaned in and whispered in my ear. "Try to sound less like a Nazi spy, hon." She squeezed my shoulder in encouragement as she straightened up.

"Sorry," I mumbled. "I'm not interested in your work—I mean, it's interesting, but that's not— We need your help."

Luke took that as a cue to take the small device from his pocket and hand it to Hedy. "We need this to project a certain frequency consistently within a twenty foot radius."

"That should be doable." Hedy took the device from him and started to turn it around as she inspected it. "Although I haven't seen this tech before. George, what do you make of this?"

The piano player leaned forward without skipping a key, squinted at the device, and shook his head. "Nothing I've seen."

Hedy shrugged at us and handed the device back to Luke. "I'm sorry. Whatever you might have heard about our patent, I'm afraid the details have been exaggerated. The military didn't believe my idea would be practical. But perhaps I can get you in contact with someone who would be more helpful."

"That's right," Dad mumbled behind me. "The tech had to catch up to Hedy's ideas. Wasn't until the Cold War that they listened."

"Excuse me?" Hedy asked.

"Could you just take a look anyway?" I asked and nodded at the device again. "It's a bit of a conundrum. See, we need to it release a frequency that technically doesn't exist yet as a sound wave. So we need someone who thinks out of the box. Like us."

She narrowed her eyes. "You want a radio to release a

frequency that's not a sound wave."

"More like the vibrational level of a rock, but through radio waves or something like that."

"Well, that is a puzzle. And an interesting one. Einstein did say that everything exists as a vibration, but a radio wave won't be able to project every vibration. Just as a piano can't play every note in existence. But the idea of projecting a vibration which mimicked that of a solid...." She took the device from Luke and stepped closer to George. "Of course, a piano could play any key it's tuned to play."

He grinned an excited let's-break-rules kind of grin and nodded at one of the well dressed men in the crowd. "Come take this piano from me. I'm getting a drink." Then he stood up. "What do you say, Hedy, back to the drawing board?"

"Come," she said to us, and the two led us to an empty table in the back of the party. The music was softened enough that we could talk, and with most people on the dance floor, we could talk without being overheard.

"Who's George?" I asked Mom as we followed them.

"Her inventive partner. They worked on the patent together. He passed before the military finally used it, though — never saw it in action — but Hedy Lamarr kept it going. Saved us during the Cold War. Penny, I think I need kudos for acting so calm. You put a museum curator in the middle of history." She showed me her hands as her fingers shook.

I chuckled. "You are much smoother than Dinah's first travel. Went full geek."

Hedy and George sat down, and we started to do the same. There was one person too many, though, and Kyle stood behind me instead. Better to hear anyway.

"What would happen if an air frequency matched the vibration of a solid?" George wondered.

"My thoughts exactly," Hedy said. "Would it break the solid or create a solid?"

"Like a high pitched sound against glass, you mean?" George frowned. "That could do a world of damage."

"We don't want to do damage," I interrupted. "It's more like this. Um…rub your hands together really quick. Focus on your hands and the way it feels. Connect with it." The bombshell inventor and the composer did as I said with mild amusement warming their souls. "Okay, now close your eyes and hold your hands out, palm out. Feel the heat? Slowly move your arms out until the feeling changes."

Hedy stopped about a foot from her skin, exactly where her aura ended. "Oh, it does change there."

"Okay, now keep moving your left arm until the feeling changes again."

She kept reaching out and paused at George's aura. "Interesting."

"I'm afraid we don't have time to explain the science behind this theory, but…." I scooted back and gestured for Luke to take my place next to her. Catching on, he leaned forward and closed his eyes. A second later, his aura darkened to that rich, amber, petrified wood. "Okay, feel with your right hand. That's exactly the frequency we need the device to mimic."

Hedy opened her eyes and raised a perfectly shaped eyebrow as her eyes fell on Luke. "You want this device to mimic your boyfriend?"

Kyle snorted. "That's one way to put it."

"On the bright side," Luke said. "No way the Nazis want that information. Think you can give us a hand?"

George frowned. "Is that possible?"

Hedy started to shake her head, but it changed to a shrug halfway through. "Maybe if you changed the keys. If every key played doubled the frequency…. You said it needs to be exact?"

"Extremely," I said. "Consistent too."

"Hmmm. What do you think? If we moved over this bit right here…." Hedy leaned closer to George, and the two whispered ideas. They seemed invigorated by the complex problem and bounced theories off each other in rapid succession. All I needed to do was keep everyone here safe until they solved the mystery, and then off to the paradox — the final battle.

It was strange how calm I felt about the whole thing like my purpose was to do this. Save the world. Protect my family. Despite what it meant for me, I was more than ready. I was anxious. Because being trapped in that paradox knowing I won, that the future was saved and no one else had to get hurt, would be so much better than this fear, this waiting. I needed it all to be over so people could go back to their lives.

The orchestra started a slow song, and people got up from their tables to dance. What would the new future be like? No more deserts, no more stealing water from your neighbor. Would there be fancy dances and celebrations? Technological advancements and collaboration between the countries? Maybe not everything would come true, but it was fun to imagine the possibilities.

Dad stepped up to me and offered his hand. "Care to dance?"

I smiled. "Sure."

He led me to the middle of the floor, and together we tried to mirror the formal dance postures of the time. "You know the waltz?" he asked.

"Luke taught me," I nodded.

Dad hummed, and we started slowly moving across the dance floor, with careful steps and an unease I think we both resented. This shouldn't have felt like dancing with a stranger, but the small feeling of familiarity between us was unstable without the history to back it up. "So, you and Luke," Dad said. "Did you two know each other before all this?"

"No. More because of all this. The Void, or Kyle before he got a body, convinced Luke to build a gateway between the dark world and this one so The Void could escape, and in exchange, Luke could go back and save his brother."

"Jack," Dad said. "And he did, correct? Jack is alive. Kyle can be trusted."

I kept quiet. Was this worth correcting? Kyle made his mistakes. He was here. I promised Luke I wouldn't ditch him. Let's move on. But my silence didn't reassure Dad.

"We can trust him?" he said again, and ended the phrase like a question.

"I mean, technically he stole Luke's memory so he couldn't go back and save Jack. Tried to kill me when I tried to get back home, although now he claims he was just trying to scare me. Then he stole some of my soul to create his own body and never willingly gave Luke his memories back. I got them back when I overpowered Kyle in a fight. But, to be fair, he taught me how to control the darkness, and he sacrificed his safety to distract The Shadow so we could save Jack." But then he destroyed the remaining trust I had in him when he withheld that vital detail about a needed sacrifice for the paradox, and then again when he refused to help on the train. Ugh. If he had even pretended to try, I would have defended him against any doubts. I had forgiven him completely, and he gave me a fresh new reason to distrust him.

"That's a lot of story and very little answer," Dad pointed out. "Penny, should we trust Kyle?"

I looked him in the eye and shrugged. "It usually comes out fifty-fifty."

Dad's frown deepened, and he looked lost in thought, confused, and I didn't blame him. Honestly, Mom and Dad were taking all of this relatively well, but I guess Luke and Dinah had been sharing stories with them before I came back.

"I'm sorry you've had to rely so much on a stranger and a traitor throughout all this," Dad said. "Your mother and I can't help but wonder how differently things might have been if I hadn't been on my business trip, or if Mom had picked you up from school instead of losing track of time—"

"Wow, rewind." I stopped dancing. "You remember that?"

"No." And he seemed overwhelmingly ashamed to admit it. "Dinah's explanations are extremely detailed. But she's got a point. If we had been better parents, maybe—"

"Oh my gosh." I rolled my eyes. "I'm gonna punch Dinah right in the arm next time I get the chance. When we traveled together, she blamed Luke for practically everything. I think it's a coping mechanism—if she can find a culprit, she can understand the problem. But that doesn't mean she's right."

"Even Luke admitted you were in this mess because you felt alone at home. As if being lonely and separated from the people you love is part of your identity. The Void used that to his advantage. I know what happened, Penny. They didn't spare the details. We begged them not to."

"Did Luke tell you that I ditched a ten year old kid in a futuristic apocalypse?" I asked.

Dad gaped at me in shock. "No, I would have recalled that part."

"I did. He's fine now, but he had a rough childhood, and maybe I did what was best, and maybe his life could have been better. I don't know. But he blamed me for a large part of his life. Just because someone blames you doesn't mean you did anything wrong, and.... Ugh."

A pain erupted in my side and I doubled over. Every muscle knotted, and every nerve was on fire. Dad reached out and held me steady. No one else seemed affected, and I didn't see any unwanted dark energies around, but by the table, Kyle had crumpled into a seat. Luke looked from Kyle to me, tore the device from Hedy's hands and flipped the lever off. Immediately, the pain ceased.

I exhaled a shaky breath as my muscles slowly relaxed. My screaming nerves went silent, and it was like nothing had happened. But, geez, that pain was intense. Worse than anything I'd ever experienced before, and I'd almost been torn from existence.

"I think you got the right frequency," Luke said. "Let's not touch the device anymore." He looked pale and almost as sick as I felt, but it was all sympathy on his end.

"Penny, you okay?" Dad asked.

I straightened up slowly, worried of some lasting effect. "Yeah. The device works. We can go now." An eternity of that. Best not think about it too much.

We returned to the table as Kyle shakily got to his feet. We shared a look of mutual shock at the level of pain and then let the whole experience stay unspoken.

"Thank you, Hedy and George." I shook their hands. "It was an honor to meet you."

"Seriously," Mom added as she shook their hands next.

"I have no idea what you plan to do with that thing, but good luck." Hedy Lamarr smiled at us.

Penny, what was that?

The Shadow's voice sounded far away, but fear chilled my blood. If The Shadow figured out our plan, it would be over. No more time for goodbyes. We needed to get out of there. Without a word of warning, I grabbed the souls of my team and opened a portal—time for the end.

Chapter 26

We landed where it all began. Long before I existed, before time travel and cute boys next door. We were at the Isle of Skye, where the humans attacked and killed the Old Ones. If anything would create a paradox, messing with this moment would do the trick.

As the physical world slowly eased back into my vision, I turned to Kyle. "I need you to get everyone home. No one needs to be here for this part."

"No," Mom said before Kyle could respond. "Don't you dare. We planned this with you. We're seeing this through, and then we're taking you home."

"I'll take us all out to eat," Dad offered. "Anywhere you want to go, Penny, but we do this together."

They didn't realize. Still. It broke my heart, and I didn't want to be the one to tell them, didn't want them to know the plan. "I'd feel a lot better if you were all safe."

"Penny." Jack stepped forward to stand next to my parents. "You risked your humanity to save my life. I'm not going anywhere until we all go home."

Dinah nodded in agreement. Next to me, Luke clenched

his jaw and looked uncomfortable. He knew how this moment would truly go down. This wasn't a moment for arguing, but for saying goodbye. I should have made Kyle promise to take them away before coming here so there'd be less time wasted.

I turned to Kyle and nodded. "Now." But he stared only at the device in Luke's hand as if in a trance. *Kyle.* I tossed the thought in his mind to wake him up. *Hello, you with us?*

Yeah. He finally tore his eyes off the device and nodded behind me. *But it's too late. Shadow followed us. It's near.*

Crap. Okay, time to act fast. "We're going to have a short window. Everyone stay back, and when this is done, Kyle, I'm counting on you to get everyone home. Luke, hand me the device."

"Wait," Dinah said and looked at Kyle. "I thought—"

Hurried steps and hushed whispers echoed from the cliffs. The army was on their way. On the other side of the cliff, the Old Ones waited, unaware of the attack heading their way. The moment I confronted the army, the paradox would begin, so I had to do it with The Shadow nearby, close enough to trap it but far enough away it couldn't hurt me before I activated the device. Because once I flipped the switch, it would be over.

"Luke." I hissed for his attention. He'd gone pale too and seemed frozen in fear, but it wasn't me he was looking at. He frowned at Kyle but blinked his attention back to me when I called his name.

"Here." He handed it to me, but when I wrapped my hands around the device, he placed his over mine. "I'm sorry."

I smiled at him, and despite the fear rising in my chest, my heart was filled with love. He promised to save me, and I knew the ending to this story would bother him, but he'd live and grow and move on. It would be okay. "I love you," I said, and leaned in to give him a quick goodbye kiss. "I love all of you." Then I tucked the device against my chest and turned to where a large blackened shape rushed near.

Hey Shadow! I mentally screamed. *I'm over here! Think you can catch me before I destroy your beginning?*

What are you doing here? You've gone too far desecrating the end of my ancestors! I will destroy you, Penelope Grace, one cell at a time!

Gotta catch me first! I said, and ran toward the army.

Here's the thing about a paradox. It started the precise second action was taken. Not when the final, conflicting act had been finalized, but as soon as it started. Just like everything else connected to the dark world, it was all about the intention. Time glitched the second I chose to move. I ran toward the army. The Shadow raced toward me, howling with a raw rage, and then....

I stood near Luke and my family as The Shadow hovered in the distance, just barely cluing in on my plan, and the race started again.

This was wrong. I needed to be able to move. I had to act outside of the glitch, but the second before The Shadow got close enough to trigger the device, time glitched, and we were back where we started. Stubborn determination kicked in, and I tried again, and again, hoping this time The Shadow would come within range, only to lose the distance covered.

After three tries, I finally clued in on my mistake. When we saved Jack, it was Luke's paradox. I had nothing to do with it, so my choices didn't affect it. But here...we were all here because *I* brought us. I chose to confront The Shadow. Luke, Dinah, Mom and Dad, and even Jack helped create the device. The only person who never helped was....

Time glitched, and this time Kyle stepped in front of me. He was free to move, unhindered by time's chaos around us. "My turn," he said and reached for the device, but I refused to let go.

"What are you doing?" I couldn't put it together. It wasn't like Kyle to take action. He was the run and hide kind of guy. And yet there he stood, smiling at me like he'd pulled his proudest trick despite the red hot fear screaming through his empty soul.

"Time to stop The Shadow, right? Thank you for trapping

it for me, but I can take it from here." He reached for the device again, and I pulled it back.

"How come you can move?"

"I never fought The Shadow, Penny. I never meant it harm or wanted to stop it. All I've ever wanted was the chance to change, to grow, and to maybe be happy someday. None of the decisions I've made or actions I've taken brought us here."

"You—you refused to fight the Shadow on the train." One piece at a time started to come together. "The Expert took you away from the group as we planned the paradox. It warned you."

"It warned me if you made the decisions, then you'd be trapped. It wanted me to take the lead, to be the one who lived."

"Then why didn't you?" Fear gripped my once numbly calm soul. I had found peace in being trapped for eternity, but watching Kyle do the same thing was not in the plan.

"Because I'd already made my choice. Penny, you're the first person in this world I've ever cared about. You called me your brother once, and I don't know if you meant it or if you were making a point, but you're my sister, and I wasn't going to let you go down because I want to be free. All of this started because I wanted to escape the dark world. It's my mess to clean up, and you're not taking the fall for me. I knew if I pulled Luke aside and told him my plan, he'd go along with it. Told the others, and they played along too. You never noticed me leave the haunted forest, did you? I didn't just check the borders. I went to your home and got them working on the plan."

"No, we made the plan after. You wouldn't have known back then."

"Merely a matter of listening to the future moments—not portaling there, but just listening. I found the moment you figured out a plan and memorized it all. Then I went to your family, got them working on the research needed, and then went back to you."

I thought it was so serendipitous that Luke and Dinah's

research matched our plan so perfectly. Only it hadn't been fate. All along, it was Kyle.

"I promised them I would take your place, that I'd wrap the paradox so firmly around you it would be impossible for you to make the sacrifice. They agreed so readily." He laughed, but it was devoid of humor. "I messed up. I tried to be something I'm not, something *more* than desperation, and this is the only way I make up for everything. It won't erase everything I've done, but it wasn't all bad. We did some good together, right?"

Tears fell when I blinked, and my insides felt ready to revolt. Panic started to take over, and a weird, shocked numbness took over my limbs.

Kyle eased the device out of my grip and held it in his hand like a bomb. "Maybe I was meant to do this. With The Shadow trapped, others can peacefully explore your world. I always felt so aware of the emptiness in my world, the dull sameness every moment. Think it'll be like that in the trap? Think my body will give in to the pain, and I'll just go back to the way things used to be? Every moment would be the same. Just me, the darkness, and longing. I hope so. I hope the pain part doesn't last forever."

I tried to talk, but the paradox glitched back before I could get a word out. The more I panicked and fought to move, the quicker the time glitches came, any argument silenced, any attempts at goodbye erased. I wanted to yell at him for not telling me so I could stop this, for tricking me, and I wanted to beg forgiveness for assuming the worst when he bowed out of our fights. It was to protect me, to take my place. All this time, I'd yelled at Kyle and revoked any trust I had in him, and he'd taken it without argument.

"I want to request one thing before I go," Kyle admitted. "Save my world. With The Shadow trapped, it should be easy to close the unstable portals between our worlds, but don't just close the doors. Take back your water, and maybe that way the souls lost in the current can escape too. We don't die, you know, which is going to suck for me if this hurts as much as it did at Hedy's party, but it means those souls are still in the currents. You just have to free them, and I know you can. I believe in you. So, that's my last request, as you humans say. Oh, and tell Shreya," he chuckled, "tell Shreya the world's better with her in it." He cleared his throat, pushed his shoulders back, and lifted his chin. "Goodbye, Penny. It's been fun."

Without another word, he turned and walked toward the glitching Shadow. I fought to run after him, to stop it, but the more I fought, the more time glitched. The paradox was firmly wrapped around me, and the more my stubbornness fought against it, the more it held me still. All I could do was watch, my aching jaw refusing to scream *stop* as Kyle stepped in front of The Shadow and set the device down between them. He glanced over his shoulder at me one last time and gave a final wave. Then, jaw clenched and all façades of ease gone, Kyle leaned down and flipped the switch.

I braced for the pain, but it never came. The radius of the device's frequency never reached me, and I couldn't see the mechanical energies, but it worked. Kyle screamed and went to his knees, and all fight left me as pure horror took its place. Time kept on, and the army continued down their cliff, unaware of the people on the other side, off to continue their fated last fight.

The Shadow, once as trapped as me in the paradox, writhed against the confines of the makeshift force field. It slammed against an invisible wall, howling and screaming in rage, and I knew it was all aimed at me. The Shadow ignored Kyle, who struggled to stay up on his knees. He swayed on the spot, skin pale and eyes glazed over from the pain, but he stared at me without an ounce of regret.

"No." My voice cracked against the strain of trying to scream. "No!" I chased after him. Arms wrapped around me and yanked me back.

"It's what he wanted," Luke whispered. "I'm so sorry." I

shoved him away and stepped toward Kyle, but Luke calmly blocked my path. "Penny, you won't be able to break through that wall, and it'll be torture to try."

"You knew." My hands were shaking, and my cheeks were wet. "This isn't right. It's not how it's supposed to go down."

"This is the best case scenario." He leaned in front of my gaze, trying to get me to focus on him, but all I could see was Kyle, who swayed on the spot as he watched me. Waiting.

His last request. I closed my eyes and lifted my hands up as I called out for all the portals in time and space. Rage and fear and shock pulsed through my mind and erased any thoughts of limitations. I had to release the souls from the currents while Kyle was strong enough to see. A sob escaped my throat, but it only made my connection stronger. This had to happen. Now.

Every single tear between the worlds answered my call at once. There were so many, a mind breaking amount, some in the past and hundreds littering the future. Clouds and streams of water leaked through the portals and drowned Kyle's world. The more I focused on it, the stronger I could feel the currents, and it was more than water. It was life, and whirring souls lost to the waves, forever trapped in undercurrents as their very selves were sliced through by unforgiving water.

On the other end, humans pled the skies for rain, anything to end the drought. So many moments in time and it should have been impossible to hold them all, but then a familiar voice echoed in my mind. The Expert called my name. There was a sad sober tone to its usual excitement, and I knew it had been watching, waiting, and perhaps mourning as Kyle made his choice. Without a moment's hesitation, The Expert added its own strength to my plan. Together we imagined the portals gathering together in those times of most needed drought, high in the sky and stretched as wide as a desert. A portal over the small towns where Zetta and Ricky grew up, over the Wild West where Ricky's ship was still stranded, and one portal over us. We opened those portals wide, and all that water fell from the skies.

Rain slammed against my skin as unnaturally dark clouds blocked out the sun. A strange, distorted energy fell with it as chaotic lightning blasted my ears. But it wasn't just rain. Thick drops puddled the ground, and while the water seeped into the mossy dirt, a darkness lingered. The more rain fell, the more darkness rose and collected like metal fillings to a magnet until they became souls. Whole dark beings free from the drowning water. They looked at their own limbs, checked their souls in disbelief. Their intense curiosity only doubled when they found themselves in a strange world, so unlike their own darkened peace. I could see the onslaught of color and sensory details to their souls.

Come home, The Expert called its souls back. *It's safe now.*

The confusion turned to gratitude once they heard The Expert take the lead. Hundreds of beings shot to the skies, and even more in the future. So many lost souls were freed. Whoops of joy and freedom overpowered the lightning as they returned home, a home free from The Shadow's rage.

Thank you, Penny, The Expert said from somewhere on the other end of the portal.

Kyle —

I know. It was his choice. And then the voice was gone.

Only when the quick storm had faded, the portals empty of water, and every lost soul back home did the exhaustion hit. I sealed the portals closed and dropped my arms as I opened my eyes. Kyle was on the ground, eyes closed, and chest still. Unmoving.

Chapter 27

Rain drenched my clothes, but it was grief that drowned me. He wasn't moving.

"Penny?" Luke whispered tentatively. He rubbed my arms as if to warm me up, but I didn't feel any cold. "Penny, you did it. You saved both worlds."

"His chest isn't moving."

Luke drew in a shaky inhale. "Let's go home. Let's get out of here."

"He's not breathing."

"Penny?" Dinah's whisper came up on my other end. "I'm so sorry we didn't tell you the plan, but we need you to come home with us. That just wasn't an option, and I get you're upset, but this was the best case scenario."

"It can't be the best case scenario if someone gets left behind." Kyle's still form burned itself in my memory. No matter how long I lived, it would never fade, and still, I couldn't look away. "We can't stop fighting just because the majority are okay with the sacrifice. That can't be how humanity works."

"I know," Luke said, but his voice was too smooth, too calm to have any idea of the storms still raging in me. My whole body shook, and his hands were too steady as he slipped his fingers between mine, and for once in my life, I resented Luke's steadiness. He'd hated Kyle ever since the beginning. They never got along, and Luke's sudden support of Kyle never made sense to me. But now I imagined Kyle speaking to Luke alone. Kyle would have told Luke how he'd be the sacrifice, and all Luke had to do was make sure I fought The Shadow and secured my place in the paradox. Luke would have agreed in a second, and I could only imagine how lonely that must have made Kyle feel. How alienating it must have been to have a whole team of people accept his plan without hesitation, to read all those relieved souls because sacrificing him was something they could live with.

The Shadow struggled to hold its form against the mechanical frequency of petrified wood, and it seemed a sick justice to have it lose to an energetic current, much like how it had allowed the souls in its protection to suffer just to make a point. The Shadow's form surrendered to just an inky haze trapped by the device, and Kyle lay there, all alone.

Always so *alone.*

"No one ever fought for him."

The words escaped my mouth, and the sound of them choked me with empathy. How many times had people fought for me? Fought to keep me safe or make me laugh when I was in a rotten mood? Luke fought for me relentlessly, and my memories were rich with Dinah's support growing up. Heck, she threatened to kill someone rather than lose me. My parents listened to Luke and Dinah's stories because they knew the family unit missed one despite logic, and when I came home, they refused to let me go. Even now, as my mind struggled to come back from the shock, they stood nearby in support. Jack was there too, watching Kyle's still form with a sickened look on his face, but he seemed resolved. He'd driven up to Cheyenne from Denver when Dinah told him I was back in town.

Then there was Ricky and Zetta, and that entire makeshift

family. They all accepted me, celebrated when I visited and worked hard to make sure I always felt welcome. Somehow, while I'd been jumping from place to place, feeling family-less, my family had grown from blood to so many people choosing me they wouldn't all fit around a table. Not one of them fought for Kyle. They barely tolerated him, and I couldn't help but imagine what I would be like if no one fought for me. If I was truly alone in the world. Bitter wouldn't begin to cover it. I'd be hardened to kindness, distrusting of a smile, and ready to do anything just to feel for a moment like I belonged. Even tear through space and time to find one person who saw me, and once I found that person, I don't think I could ever let go.

I'm sorry, but I need a fresh start. Those were the first words Kyle ever spoke to us. Memories of conversations rushed through my memory as all Kyle's thoughts and choices finally made sense.

Friends who left you alone? Who don't see your powers? They abandoned you. They distrust you. Everyone will, eventually. Your friends, your parents. Even your sister. He said the words to me once, but only now did I understand why. Not because he understood my family or that he was playing with my deepest fears. It was how the dark souls treated him for how different he was, how he struggled with their stillness.

Could be that's why I always liked you, Penny. You get how it feels to call a place home and know you don't belong there. To see the world so differently from everyone else and not be able to share the beauty of it with anyone.

The guy who once said that to me still hadn't moved, and it had been too long to hold hope anymore. If The Void remained, it was lost to the inky haze with The Shadow. No more red fear behind a cloudy darkness. Just a body.

"They can't die," I frowned. Something didn't click right.

"He was half human," Luke sighed. "Which was merciful, I think."

"No, they can't die. They can separate like the souls in the water or The Shadow in the trap, but they don't die. I remember something The Void told me. To die is to be a part of life, and the dark souls exist outside of life." I turned around to where the army was long gone to destroy what they believed to be demons. "The Old Ones."

Luke gasped as he caught on. "They're not dead. They're just in pieces."

"We can save them."

Chapter 28

"Where are we running?" Jack matched Luke's and my hurried pace as we raced up the hill to the basin. Mom and Dad slipped their way up against the wet moss, and Dinah's analytical blue soul tinged red with disdain for cardio. "What's the plan?"

"The Shadow hates this world because some humans attacked its elders. A massacre right in front of it, and I think it was young, like a kid at the time. It led the dark world alone, and it refused to let anyone enter this world for fear it would happen again. That fear turned to an unreasonable rage, and when Kyle snuck through, it was willing to sacrifice its own people just to make a point of how dangerous this world is.

"The Shadow isn't evil. It was hurting and spiraling in thoughts of anger and fear, and somewhere along the way, it lost reason. But who wouldn't? All alone with no one to understand and pull you away from the spiraling fears. Humans do it all the time. But the Old Ones aren't gone. I can save them." And if I could save them, and heal the rage which kept The Shadow so dangerous, maybe we'd save Kyle.

We reached the top of the hill, and the destruction of the battle tore up the land below us. The mudslides, fallen cliffs, and torn land. Mom gasped, and Dad cursed. "The energy is so strange here," Dinah said, and she held her palm out to read it, only to pull it back in a second later and shake the energy away.

Luke reached out his hand and felt the air. "I almost feel something, but it's so weak." He shook his head. "See anything?"

"No. If I had last time I was here, I wouldn't have left, but they have to be here because the empty souls don't die." Panic cut through my voice, and Luke gave me a concerned look. "Please don't tell me this is a part of grieving, and I just have to work through it, okay?" I snapped at his uneasy side eye at me.

To my surprise, Luke smiled. "What about any of our time together makes you think I'd say that?" He glanced pointedly at Jack. "Listen, I know we can't save everyone, but if you have an idea, let's try it out."

"Wait," Dinah said, "let's think this through a bit. Say Penny's right, and she can bring back the Old Ones. They've just been attacked by humans they trusted. What would stop them from killing us on the spot?"

Dinah's cold reason stumped my hope. Nothing. They'd attack first, and there'd be no time for questions later because, unlike the dark souls, humans could die. On the off chance they didn't strike first, what were the odds of successfully disarming the device and talking reason into The Shadow? And in those small odds alone, even less likely was it that Kyle and his now mostly human self survived enough to be saved. Was it worth risking my entire family? The two worlds I just saved? Because if the low chance of saving Kyle wasn't worth the risk, then I was as bad as everyone else. Then I couldn't blame anyone, because I would have done the same thing, and the thought that I would have even considered…. I understood why my family made the choices they did, but if I went home, I would be making the same choice. The idea was almost fully formed in my mind. If I turned away now, I, too, would be sacrificing Kyle. Somehow, that felt the same as turning my back on myself. But convincing the Old

Ones that we meant well seemed more difficult than breaking the laws of time.

"The Expert. It knew the Old Ones too, right?" I turned to Luke, only to remember he wasn't with me when I met The Expert. Kyle had been there, but no one else. "I think I remember that. If we could get The Expert on board, it could act as a negotiator if emotions get high. Of course, that's assuming we can find enough of the Old Ones to put them back together."

"That's a lot of ifs," Mom pointed out with an uncertain frown. "Are we sure this is worth rocking the boat over?"

Speaking of boats... Ricky and Zetta's family were trained in meditation. Luke widened his eyes and looked at me the same time the idea flashed in my mind.

"If they helped —," he started.

"We'd find the essence of the Old Ones in half the time. And with The Expert and any volunteers from the dark world helping out —"

He grinned. "The Old ones will have souls they trust, and so will The Shadow when we turn off the device."

"And Kyle will have everyone who knows him there too." Hope jump-started my energy. I practically bounced on my heels. "We could protect the worlds without trapping anyone." Mom and Dad seemed confused, while Dinah and Jack shared a look of fearful knowing as if recalling the last time I got this stubborn.

Luke caught their look just as much as I had, and he sighed, scratching the back of his neck. "Maybe we should take a step back, really consider our options before we do something we can't take back." His words drenched the small hearth within, but then he followed up with words I couldn't argue. "Ricky and his ship are still stranded. Why don't we get them back where they belong first?"

"That's a great idea," Dinah rushed in. "These cliffs creep me out, and I haven't seen Ricky in ages."

"That's the pirate dude that crashed our party, right?" Jack added. "I'm down with a reunion."

"Ricky." Mom nodded. "We've heard that name tossed around. I'd like to meet this…pirate dude."

Dad squinted. "I thought Ricky was the Shakespearean era kid."

"He's eclectic." I knew what they were doing, trying to distract me, but they also had a point. With The Shadow gone, they could return to sailing the seven seas in freedom and relative safety. "Okay, we'll go visit the ship and then go from there."

I closed my eyes to make the connection but hesitated as the memory of Kyle laying on the mossy ground slammed to the forefront of my mind. I couldn't help, couldn't check for a pulse or even properly bury him. Still, it felt wrong to just leave. *I'll come back.* I mentally shouted the words to him. *I promise on my life I will get you out of there.*

Connecting to the door hovering over the Noble Pirate Ship was as easy as stepping into one's favorite uncle's house — muscle memory at this point. I couldn't just portal us there, so I envisioned the door coming to us like I had in the beginning days. "We're going to have to enter one at a time. I couldn't connect directly onto the ship, so there's a bit of a drop."

"Just as long as we're not doing a two day hike again," Dinah mumbled, and everyone gathered behind me. With a long exhale to shove the regret of leaving Kyle away, I swung open the door. The desert sunset slipped into view, a breathtaking deception to the petrified wood rich land underneath. I stepped forward and leaned in to look below. Ricky hurried from one side of the ship to the other in a tense game of tennis against Shreya on the deck.

"Can we drop by?" I hollered down.

Ricky looked up, and the tennis ball flew over his head and right over the deck. Oops. But instead of being ticked at the interruption, he burst into a smile and waved. "Hey! Penny's back!" Then he pointed his tennis racket at me. "I distinctly recall telling you not to leave in the middle of the night!"

"You know I never listen," I teased back as I looked for the best way down. It must have been a few weeks at least since I'd left because the makeshift elevator had turned into a much more sophisticated staircase, with a dolly system for groceries or water. Luke helped me step down, and I took it two steps at a time. The last few minutes had been too big of a shock, and I needed one of Ricky's giant bear hugs. Maybe I ran too fast or desperately, or maybe he just saw it in my face because he dropped his tennis racket and wrapped his arms around me so tight. Then he straightened up, and my feet left the ground. I clung to his neck. "Kyle stopped The Shadow. He…he sacrificed himself."

Ricky's grip tightened around me. The only person who knew Kyle as well as me was Ricky. The two had been friends in Ricky's teenage years, and while Kyle may have lied about his name and background during those times, he probably shared much of his truth with Ricky. Ricky eased me back to the ground as he let go of the hug. "I didn't realize he had so much heroism in him."

"I never even considered it an option." And I'd been so rude to him. I had so many things to apologize for, and I would. I had to. "Ricky, I think we can get him back. It'll be tricky, and it might involve releasing The Shadow again, but there might be a way to revive the Old Ones who The Shadow loved, and if they're there to reason with The Shadow, I'm sure—" I stopped at Ricky's face. So much sympathy and not an ounce of belief. "I can do it."

He glanced over my shoulder, and I followed the path. Luke was already on deck. Dinah stood beside him while Jack, Mom, and Dad slowly stepped down the stairs, mouths open at the bizarre scene in front of them.

"Parents?" Ricky asked. "They remember you now?"

"Not exactly, but they know I exist, which is a step closer." I was downplaying the importance of them here now. It was worlds colliding. My old life where I was forgotten and lonely, and here where I made the rules, people trusted my powers and accepted me.

"Penny, that's huge." Ricky looked back at me. "Isn't that huge?"

"I guess." I never thought about what happened after.... I wasn't supposed to be running around free and having to make up plans. The family trip to Hedy Lamarr was supposed to be the last goodbye. Now what? Go to school? Would they give me my old room back, or would they expect me to share with Dinah? Or maybe I was just supposed to visit every now and then? Mom and Dad might not want me around all the time. What would they want? What did *I* want? But I didn't need to think about it right now. After we got Kyle back, then I could focus on my future.

I wanted to keep talking to Ricky, but Mom and Dad reached the deck and walked up to us. Dad offered his hand to Ricky, who gave it a generous shake.

"Nice to meet you."

"Welcome to my ship. And you must be Penny's mother."

"We've heard so much about you." Mom smiled politely.

"Jack." Ricky grinned and pulled Jack into a one armed manly hug, the kind where they hit each other's back like a competition. "Still alive, I see."

"I finally get to see the famous Noble Pirate Ship." Jack looked around, nodding in approval. "The tiki lights are a fun surprise."

I tried to stand there and patiently let people meet as long as I could, but the evening wind stirred thin slices of petrified wood into the air, and it slammed against my skin. My fingers shook, and my strength drained away. If I was going to get them out of here, I needed to do it now. "Is everyone on the ship?"

"All home and accounted for," Ricky nodded. "Are we going sailing?"

"That's the plan."

I stepped to the middle of the deck and closed my eyes. Wow, this ship was big, and there were so many people inside.

So many souls who needed to safely take the trip too. Not only that, but the ship was half buried in my very own kryptonite, and flecks of the stuff dusted every room. It was in their clothes and the air. I hadn't even brought them here alone, hadn't been strong enough. Kyle had come to rescue then. Another time he had my back. Did I ever thank him for that? I couldn't remember. It wasn't important then.

How was I supposed to do this? Okay, Penny, shake it off. You recently closed multiple portals in different moments of time simultaneously, so you can do this.

A gust of wind hit my side, and flecks of dust stung at my aura. I flinched and shuddered. *This is nothing compared to what Kyle went through. Suck it up and do your job.* That thought brought a surge of rage. I sent my dark energy out like a fabric around the ship, covering every body, every item, forcing it down into the sand and dirt until it wrapped under the ship and met the other end.

Sweat cooled my forehead, but I refused to acknowledge the difficulty, afraid if I let one thought in, I might crumble and lose all the progress I'd made. *I've got this. This is simple. Now just make a portal out of here.* But my hands were shaking, and a pounding headache started against my temples as if I could feel the effort of my blood pulsing. Just gotta connect to the sea. Come on. Come on. There!

Not wasting a breath to warn anyone of the jump, I made the connection and lurched the ship through. There was a dizzying buzz when we went through the dark world like it was suddenly alive with cheers and celebrations and a strong undertone of *why is one of us missing?* And then the deck below me started to sway. The air shifted from stifling hot to chilled.

I opened my eyes and took in the whoops of cheer around me — so many souls beaming in bright yellow joy.

"We're back, baby!" Ricky whooped somewhere from my right.

Little Davy's voice came from the other side of the deck. "Oooo, so much water."

Relief settled into my bones like a drug as determination and rage faded into exhaustion. I blinked, expecting the physical world to slip into view any second, but instead, the pounding in my head got louder and black dots disoriented my vision.

"Penny?" Luke and Dinah asked at the same time.

"I don't feel so good," I mumbled. Then the pain and disorientation turned into an uncontrollable wave of surrender, and I passed out.

Chapter 29

The bird woke me up, some irritated robin screaming like an old man warning a kid to get off his lawn. I groaned and opened my eyes, only for a pounding headache to surge back into action. But the headache soon took a back seat to a major freak out as I took in my surroundings.

This was not the ship. Somehow I'd ended up tucked in bed, but the bed didn't sway with the ocean waves. Light purple pastel painted the walls. A small desk was littered with papers, and in one corner was a little meditation set up: a soft round rug, a pillow to sit on, and a notebook for thoughts and inspiration. A poster hung on the wall with the silhouette of a person and the major chakras aligned in fun rainbow colors.

I set my hand down on the duvet covering my legs. It was designed like the universe, black and all spotted with stars, but there was a stain near the edge from when I fell asleep doing homework and the blue ink of my pen absorbed into the fabric.

This was my room.

I flung the duvet off me and leapt out of bed like it would burn. This was impossible. I didn't exist. My stuff was erased months ago. And yet....

Band T-shirts and comfy sweaters filled my closet. Fuzzy slippers on the floor. Tears from all the familiarity filled my eyes. Ugh, my clothes! My comfortable, oversized clothes! I tore off the ratted mess of fabric I was wearing, full of sweat and dirt from the Petrified Forest, and slipped on my favorite black shirt from the LoveLoud Festival. The festival symbol decorated the top, and the back listed off all the bands and speakers from that day. I changed my pants for some baggy sweats and the slippers for my shoes. Ah, yes, that felt right.

None of it felt real, like I was disconnected from it all. My fingers pinched the fabric. I heard the annoying robin outside my window, saw the colors of my old room, but it all got muffled before it reached my brain. I wanted to embrace it all and never leave again. Spend weeks going through my piles of random stuff, wondering if I should keep or toss for hours as I listened to my music playlist. There was a small mirror on top of my homework desk, and I stepped to it. My hair was nearly dry from the rainstorm, and I brushed it out to smooth the ratted bits on one side.

Look. There I was. All me. My face, my hair, and my clothes. Everything was exactly the same except for my soul, still blackened by the dark energy. How had this happened? And how did I get here?

But then it clicked. The Shadow was gone. Its efforts to terrify and back me into a desperate corner no longer made sense to the timeline, and time corrected itself.

Oh no. Jack. Ricky. His entire family.

I raced out of the bedroom, heart racing. No, no, no. This can't be happening. Please tell me not everything went back to the original timeline.

I stopped as soon as I reached the living room. There, squeezed in the middle of the couch, his fingers pinching a small teacup, sat Ricky. Jack stood next to a chair where Luke chewed on some cookies. Mom and Dad, and Dinah were there too, and they were all staring at me.

"What happened?" I asked.

Ricky stood up. "You passed out after the travel. Overdid it, I think, but everyone's fine. It's all smooth sailing." He chuckled. "We still had that door connected to a portal, so we took you home."

"Your room was just *there*." Mom smiled.

"We think it's because The Shadow is gone," Dinah chimed in. "It was the one who stole your past, so when it got trapped, it must have had to release the past back. Or maybe time just righted itself, I don't know. But…." She grinned with so much excitement her lips looked strained to contain it. "You're back."

"I'm…." I tried to say the words, but they got lost in my throat. For all the happy endings I'd seen for other people, I never imagined….

Dad cleared his throat. "Now, that being said, there's some new rules I'd like to set in this house. No more running away from home, no more time traveling unless you notify us first, and don't think I've forgotten about that tablet you 'borrowed' when I was on my work trip. You owe me yard work, young lady." He waved his finger at me, but his eyes were twinkling with mischievous glee, and it took me a second to catch up. *Don't think I've forgotten.*

"No way," I whispered. "You have your memories back?"

"A little." He shrugged. "They're slowly slipping back in this old filing system up here." He tapped his temple.

Mom apparently couldn't take it anymore and rushed from her chair. Her arms were around me in a second, and she hugged me so tight I couldn't breathe. There was a splattering of chuckles in the living room. It was like a weight had been lifted off the entire household. That lingering tension and uneasiness between us all had faded away like a handful of sand against a windstorm. Relief and love and home warmed my chest, and I smiled so hard my cheeks hurt. There was no holding it back. Happy endings were possible. I could have it all.

Mom and I finally let go, and I went over to hug Dad next. "I was just kidding about the yard work," he whispered with a laugh. "I was just excited to remember our fight."

"Actually, I'd probably enjoy helping you set up the garden," I confessed, and then gave him a warning look as I let go of the hug. "But just this once."

Ricky slurped the last of his tea and stood up. "Well, I better be off. Let you all settle back into your norm."

"Actually, can I talk to you for a second?" I asked. "In private?" He nodded and followed me back to my room. I closed the door behind us. "Listen, I need to ask you something."

"Anything, Penny." He smiled.

"I think I can get Kyle out of that trap, but I need your help."

Ricky's smile faded. His aura stiffened with apprehension, and he immediately shook his head. "No—"

"Listen to my plan. I think it can work—" I started, but he held up a hand for me to stop.

"Penny, I owe you everything I have. You know that. But you just passed out from exhaustion because you don't stop."

"You needed help," I said in confusion. "What was I supposed to do?"

"Tell us you were too tired or that it was too much. We were surviving there. Sure, it wasn't our dream location, but we were making do. And if we really needed to leave, we could have left the ship there. You take on too much. And yes, you've accomplished many miraculous things. I can't even name them all, but there's such a thing as stretching yourself too far. *Going* too far." He leaned in and grabbed both my shoulders. "Quit while you're ahead. It can't get better than this. This," he gestured around us, "is a better ending than any of us could have imagined. But it can be undone. Remember that."

I frowned at him. "I can do this. I know why The Shadow is so angry, so destructive, and I just need a little help here."

He dropped his hands from my shoulders and gave me a sad frown. "Anything else, Penny, and I'd say yes. Not this. I'm sorry."

He turned away and walked back to the living room, signaling the discussion was over. Wow. He'd told me I needed to ask for help more and refused to help me in the same breath. Irritation jittered at the tip of my tongue, willing me to lash out and yell at him, to list all the things he had because of Kyle and me. I bit my lip and closed my eyes, forcing myself to see it from his side. He had a family, a home, and a responsibility to many more people than me. Saying yes would put every single person he loved at terrible risk.

But attempting this without an army of people who had been meditatively trained only increased the risk of failure. Could I do it with just my family? Well, they weren't all. I could still reach —

Penny.

The Expert's voice slipped into my mind just as I thought of it. I smiled. *Hey, listen, I need to talk to you.*

I know your plans. Your desperation has shouted them across the worlds.

I need your help to save Kyle.

The Expert's sigh rattled my brain, and I tensed, already knowing the answer. *We've lost our leader and one of our own. Who you call Kyle once had a place in our world. The souls here have never experienced change, and now they're traumatized by memories of that water, and the idea of death has implanted itself in their minds. We are our thoughts, Penny. Do you have any idea how dangerous the word death is here? We cannot spare time on your adventures. I'm sorry, I truly am, and I am grateful for what you've done. Now it's time to return to our normal lives and try to forget.*

Forget? I winced. *We can't forget Kyle.*

Penny. I must go. Please, let peace take over your mind now. The war is over. You won.

And then the connection was lost.

Just like that, the chances of this plan succeeding decreased even more—felt like less than five percent. Was it worth it? I looked in the mirror, half hoping the obvious answer would be written on my face, but instead, I just saw my eyes, my skin, and my hair. The same eyes and skin and hair as Kyle, who lay abandoned and alone centuries away. Was he dead, or had he mercifully passed out? Would he wake up to that same pain we felt at the party? Would he become numb to it, or would it forever be sharp? Could he make peace with his fate, or would he lose his mind? Feeling alone had made him tear through his own reality in a desperate search for someone who saw him, who understood him.

Who'd remember him.

And now, he was even more alone than before. Truly, torturously alone. I studied my bedroom, all the little trinkets from my old life. It was so good to see them again. For the first time in months, ever since this whole thing started, I felt at home. And it could be better this time. Mom and Dad seemed genuinely determined to remember me, to not let me get lost in the shadows of their to-dos lists. I could go back to school, graduate, and then…. I didn't know—anything I wanted. Maybe I could take business classes and then open up that psychic shop, help people face their inner fears in a safe environment so they could grow. I could teach all the meditation techniques Zetta had taught me. And I'd have a little place in the store, like a shrine to honor Kyle's sacrifice. There'd be a candle to represent the burning house he ran into with me to save the very people who'd held him hostage at one time. And a feather to represent how much he loved the wind. A water fountain for all the souls he sacrificed himself to save.

I could see my older self clearly. The business would be a success because I was extremely accurate with my energy readings. People would walk by that shrine every day and not know what it meant, who it was for, and I'd just smile sadly because no one would believe the truth. After work every day, I'd turn off the lights, hear the running water fountain, and think to myself, *He was so alone.*

That did it. I clenched my jaw as the decision settled into my bones. Kyle used to be alone, true. He had no friends and no one in his old world who understood him. But that's the thing about change. You could never truly go back to the beginning. Kyle would never be alone again because we chose to be each other's family, and I wouldn't let it happen. Someone had to have his back, and who better than his sister?

I thought back on everything Dinah and Luke had done to keep me safe, to support me. They risked their lives, their plans, put their personal goals on pause for me. If they hadn't, I probably would have died ages ago. They didn't have a team of backup when they protected me. They just did the best they could, and it was enough. Now it was my turn to be the backup.

I stepped back into the living room as Ricky said his goodbyes. Maybe he thought his presence would no longer be welcome after his refusal to hear me out, but he claimed it was so we could catch up as a family. He went to the front door and put his hand on the knob but stopped and turned to me. His aura churned with conflict as his love for his family, and his loyalty to me battled, but it was like a seasoned wrestler nudging a trainee out of the way. "I'll see you around," he told me and stepped through.

The room went quiet. Even the ones who weren't trained in reading energies could tell that something was wrong. Mom and Dad creased their eyebrows at me in this joint look of concern. Jack shifted on his feet while Dinah pretended to thumb through a book on the coffee table.

"How are you feeling?" Luke asked.

"Tired," I admitted. "Ricky's not going to help. And The Expert already contacted me—apparently, it overheard us thinking about the plan."

Luke gave me a sympathetic grimace, like he already guessed the answer. "And?"

"Looks like it's just us."

Mom and Dad shared a glance, and Jake actually winced, but the final nail in the coffin was when Dinah and Luke nodded at each other like they knew what they needed to do. I could only guess that while I was in the back, trying to convince Ricky to help me save Kyle, my family made a decision of their own.

"Looks like it's just me," I rephrased.

"Honey." Mom stepped forward and wrapped me in her arms, but I wasn't in the mood for hugs, so my hands stayed at my side. "We just got you back. You have to understand why this plan doesn't sit well with us."

"I know sacrifices are rough," Dad continued. "But that's a part of life. You did so much, fixed so much. Let it be enough."

Mom let go of me and straightened up. I felt bad for not hugging her back, for not looking Dad in the eye as he spoke. It made sense, and I could see their point of view. They didn't know Kyle. There's no way my parents could understand the change he'd gone through, how significant it was that he even thought about taking my place.

But no, it wasn't just about Kyle's transformation, his untapped potential. His last act came out of the blue for me. I never once thought he'd do anything so...selfless. Saving the world, that would happen one way or another. I would have done it if he hadn't. And saving the lost souls, returning the water to this world — he could have done it if I had been trapped. So taking the device, taking conscious steps to avoid the paradox, forcing me to be trapped in said paradox by making me act in those tiny moments, at the train and who knows when else, all those choices Kyle made were for *me*. He was in agony right now for one reason alone: to take my place. So, no, I wasn't going to forget about him.

I looked at Jack, and he seemed to know why before I could

say anything. "Penny, I...." He shrugged. "You saved my life, and I'm grateful, but I made the choice to protect that woman myself. And I'm a cop. I'm ready to put my life on the line to protect my community every day. When someone sacrifices for you, it's an act of love, a gift. Sometimes you have to respect it. Even if you don't want to."

I nodded and looked at Dinah and Luke. "I'm guessing you're out too?"

"It's just not a smart idea." Dinah gave me an apologetic cringe.

"You know where I stand," Luke said. "I want you safe. Saving Kyle just isn't worth the risk."

I opened my mouth to point out Jack was only alive because Kyle ripped through the fabric of time and reality and made it possible, because Kyle distracted The Shadow long enough for us to go back and save him, but then Luke caught my eye and winked.

Oh. I could have kissed Luke but forced my face not to react. "You all make valid points." I nodded and shifted my weight from the heels to the balls of my feet. A rush of anxious energy surged through me. This was happening. Penny and Stranger out to save the day. One last impossible mission, just like all the last impossible missions we'd gone on before. Some things never changed.

Dinah clapped her hands together. "Well, now that that's all figured out. I'm starving. Let's order some delivery, shall we?" She waved for people to go in the dining room, where I knew a drawer full of local menus was stored. Mom and Dad took the initiative and started out of the living room. Dad squeezed my elbow in comfort as he passed. I felt a bit bad for the trickery, but not enough to stop. Jack gave me a supportive smile before heading into the dining room as well, while Luke and Dinah headed to me.

Luke took his place by my side, and Dinah stopped in front

of me. She leaned in and whispered, "I'm giving you two a ten minute window. If you're not back, I'm calling the alarm and screaming for Ricky to help."

"He said he's not interested," I reminded her.

"He's not interested in saving Kyle," Luke pointed out, and he spoke with a level-headed confidence. "If we don't make it back in time, he'll come for us."

Dinah pulled me into a too-tight hug. "I'd go with you in a heartbeat, but if you do need backup, someone has to guilt trip everyone else into gear."

I hugged her back, and it didn't feel like a goodbye hug. Running into danger, defying the odds, it was what Luke and I did. It was natural. Home even. I loved Dinah for understanding that.

"She's terrifying enough to make sure we'll get the muscle we need if it comes to that." Luke smirked. "Not that we've ever needed help." He nudged my shoulder with his. I smiled at him, and tears of relief blurred my vision. A tsunami of gratitude for every weird, terrifying, life-altering moment which had led to us finding each other came over me, and I reached out for his hand.

Dinah glanced behind her at where our parents and Jack chatted about food preferences. "I'm going to tell them you're still tired and Luke is in the bathroom or something."

"For ten minutes?" Luke asked, raising an eyebrow.

"I don't know your fiber intake." Dinah shrugged indifferently. "Besides, it's not going to take ten minutes, is it? You two are going to get in, resurrect the Old Ones, stop the device, let the Old Ones deal with The Shadow, and bring Kyle back to the same moment you left." She started to talk fast as a flush of fear reddened her aura. "Right?"

"They won't even notice we were gone," I promised.

She nodded and turned to the dining room, leaving me alone with Luke.

"Ready?" he asked.

As much as I wanted to get going and just trust that we were doing the right thing, I had to give Luke a chance to change his mind. This was too big, and it was nothing like anything we'd done before. Honestly, as much as I felt calm about this like it was what I was supposed to do, I understood I might not come home. It was the life I'd chosen, and I'd chosen it so many times it had become natural. But that didn't mean Luke felt the same.

"Are you sure about this? You're not going to tell me we should leave time alone?"

He made a face and nodded toward Jack. "That's hypocritical, don't you think? You never once asked me to give up on Jack. I'm not going to ask you to let go of Kyle. Not while we have access to time travel. So let's revive a whole bunch of ticked off souls, release an enraged darkness, and save that annoying Void, shall we?"

"That's the spirit," I chuckled. We slipped into the hallway and out of sight. I closed my eyes and started to search for the right moment to travel.

"Wait," Luke whispered, and before I could open my eyes, he kissed me, a long, deep, just-in-case kind of kiss that affected me from head to toe. The kind of kiss that solidified the importance of what we were doing, of who we were to each other. His hands were in my hair and at my waist like it might be the last time we touched. I wrapped my arms around his neck, every cell buzzing with love for him. Luke Hendricks. My Stranger. The boy who always supported me, who stood by me, helped me overcome so many impossible rescues.

He ended the kiss with a sweet peck and rested his forehead on mine. "Okay. I'm ready now." Both of his hands found mine, and I clung to them as the significance of this choice settled into my mind. One last kiss. One last look. Time to go.

Chapter 30

We landed where the Old Ones had fallen. Luke waited, not letting go of my hand until my vision cleared. The broken rocks, moss, and the general uneasy feel seemed familiar now. This was a place of trauma and tragedy, and I wasn't afraid to confront it anymore.

"I'll try to pull the dark energy out. Think you can locate concentrations of the energy with me?"

Luke's sunshine aura shone with a stubborn strength as a whispering doubt threatened to question his choice, but he'd gotten just about as stubborn as me lately. His jaw tensed, and he nodded.

We split the area in half. He took the left, and I took the right, hands out, slow steps, as we read the energies. The general miasma in this place was more than memories of a betrayal and consequent murders. It was the remains of the Old Ones scattered around. We collected sticks and placed them where the general unease changed into a more concentrated feeling of horror. Like human metal detectors, we slowly moved our hands from side to side and covered the length of the land.

There came a thought halfway through that my theory was

wrong. The Old Ones might be their equivalent of dead, too far gone to revive, and that this was all a waste of time. But on the other side of the cliff, Kyle waited for me, so I had to try.

Luke and I met in the middle. Without a word, he nodded at me to do my thing. I knelt down on the soft, damp moss and placed my fingers in the green. Luke stood to my right, his aura a deep, golden heat. His eyes were open, but I knew he focused on feeling the energies around us, arms tense, the energies by his hands already set with whispers of rich petrified wood in case something went wrong — my protector.

I closed my eyes and let the energetic world take over. The residual energies from the human armies lingered in the moss. Where they stepped scarred the land with red hot fear and determination to be rid of the devils. The Old Ones hadn't seen it coming. They'd helped and fully expected to be helped in return. They didn't know about devils and Heaven and hell. How could they when they didn't know about death?

Brushing the thoughts aside, I dismissed the residual energies from the humans and looked deeper. A hint of sunshine aura from Luke's hands kissed the sticks he'd dropped on the ground, but where I'd searched, the land was dotted not in color but darkness. My own residual energy.

Around those sticks, both mine and Luke's, the air was different. It was so subtle that, at first, I didn't even notice, but it was darker there. Like slivers of storm clouds struggling to hold their form. I mentally reached out and connected with them.

The instant wave of trauma slammed into me — raw fear, enraged adrenaline, and desperation to survive as the introduction of pain pulsed through these souls. I tugged on the energies, lifting them from the ground, and collected them together about ten feet in front of us. The clouds thickened and grew but were nowhere near the black-hole like darkness I'd come to associate with the dark souls. They separated on their own as if the energies intuitively knew what was part of the self and what was someone else.

And then it happened — a shift.

I tensed and paused. One of the clusters deepened and darkened as a conscious awareness settled in. Next to me, Luke felt the power shift. The energy of petrified wood slid from his hand to his entire soul.

A deep, venomous voice slithered into my mind. *Humans.*

We're here to help.

The Old One responded with a deep, distrusting growl. It was done talking.

I trapped Luke's hand. "Lower your shields. They need to know we're on their side."

"You've got to be kidding me." Luke's voice shook with adrenaline and fear. He took a deep breath and forced the instinctive protection to lower.

Our minds are open to you, and you can see we mean no harm. We want to help.

There was a moment of tense silence. I didn't know if it had the capabilities to go through our minds, to see our memories and hear our intentions. It had to be weak and disoriented.

But then the Old One shot out what looked like hands, and thick walls of darkness encased the area. A wide net wove around us on all sides, blocking out the sun and erasing any chance of escape.

"Penny," Luke warned.

"I see it," I said. "It trapped us. I'm sure it's just temporary. It'll let us go when I finish." It was a lie, and we both knew it. Luke could feel the rage in this trap as clearly as I could see it. It was betrayed once. It would not be taken by surprise again.

Finish.

I obeyed, freeing more of the loose, thin clouds of souls from the earth with as much care as I could, even as my mind struggled to think up the next steps. Luke and I were sitting ducks. The Old One might wait until the others were revived and then step on us like bugs. Why had I brought Luke here? Why did I even ask to bring everyone I loved? They were smart enough to refuse. If only Luke had done the same. And yet, it seemed a fitting end somehow. Luke and I fell through time together what felt like ages ago. We would go down together too.

But I forced the thoughts down. If the Old Ones were coming back, then they needed to know humans could be good or else I risked leaving the world worse off than before—with more embittered Shadows and less curious Voids. I could feel the first Old One's attention on me like hawk eyes on prey, and it made shivers run down my spine, but I kept to my task. A second consciousness started to stir, and before I could even think *We're on your side,* the first Old One connected to it and, after a private word I failed to overhear, the second one added its energy to the net around us.

"Oh, geez." Luke flexed and unflexed his fist, ready to fight but careful not to make the first move.

Then the third one woke up, and the power of the net tripled, quadrupled. There was a grunt, and Luke's aura crumpled. I snapped my eyes open. He was on his knees, skin pale and sweaty. His breath was shallow.

"Luke—," I started, but he shook his head.

"They're not doing anything. It's just the energy. They surrounding us?"

"Yeah."

"Penny, if this is how you felt around petrified wood, then...." But he couldn't finish as he struggled to breathe. I wrapped an arm around his shoulders to hold him steady.

All right, you're back. Release the walls, I demanded. No one said a word, but a thought slammed into my mind. A young soul, naïve and trusting, watching and learning. There had been a fifth. Who I'd trapped. Crap.

I thought of my entire adventures. The Cheyenne Circles which The Shadow consciously made, stealing our water and not caring when the waves drowned its own souls. How both our worlds had an expiration date, how, for the safety of everyone, action had to be taken, and most importantly, how I wanted to fix it.

The Shadow, the first Old One, sneered.

That's what I call it, I admitted with a cringe. *We humans use names.*

Labels. Restrictions. The walls shifted, widened, and Luke's shallow breaths became a touch more steady, but they didn't release us. No, the walls moved toward the trap, and I knew intuitively that it shifted to give us access. *Continue,* the first Old One ordered.

There was no other option. "Think you can walk?"

Luke nodded, and we slowly got to our feet. "I'm okay," he said and quickly repeated the words as if to believe them. There was almost no color to his face, and concern rattled my mind. I had enough darkness in me to create a portal around both of us. If I moved fast, maybe we could get home before the Old Ones could react.

And then we'd spend the rest of our lives in fear.

"Hey." Luke grabbed my hand and gave me a weak smile. "Let's finish this, huh? Then let's go home and take a nap."

I smiled. "Yeah, that sounds perfect."

We walked around the cliffs with careful, steady steps so Luke wouldn't trip on the rocks. Even as his body reacted to the air saturated with darkness, his soul remained strong and watchful, ready to throw up a shield around both of us if needed. The Old Ones followed us, matching our pace with an ever-looming energy.

And then it came into view. The trap. The pulsing synthetic petrified wood and the body on the ground. The darkness within had stilled, but as we neared, a strong tendril slammed against the force field. I jumped, half afraid the hold would break against the onslaught, but it remained steady.

"Looks like The Shadow is as ticked as when we left."

Luke chuckled and coughed. "Wouldn't expect it any other way. Keep to the plan?"

"Yeah."

"Here's my question. How did you plan on turning off the device? Neither one of us could survive walking into that thing. The Shadow would tear us up."

I stepped closer to the device and eye-measured the distance between the device and Kyle's body — about two feet. "If I made a portal right above the device…," I said to myself. "Yeah, I can do it." *And when I do, you take The Shadow and leave our world. That's the deal. We go our separate ways.*

No more deals with humans.

Rats. Not that that changed anything. The plan was still the plan. I turned around, searching until I found a heavy looking stone roughly a foot wide. "Ready?" I asked Luke.

"Do it."

I traced from the device to directly above it and the force field and opened a portal. Keeping it steady, I sent a tendril of my own darkness to the rock and wove a portal under it too.

The rock fell through the portal and crushed through the device. Pieces scattered and the synthetic energies holding The Shadow back dissipated.

Before anyone could react, The Shadow charged. I stepped back, and Luke raised his arms, but there wasn't enough time. The Shadow increased speed and slammed right through me.

Chapter 31

Pain tore through my chest. I stepped back to steady myself but couldn't feel my foot. My knees gave out, and I fell back first, to the ground. My skull hit a rock, but I could barely feel it over the agony. Every cell was screaming. I'd felt this before, this agonizing inner war, back when we tried to save Jack and the paradox threatened to rip the darkness from me. But it was a part of me now. To lose my darkness would be to be torn in half.

Which was exactly what The Shadow intended.

"Penny?" Luke knelt down next to me and grabbed my head. I tried to meet his gaze, but my eyes wouldn't focus.

You'll pay for that trap, The Shadow screamed in my head. *You'll pay for all the deeds of you humans!*

I gripped Luke's wrist, my fingers digging into his skin as I fought to stay conscious. Black dots blurred my vision as my body threatened to give up. Luke slipped his hand behind my head as if to cushion me from the hard ground, but he soon withdrew. A deep red lined his skin, and a fresh horror distorted his face. "You're bleeding."

I didn't bleed, not since the darkness took over. If I got hurt, my body acted like the darkness and wove itself back together.

So if I wasn't healing, if my blood was red....

Above us, the Shadow hovered, enjoying the view as I struggled. There was a sound like a whisper, and the wall of blackness surrounding us dissipated.

Your actions to revive us have been noted. The first Old One's voice rattled around in my unsteady mind.

The Shadow hadn't expected that voice. It tensed, and the overwhelming power which made up The Shadow's silhouette shrank before my eyes. Dark souls were their thoughts. And that voice made The Shadow feel small and young, a child.

But then it must have fought against the thought because it towered up again as if puffing its chest.

You have done your souls wrong. The Old One spoke low and with warning. There was a whoosh, and all four Old Ones rushed The Shadow at the same time. A portal wrapped around them.

It was over. The Shadow was gone. The Old Ones too. Back to their own world where I prayed they'd stay, at least until they could be less intense.

Now, if I could just get my body to move. I tried to shift my weight, to move an arm or leg, or speak, but all I could manage was a twitch or a grunt. Luke knelt over me, his hand back between me and the ground, pressing against a wound I could barely feel. It was like everything hurt so much it made me numb.

"Penny, you need to heal," Luke pleaded. His other hand found mine and gripped it tightly. "Come on."

I shook my head. I didn't know what was happening. Everything was wrong. Half of me was missing.

A thick blackness covered my eyes. At first, I thought I had passed out, but the pain was still too strong, and I was much too aware. The sensation was strange and yet oddly familiar. Curious and determined, how a strong orange willpower might feel. There was a warmth to it, too, like a hearth, like family.

And then the screaming in my cells quieted. I could feel the cool dampness of the moss against my clothes, Luke's hand in mine, the jarring sharp pain in the back of my head. I blinked and the dark covering over my eyes faded. Luke looked half-crazed with concern as he leaned over me, but he sighed in relief when my eyes focused on him. He cursed and bent down, his forehead on mine. "I thought you were gone."

"Can't...get rid of me that easy." My voice croaked, but I got the words out. I moved my arm, and it obeyed.

Luke helped me to a sitting position. His hand tightened in mine, and he frowned. "Penny, you feel different. Your soul."

I held out my hand. There were blues and greens and a bright, intuitive purple shining back. No blackness. I reached my arm out and tried to connect with some darkness, to create a portal, but nothing happened. "The Shadow ripped the darkness from me," I said. "It's...gone."

"But wouldn't that kill you?"

"I think it almost did." Until a darkness covered my eyes and that warm hearth energy came.

Luke angled me to the side and studied the back of my head to take inventory of my head injury. "It stopped bleeding."

"I think.... There was this energy — it healed me." I shook my head, and the injury barely hurt. Who could have — ?

Kyle.

I scrambled to my feet only to crash hard on my knees ten steps later, where Kyle's body lay. He hadn't moved once. Not a groan or an inhale. And where his dark soul should have been, there was nothing, not even that void-like gap of unearthly energies. My fingers trembled as I reached out, praying to find warmth to his skin, but before I could reach him, a strong breeze rippled through the Scottish land, and he just...crumbled. Like sand in the wind. Gone.

After all that, he was still gone.

Luke wrapped an arm around me, and I leaned into him, blinking weirdly dry eyes. There wasn't even a threat of a tear because it just didn't make sense.

"We freed him," I said. "Dark souls don't die. Even if his body— He should still be free. He should be *here*. Where'd he go?" It didn't make sense.

Luke's grip tightened around me. "Maybe he was human enough to—" He stopped, and the empty silence screamed at me. No taunting shadows. No trickster Void ready to make trouble and run from the consequences. Just Luke and me staring at the empty spaces.

"Penny!"

I jumped at the sound. Mom, Dad, Jack, and Dinah were running between the cliffs. Ricky raced behind them. "What did you do?" He gasped, looking around us.

Dinah's eyes landed on the shattered device. "You took over ten minutes," she explained. "Did it work?"

I shook my head and opened my mouth, but nothing came out.

Luke squeezed my arm in comfort as he took the lead. "Penny did amazing. Everything she said she'd do. The Old Ones are revived. They took The Shadow with them. It's over. For good this time."

No one asked about Kyle. The answer was there in the silence, in the way Luke and I couldn't celebrate our success. Dad knelt down in front of me and leaned until he was in my eyesight. "Hey," he half whispered. "Why don't we go home? Plan a ceremony for him. To honor him."

"We can do it on the ship," Ricky offered. "A full memorial."

I tried to think, but everything felt numb. A strange, different numb I'd never felt before. "Yeah, okay," I played along. "Wait, if the darkness is gone, how did you get here?"

"You left the door connected to the darkness in my ship," Ricky explained. "It's still open. Perhaps the dark world hasn't left us completely."

I thought of how The Expert helped us, how it cared for Kyle and broke the rules of the land to help him find his happiness, how The Old Ones had traveled between the worlds before that horrible day and how those travels resulted in a magical mythology. Would magic come back to my world if Earth and the dark world once again live in harmony? Would I be a part of it, or would I have to watch on the sidelines?

Luke helped me to my feet, and Ricky led us to the door he'd used to find us. I walked through and braced myself for the blinding nausea, but no overwhelming disorientation took over. No dizzying effects, no temporary disconnect from the physical world. There wasn't enough darkness left to overpower me, and yet…when I passed through the threshold, the confused celebration of the dark souls chattered in my ears, and when my mind tapped the darkness, it responded. Maybe my connection with the darkness hadn't been closed forever.

Chapter 32

"We're here today to celebrate Kyle Tullet. The Void. And whatever other names he went by during his existence." Ricky stood at a makeshift podium at the bow of the ship. The deck was full of humans dressed in black, and black souls. Dry eyes and bowed heads. I wore a black dress Mom had taken me on a shopping trip last week to purchase just for this occasion. I'd bought a cheap Indiana Jones hat from the costume store too, and set it next to the flowers. Kyle, the explorer. The free spirit he could have been. All those things he might have discovered. Those would haunt me, too, somehow. My arms were tightly folded across my chest. I hadn't cried yet, and people told me it was okay if I did, okay if I didn't, but it felt wrong not to cry.

Luke said it was shock. It took him a few days to cry after losing Jack, back in the days before Kyle made time malleable. But it wasn't just losing Kyle that hurt as much as knowing no one really knew him well enough to mourn properly. People shared stories that never fully captured him. I knew him the best, and not even I could muster up a tear. It made me feel guilty.

A lot of people showed up, though, and that was nice. I wasn't sure how many were here to say goodbye to Kyle or how many were just humoring me, but the number in attendance was a compliment. Everyone in Ricky's family, my family, Luke and Jack. The entire population of Zetta's hometown in the future showed up. They'd known Kyle for a year back when he hid there and was friends with teenage Zetta and Ricky. It had rained there, for the first time in years.

Even some dark souls showed up, hovering around the edges so as to not accidentally walk through anyone. The Expert politely shared details from the dark world with me, but I could tell it was uncomfortable. Funerals weren't a concept it wanted to linger on. *The Old Ones' return has helped ease the trauma of many souls. Death has lost some of its fear now that they are back. We have a word for resurrection now, which is strange. A good strange. Thank you.* I could tell by The Expert's voice that it was smiling as it spoke. *The Shadow is being properly punished for betraying the safety of our souls for a personal vendetta, and…for what it did to you.*

My soul wasn't dark anymore. Where once only an emptying blackness resided, now brilliant colors took its place. Blues and purples and yellows. It took a while for me to figure out how to connect to the darkness without some within me, and I wasn't quite skilled enough to travel yet, but every now and then, when I meditated really hard, I could feel the darkness respond. It would take time to retrain my soul to work with the dark energy again, but that was one thing I had plenty of now. Time, it seemed, was finally on my side.

The dark souls didn't linger long, afraid of letting the human limitations slip too much into their reality. Mom and Dad said a few words about how they never really knew Kyle personally, but they knew what they'd have lost if not for his sacrifice. Their memories were slowly but steadily returning, as was proof of my existence. Mom found my birth certificate in with her piles of letters. And the school called last week asking why I hadn't been to class for the last month. Summer school officially became a part of my new linear future.

The talking and sharing stories at the podium part of the evening ended, and people went to the buffet, checking out the various entrees and desserts, and wondering how soon they could leave without being rude. I'd lost my darkness, not my empathy, and could still read everyone like a book.

It was strange. I had been so lonely before, grew up feeling so separated from the world. I saw the world differently, knew too much, and was known as a freak. But now…. I'd never felt so loved in my life as at this moment. All these people from different worlds, spanning time and space to mourn someone with me. Of all the things Kyle did, this was my favorite. Somehow, all while intimidating me and irritating me, he'd surrounded me with love and family. A tear fell when I blinked, and I wiped it away.

"Ah, no crying. You'll make this place feel like a funeral."

I turned at the unfamiliar voice. A guy stood there, around my age, with wild dark hair and pale skin. He wore a leather jacket and combat boots, which looked too new and scuff free to be intimidating. He smirked at me and stepped closer, glancing over the food. "Aren't there supposed to be these cheesy funeral potatoes at these things?"

Shocked at his brash words, I pointed at a casserole dish on the other side of the table.

"Ah, thanks." He picked a grape and tossed it in his mouth. Who was this guy? Did he belong with Zetta's hometown? Did Ricky and Zetta adopt another homeless kid who lacked even a bit of decorum? "Cool colors, by the way." He gestured at me.

I looked down at my dress. "It's black."

His smug smirk never faltered. "So what's next for you?"

"Um…summer school, I guess." I frowned at him. Something about him was weirdly familiar. I scanned his aura for clues. A strong, unique orange dominated his aura. An excited, near giddy willpower to try everything, explore each corner, leave no experience untouched. "I'm sorry, do I know you?"

"I don't even know me yet. But I look forward to figuring

it out." He smirked at me, grabbed a plate, and headed for the funeral potatoes.

Luke worked his way to me through the crowd with two glasses of fruit punch. "Who were you talking to?" he asked, handing me my glass.

"I have no idea," I said. We watched the strange guy toss some potatoes on a plate and move over to the flowers for Kyle. He leaned down and smelled the flowers and sneezed once, but when he reached the hat, he paused. The guy pinched the top of the hat between his fingers and picked it up. He set the hat on his head, wiggled it to position, and turned to look at me over his shoulder. Then he winked. Someone walked between us, and by the time the view was clear, he was gone.

No way. No friggin' way. And yet, it seemed like the kind of thing he'd do. Wait until I was crying to show up. The relief and hope mixed with sheer annoyance for his signature selfishness. "Kyle," I growled in a rush of emotions, and downed the fruit punch in one chug.

"Huh." Luke tilted his head. "Take the hat and leave. Sounds like him. So he didn't die. Just needed to make a new body."

"New soul too. All colors, like mine."

"Must have seen how The Shadow tore it from you." Luke sipped his punch. "You realize we'll have to deal with him for the rest of our lives, right? Every family reunion, he's gonna be there. Popping in and out." He spoke with an irked tone, but when he met my eye, he had a sexy half-grin.

Yes, Kyle was gone. Whoever came through here and took the Indiana Jones hat was someone new. I'd have to meet him all over again, but this time it would be the real him. The pure soul free from the past, able to chase that curiosity as long as he wanted. And when he needed a place to crash? I'd make sure we always had a setting for him at the dinner table. Heck, once I figured out the trick to time traveling with my multi-colored soul, I'd be up for joining him on an adventure or two. We could go back to the forest, figure out what those blasted blurs were.

After this ceremony, Luke and I would go home, back to our normal, daily life, and the weirdest thing was I couldn't wait. It was time to say goodbye to the life of time travel and adventure. Time to live for the present and the future. We were all free to chase the impulses of our souls, to learn and grow, and then race home to tell family about it all.

Home. Family.

Finally.

Acknowledgments

My life is rich with love and support, all of which I had to choose and accept. My eight siblings have all been great beacons of encouragement, and it often seems silly to add the "in-law" after the siblings who came along later. To my nieces and nephews (and great nieces and nephews), I love you with all my heart and am endlessly proud of you. Thanks to all my friends who love me and accept me like family. Cassandra, Ahmani, Elena, and Juan; you'll be a part of my life forever, no matter what happens.

I also couldn't have done this without the expertise of Karen Fuller and Maxine Bringenberg at World Castle Publishing. Thank you for believing in me.

Aspen Bassett lives in Boise, ID, with her sister and a very spoiled cat. She grew up learning about chakras and auras and the true power of imagination, which slips into her writing whether she intends it to or not. In college, in addition to earning her degree in Creative Writing, Aspen received her certificate in Women's Meditation. Now, she's certified in Reiki, Hypnotherapy, and Ho'oponopono. When she's not working, she's usually sipping tea or hot cocoa and wondering what would happen if she had superpowers. In addition to her Penelope Grace Trilogy, Aspen has been published in multiple anthologies, including Oomph: A Little Super Goes a Long Way and Inaccurate Realities.

www.ingramcontent.com/pod-product-compliance
Lightning Source LLC
Chambersburg PA
CBHW030131180626
46812CB00002B/645